LEATHER
AND
SAGE

LEATHER

AND

SAGE

Taylor Shepeard

Cursed Dragon Ship
PUBLISHING

Copyright © 2021 by Taylor Shepeard

Cursed Dragon Ship Publishing, LLC

6046 FM 2920 Rd W, #231, Spring, TX 77379

captwyvern@curseddragonship.com

Cover © 2021 by Stefanie Saw

Developmental Edit by Kelly Lynn Colby

Copy Edit by S. G. George

ISBN 978-1-951445-14-0

ISBN 978-1-951445-13-3 (ebook)

Grandma,
Thank you for always believing in me. This first tale, and all the ones to follow, is for you.

Forespoken
Sweet child
Of the orchard
Sighting apples
Before they bloom
Already ripe
In the place of fertility

Witchling
Still yet to breathe
It is us creators
That sound in dreams
Not yet come to
Listen, willow moss and
kindling

We are here
Here for you
You will see

We all fear
Fear for you
You will sting

Daughter
Juice froths beyond
Your barren toes
Our rooted souls
And stains maroon
The stone of rested
ancestors

Sweet Child,
Daughter, Witchling
To see ripe apples not
there
And hear screaming
souls gone
The Bloodbud won't be
undone

We are near
Near to you
You will know

I am the Coven
You are Infected
We have Fallen

PROLOGUE

(ROOTED DEEP, THIS FORSAKEN)

HOWLS FILL THE WOODS. They wrap 'round trunks of birch to curdle the disposition of the Inner Circle and the Matron. I watch them figures, hunched together as the wails heighten. I just want them screams to stop—those of my mother.

A fire burns 'tween the huddled witches, and over it sits a burnished, black cauldron. The flames flicker and flare, then paint the Inner Circle's faces with oranges and yellows and blacks like they a field of sunflowers trapped under a bog.

'Nother shriek sounds, and I twist blue-dyed fingers into fists that quake. Beatrice, a witch and Elder of my clan, the Orchard, fits her hand over my shoulder, gripping tight. It's too soon. The spirits have found they way into Mother's mind, and once they in, there ain't nothing to be done. I swallow, my throat a wasteland, and wait for the Matron to reach a decision. Are we to give my mother to the spirits as an offering, or do we put her to rest with a knife at her throat?

Beatrice's hand near my nape don't leave, its bony strength covered in a thin lining of skin and blue veins. She watches the figures, her eyes black 'gainst the night that shrouds us. When the others remain together, she leans to murmur in my ear. "Did you collect the ingredients during a full moon?"

I nod, not trusting my lips to move without cries escaping. A full moon's best, though an absent moon is still a strong celestial time to start the poultice. She pinches her whitened lips together.

"And the Last Lamentation ... you chanted it?"

A nod.

"How many times?"

Ice churns in my chest as I choke out a response. "Just the one. Recipe don't say more than one."

Beatrice gives a curt tilt of her chin. Her eyes close, and the lids twitch where the bulbs slide and work 'neath them. "It's too soon. The spirits, they ain't taking as long as they used to, weaseling they way in to root down in our minds. Your mother only has two girls. Won't be long 'fore the birth of a daughter don't mean nothing. They'll get in 'fore the gift is shared."

I shudder as the sacrament of her words slices down my spine. We were once the most powerful creatures of all, with hands made to weave life from nothing, eyes to see beyond sight, and ears to hear the unspoken. *We are the Coven.* It's just a mantra now.

Words with no power. Titles with no potency.

Another howl, deep and disturbed, drifts through the forest. My breaths stutter. Not even our poultices work to block the spirits that hunger after us from the Beyond.

The pressure from Beatrice's hand lifts. She moves aside, head bent down to search the ground 'tween her feet, and I know the Blackwoods come. They hushed voices that were masked by the crackling fire lie silent as they approach. I don't make move to watch.

"Miriam Hallivard," The Matron calls out, voice dry like the warning of a rattlesnake, "Daughter of Gretchen Hallivard, who is the Matriarch of the Orchard Clan, we have decided."

They want me to look to them, but there ain't no way I can. They gaze be nothing but a sentencing 'cause, whatever they say, my mother dies tonight. I should know which I want—a quick death or a sacrifice—but I cain't think on it. Shifting my eyes from Beatrice's feet, I tilt my face up to the Matron.

Her eyes are of willow moss and kindling—just like mine and all the women of every clan—deep set in a face with shrunken skin and pointed bones. She seems a spirit herself, but she ain't. We're witches, all of us here, though the Blackwoods be the first of our kind. It makes them stronger, the magic drawn to them more than it is to any of us other clans that form the Coven.

A knife glints in the Matron's hand. It looks warped, the way the fire reflects off it so. They've chosen a quick death for Mother. My chest leaps, but I don't know if it's good or bad.

Everyone waits, watching, and I think on the words I'm s'posed to say. My throat's still dry, a plow field in the winter. I swallow. Once. Twice. Then, I speak.

"Matron, Blood and Kin, how will my mother, Gr—" I cut off, tears clenching my throat, then inhale deep. Beatrice's hand don't return for comfort, harsh a support as it was. The Matron's here. "—Gretchen Hallivard, Matriarch of the Orchard Clan, serve?"

The Matron pulls her hood back to reveal wiry, silver hair, like spiderwebs drifting back. Her gaze be a bright beam, like gator eyes caught in the moonlight. I clutch my hands together and shift, not liking the way she watches me. My willow moss and kindling flashes to the three 'round her, then to the two that still stand near the cauldron: the Inner Circle, who place highest in ranks among the Blackwoods and support the Matron in all she chooses. We only see them when something big has happened, and I don't want them 'round no longer.

If only Mother would come back, none of this would need be.

3

At last, the Matron answers. "Gretchen Hallivard, Matriarch of the Orchard Clan, will serve by giving the Coven protection against the spirits from this night forward."

The words settle in the night and tap at my skull. My lips flit down as my nose wrinkles. Tears still glisten on my cheeks even if they ain't running no more. A Blackwoods steps forward to hand over a piece of parchment.

It's a Creation recipe. I skim the lines, taking in the ingredients, while Beatrice stands behind me to do the same, her chin just high 'nough to reach over my shoulder.

A flower? My teeth dig harsh lines into the flesh of my cheeks. "This … it'll work? What're we gon' do with a flower?"

The Matron don't answer at first, staring at the parchment, then she removes it from my grip and slides it from sight.

"It will be planted around our homes as a protective shield. The spirits cannot cross over a barrier made of this particular bloom, as that is how we will create it. Your mother's blood, imbued with the gift and tainted with the spirits, will be the binding agent for all the ingredients. You, of course, will give blood as well, since you are her first-born daughter."

It's all too much. Mother's screams light the night 'gain, followed by the chime of hysterical laughter. This is it. Soon 'nough, she'll be gone regardless, her body a vessel to whatever spirit got her mind in its grasp. I nod then push the Matron and her Inner Circle 'way with a wave of my hand. I wave and wave and wave, wanting them gone from me, wanting Mother back, wanting this night to be over with and never come 'gain. They retreat as Beatrice kneels beside me.

Her hands clutch my wrist, and she hisses in my ear. "Did you see the poultice? Those ingredients … they don't seem like ones that gon' protect, Miriam."

My mind beats at my skull like it's iron that needs tempering.

"I ain't never created a poultice that wasn't already written down. How is we to know what should and shouldn't go into a new one?"

Beatrice chews her lip. Her grip tightens. "Still, I don't like this. I think this be bad. They've dabbled in something dark, and we 'bout to be part of it. This feels like black magic even though I didn't see a splinter of soul as an ingredient."

I try listening to Beatrice, but the screams and howls and wails and shrieks and wild, rough laughter of Mother rings in my head. The sounds toll 'gain and 'gain, a rooster come to force my mind awake. If only that were true and this was all a nightmare; I'd open bleary eyes to a day where Mother's laughing in the kitchen while she strips poultice ingredients and bickers with Paw. But this ain't. I shake Beatrice off my arm. "They the Coven."

"We the Coven, too," she counters.

"But they the main clan. They the blood of the first witches, the Blackwoods. We ain't never learned how to craft stuff to new medicines or weave life or create. We just got the gift and the way it lets us see things that ain't there, hear things that don't make sound, and feel gooseprickles of warning. Madness from the spirits is a big price to pay for it. They can take that price 'way."

Her hand hovers near my wrist, a slated glint in her eyes. For a moment, I think she might grab me and run. Then, her palm lowers, and she casts her gaze to the Matron.

"Bloodbud," she says, the word a curse. "Ain't no good gon' come of a flower named Bloodbud, you mark my words, Miriam Hallivard."

"All we do is dealt in blood, Beatrice. Mother's medicine to ward from the spirits took mine, and I'll need my daughter's once I got one. There are worse names. Deceitful names. Wintersweet can kill, but it sounds all happy and innocent. Sweet, it says."

The Blackwoods start to chant. They graveled voices rise

and fall in a harsh, guttural tune that hurts my ears to listen to. The Old Language. Beatrice's face falls blank, so I 'ssume she don't know the words, neither, despite being an Elder of the Orchard. As they speak, the Inner Circle adds ingredients to the cauldron nestled over the woodland fire. When they gathered, I don't know. They must've hoped I'd agree to this and prepared.

A powder gets poured in, either the dirt of a dead man's grave or the crushed bat skull. Next, they hold a rattler over the poultice. It wriggles in anger 'fore a knife plunges into the soft of its belly and rips through. Blood and entrails fall out. The serpent's body gets discarded to the side, and the Blackwoods keep pouring ingredients: meadowsweet, claw of salamander, sage, web of a journey to the Beyond.

Beatrice paces beside me, a cat with its back arched at some unseen noise in the dark. I wonder if she gon' hiss, too, her tongue tucked behind front teeth. It don't matter. I close my eyes, the lids bright red and flashing blues. They stay closed 'til I hear her. Mother. The colors disappear as the forest snaps back to sight.

Oh, Mother.

She steps closer so the fire no longer blacks her from sight. Blood's raked 'cross her face from the claw marks she's left there. She's almost gone, the last pieces of her sanity and her mind holding to what little portions of this world remain to block the insistent talons of the next life. The Beyond. She spots me 'cross the way, eyes crazed, the tint muddled and gray, no longer willow moss and kindling. I plunge my fist into my mouth to still my own wail. The Matron watches on as Mother's forced to the cauldron.

Beatrice and I step forward. Mother keeps her gaze on me and clicks her tongue. Her fingers twitch, and she chomps her teeth like she's gnawing on cud. We're too late to make the flower 'cause this ain't Mother no more. The spirit that has her now cocks its head left then right, left then right, left then right, like a nervous habit. Together, voices aligned, the Inner Circle resumes they chants. The Old Language churns in the air and scrapes at my ears.

Then, the Matron moves behind Mother, knife in hand. I meet Mother's gaze. Wrong eyes—gray eyes—stare at me. All that can be heard is the low grumble of the incantations and the crackle of the fire. My heart beats a flurry of hummingbird wings.

I hope she still hears the unspoken. I tell her she's a good mother. I let her know how I love her and how I know she loves me.

Tears blur my vision, but I brush them 'way before the Blackwoods see. When I look up, I'm met by eyes of willow moss and kindling. Mother's eyes. They crinkle 'round the edges as she smiles, a soft curl of lips that hides her teeth and warms her cheeks. She heard me. I grin back and reach out as though to brush her hand, though she's too far 'way to touch.

Silver flashes, followed by crimson, and those eyes turn gray again. A roar wrenches out of her throat as she bears her canines. Beatrice slaps my hand back to my side, and I drop to the ground. My knees hit the earth with a crack. The Matron holds Mother's honey wheat hair in her hand while two more of the Blackwoods keep grip on her limp arms to lean her bleeding neck over the cauldron. The flesh yawns wide as blood guzzles and spurts a steady stream into the poultice; they got they binding ingredient.

The life leaves her, 'long with the spirit. My hands grapple at the dirt, fists clenched as I beat the ground and moan.

She had heard; she had looked at me. She was *there*.

The chants swell 'cross the clearing. I think my ears may bleed with the pain the Old Language causes them as it turns to a graveled pitch.

"Miriam, it's time for your blood." The Matron summons me.

She moves from behind Mother, knife still in hand, while two witches lift 'way the lifeless body. In front of me, the poultice boils and pops and grumbles. My teeth clench 'gainst the anguished cry I want to let out but cain't. I drop the dirt in my fists. It's done. Mother's gone and this flower needs to come into creation so that no other witch will suffer our fate. My daughter won't need a Requiem to slip a knife 'cross my throat.

Beatrice moves to Mother, whose body is laid out on the ground some feet from the fire. Her veined hand reaches to close the dimmed eyes, and she pulls the sage forth from her robe. Once I give blood, I'll join her in the burial rites.

The Matron beckons me, and I avoid the fresh puddle of burgundy on the ground as I walk to her. She hands me the knife. It glimmers, unclean. I slice it 'cross my palm. There should be pain, but I'm too numb.

"How much it need?" I ask as my blood drips into the kettle. The poultice bubbles up, green like swamp water and thick like syrup.

"Until the buds can be seen."

The Matron don't say more, so I rub my shoulder to keep the blood flowing. Beatrice mutters behind me, and I twist my neck to watch her light three candles 'round Mother's head as the smoke from the sage hovers 'bove her body. Her throat's been wrapped in ribbon to hide the wound.

"Enough," the Matron states.

I jump back and pull in my wrist. The voices of the Inner Circle halt, and goose prickles raise on my arms at the sudden silence. Beatrice looks up from the rite, her hands wavering over Mother's face, as the Inner Circle bounds forward. We watch the Matron, all of us. A fog hangs heavy 'round our gathering as we wait to see this flower that will protect the Coven. I back 'way to give the Blackwoods room and kneel beside Beatrice as I grip Mother's stiff hand in my nimble one.

The Matron frowns into the kettle, her body rigid.

"Forespoken," she whispers, her sight on the contents I cain't see. Those gator eyes flash and spark. "Forsaken."

"Matron," one of the Inner Circle begins, "is it done?"

She keeps quiet as we breathe ragged in the silent night. There's no sound and no breeze, just a stifling heat that folds down my nape.

"Pour out the poultice. It is done," she says at last. Iron coats her tone.

The Inner Circle moves to meet her command and dump the poultice onto the ground. It's tar-like and bubbling as it leaks out at her feet.

"And ... the Bloodbud?" asks 'nother.

The Matron's face screws tight as she turns to us, then twists in rage as she sneers at Mother.

"There," she says and points.

I look down to Mother's hand clutched in my own, eyelids closed to hide the poisoned color. "Mother is the Bloodbud?"

"No, you stupid child," the Matron hisses. She reaches down to rip the cloth from Mother's throat and exposes the fresh wound. I lunge at her and shove her back while the members of the Inner Circle grapple to yank me 'way.

From the ground, Beatrice shrieks in distress. "You cain't disturb the body during a rite! Her soul is searching for entrance from this vessel into the Beyond! So it is that the Blackwoods have lost respect for those clans at the borders."

The Matron ignores Beatrice. "Look."

Caught in a rage and still fighting 'gainst the hands that grip me tight, I turn to Mother.

There, I see it.

The petals are gray, gray like Mother's eyes had been with the spirit at her mind. The leaves are red as the life that spilled from her throat. It peeks out from where the knife sliced through.

"This the flower to protect us?" Horror peels Beatrice's lips back.

"No," the Matron snaps. "This is the flower to destroy us."

"What you mean?" I snarl at her. "What you mean this flower gon' destroy us? You said it would save all the witches! You said Mother's sacrifice would bring us protection from the spirits." Venom coats my voice as I spit out the words.

The Matron's face remains placid. She looks down at me like I'm a child in need of discipline. I ain't a child. My gaze snaps to the rest of the Blackwoods. They all glare at the flower sticking out Mother's throat with furled lips and crinkled noses. I want to gouge they eyes out so they cain't look at her like she a disappointment.

I turn on the Matron, her beady gaze and flat cheeks fuel to my anger. "This be on you. Whatever you've created, whatever it gon' do to destroy us, you is to blame. Not my mother, not our clan, but you. Now go, and never come back."

Beatrice grabs my forearm, eyes cowed wide. "Miriam," she snarls at me, "what you doing? You cain't send them 'way. We still need them!"

I yank free from her. Need them for what? What they done but trample over us and control the way we live? They'll not step foot in the Orchard 'gain, so long as I breathe. I lift my chin to Beatrice and turn to the Blackwoods, my gaze a curse on theirs.

"Matron, Leader of the Coven, Matriarch of the Black-woods, you are fors—"

"Miriam!" Beatrice shrieks. She rushes forward like she's gon' put her palm over my mouth, but I push her 'way. "My mother was Matriarch of the Orchard, and now she's dead, that title belongs to me. The Ancestor's already gave they assent," I hurl at her.

Beatrice whimpers but don't say nothing more. When I turn

'round, the Matron glowers at me, her hands clasped in front of her like she might smack me with them.

"Think on what you're about to do, Miriam Hallivard of the Orchard Clan. Though you're not Matriarch yet, should you assume the title this vow will be taken as an oath. Do you want to isolate your witches from us? Will they ever forgive you, assuming they survive the spirits?"

I think on the other families, all of them no doubt awake in they beds and terrified of the Matron and the fate of my mother. We'll be better off on our own. I straighten and roll my shoulders.

"Matron, Leader of the Coven, Matriarch of the Black-woods, you are forsaken from the witches of the Orchard Clan, from this breath 'til my dying breath and the dying breath of my first-born granddaughter."

Knife still in hand, I slice it 'cross my palm, a new line next to the one used for the poultice. The blood drips onto the ground they've been banished from. The oath is sealed. In three generations time, they may return, unless my granddaughter decides 'gainst a Reunion of Kin. There's a thud as Beatrice falls to her knees. The Matron don't move, her teeth working behind closed lips.

"Burn the flower, lest it spread," she says to me, voice dipped in ash, then they leave.

They silhouettes vanish 'tween the shadows of the forest that surround us. Only the rustle of they cloaks make a sound in the dead, dark night. I turn to Mother and the flower that peeks out from her throat as the candles lit 'round her head start to fizzle out.

"It's done," I say to Beatrice.

She snarls up at me. "So it is. We're no longer protected."

"We were never protected. That much was made clear tonight with this creation gone wrong. And what's it done? We got a flower that turns even the Matron pale in fear."

Beatrice stands slow, her knees popping as she rises up and looks at the bloom, all gray and red. "Poison, you think? Or perhaps the spirits be drawn to it, the way bees are to pollen."

There's a beat at my temple like a dog scratching at a closed door. What's it matter now? Our only hope is that the gift will whisper warnings of the bloom, give us sight of what it will bring or tingle our senses when we need fear. The flower's been created and the Matron didn't pour the poultice onto Mother. No. She poured it into the land. Our Orchard. I doubt burning one body will stop its spread.

Even still, it's best to destroy this one. I grab a fallen branch, thick with dead leaves, and dip it in the fire 'neath the cauldron. It lights, and I hold the limb out to Mother. My arm falters as I hesitate, but the bloom leers at me, a curse, and I bite down on my cheek as I lower the flame.

The blaze dances in Beatrice's dark gaze. In the shadows here, it's more graphite than willow moss and kindling. "You ain't never gon' be accepted as Matriarch after this. The Orchard will not stand for it."

I don't respond, and she leaves with nothing more to say. No, I won't, but it takes the blood of my kin to reunite with the Blackwoods. They'll not have a choice, even if they hate me.

In front of me, the flames crackle, and I imagine I can see Mother's soul drifting up as she burns. I kiss my fingers and hold them out to her, the way she would kiss her fingers and hold them to my temple before she'd send me off to sleep.

"Be well in the Beyond, Mother. I'll see you 'gain."

The words are eaten up by the crackle of the flames, but I know she hears them. She hears them the same way we see things not there and catch things not said and feel things without presence.

We are the Orchard Clan, rooted deep. Whatever this flower be, we'll stand 'gainst it.

1

GRAY LIKE THUNDER, RED AS THE SETTING SUN

Ellie Hallivard

MAMA ALWAYS SAYS we'll go crazy, that we need to live in the now, but I like to think 'bout the future. Guess it's 'cause I'll be Matriarch one day: leader of the Orchard Clan, our clan. Cain't think 'bout the me in *now* when I've got to worry 'bout the everyone during *soon* and *soon enough* and *years to come*.

As Lillian grabs a ladybug off the kitchen table and squeezes it 'tween her fingers, nose scrunched up, then pouts when Kylie hits the bug 'way, I wonder 'bout the *we* and the *here*. And the making it through this one lesson. Just this one. *Ancestors, guide me.*

"How much you got left to read," Lillian whines, that eight-year-old trill on the verge of bellows and tears.

The pages of Grannies grimoire ruffle as I count in haste. A subtle catch-and-drag makes them hiss for every one that I pull forward, an entire history told on this bound parchment in the blood of the Matriarchs before me. It's technically Mama's now, but I still call it Grannie's. She had it longest, before she passed it on. It'll be mine, too, one day. Mama keeps a full pot of the self-formed ink, tinged in red, on the desk in the corner of the common area. For now, I sit my sisters in the kitchen, Kylie just a few years shy of myself at her fifteen, and read.

I shuffle the pages, and the scratchy parchment shifts back to the place I've held open. "Got a few pages, so cross your legs and tuck in. This important."

Lillian puffs her pinkened lips, hair all red and angry 'bout her face. I think she might start in at her wailing, but Kylie flicks a mint leaf down for her. She squeals, then pops it in her mouth to chew, content for now.

"Get on, then," Kylie huffs.

I cain't help but purse my lips at them both, then take the bit of time I got left of they attention. "This Grannie's writing, so you listen up. She still talking 'bout the Bloodbud and her mama. It say here, 'Per the Ancestors, Miriam Hallivard foretold that the curse to return every hundred years, seeking the blood of her kin to fulfill the prophecy of the Forespoken. Those of her brood are to turn and run at the sight of any flower with petals gray like thunder and leaves red like the setting sun. Always run. If the Hallivard blood make contact with the curse, the Forsaken shall be born, and the Coven shall begin the descent to destruction—'"

"What that," Lillian interrupts, eyes bright as she gnaws at the herb in her mouth. It's like she's chewing cud, just the way them cows do.

Kylie glares at our younger sister, arms crossed. "Don't make them noises, they rude. And it means to break apart so it cain't be fixed."

Lillian waves Kylie's words off, and they eyes of willow moss and kindling bore into one 'nother. We all got them eyes. Those ones of hickory and umber and amber, of grays and greens, like they made from the barks of trees or taken from the shadowed copse of the woods. Kylie's honey wheat hair glints in the sunlight that streams through the kitchen window, a contrast to Lillian's flames. "Not destruction. That other one. The de- deesent one."

A bead of sweat drips down my neck, and I brush it off. Ain't no use, though, as 'nother slides right after it. I huff, then pull my own hair from off my shoulder and tuck it 'way. It's more like Kylie's hue, though it's gotten a twinge darker as I grown. "Means to move down. To fall."

"So," Lillian starts, a tilt to her head, "the Coven gon' fall, and then it gon' break 'part?"

"Yea," I say, just as Kylie grumbles. "What it matter?"

I snap the book up and return it to the shelf Mama keeps it on. We're done for the day. I'm sick and tired of wrangling the two of them, and the grind of Lillian's teeth on that mint gonna drive me madder than the spirits, those ones that burrow they way into the minds of witches and turn they eyes gray like wilted weeds. Like ash. "It matter 'cause the Coven made up of all our sister clans. The Springwells and Hammerbrews and Everglades and—"

"And them Blackwoods," Kylie grouses.

Why they talking over me today like this? No one taught them to be rude; I know that for sure. Kylie's shoulders set at the glower I flash her way. "Yea, and the Blackwoods. They the head of the Coven, Kylie. You cain't pretend they don't exist."

When my sister leans forward and sucks on her teeth, her hair lit in gold as the sun hits it right on, I know I 'bout to be in a rage. Even Lillian sits taller, her legs bouncing in anticipation. Kylie's stubborn eyes of willow moss and kindling flash an aching ire.

"They sure as spirits pretend the Orchard don't exist, so why cain't I do the same thing 'bout them, hm? Done and cursed our family then left us to rot. I'll be," Kylie chokes back a word, eyes a quick flash to Lillian then back, "burned 'fore I acknowledge they poisonous clan. We ain't even really a part of the Coven no more after Great Grannie Miriam exiled us."

A scoff sounds, and I whip my head 'round to the threshold that separates the kitchen from the common room. Mama stands there, leaning 'gainst the pine molding, her auburn hair piled and pinned atop her head, face flushed. The gift bubbles up from my sternum to greet her magic, then settles back down, curled up like a cat dozing in the sunshine.

She must've been out helping Papa. I tilt my chin up at Kylie, a smirk on my lips. Suits her right to be speaking nonsense when Mama shows up. Even Lillian's stills a hair, and our youngest sister don't never stop her twitchy movements.

"The Blackwoods Clan," Mama starts as she raises a brow at Lillian, whose jaws slow they work on the mint, "is the Coven's head, and from it comes our Matron. Only the Matron can perform the Reunion of Kin to allow us back into the Coven so we might rejoin our sisters. It would be unwise to pretend they don't exist." Her hand lights my shoulder, and she settles into the chair beside me. It groans, and she frowns, then huffs and squeezes me. "Could you have your William take a look at this? Your Papa will make it worse in trying to fix it, and William always mends the furniture to better than it was when it was new."

Kylie shoots me a grin that's all teeth, her cheeks balled up to rosy points. Lillian don't seem to pick up on the tease, but she does notice the flush that rises to my cheeks and takes the chance to speak through her mint. "Yea, Sissy. William ain't been 'round this week, and he always gots some sweets for me from that lady in town. When he gon' come back by?"

I duck my chin and ignore Lillian, then turn to Mama. "Yes'm, I'll ask if he can come by to get that creak out. I got a cider for him, anyhow."

This time, it's Kylie who snorts, but she don't say more when I curl my lips up at her. She bites her cheek then glances 'way, eyes still bright. She knows I've been slipping a Poultice of Strength and Prosperity into William's ciders. We ain't supposed to—the townsfolk don't know 'bout the Orchard Clan and us witches, and it's best to keep our practices to ourselves.

Mama chuckles, then strokes my hair back from my neck and forehead. There's a tug, the band pulled from the end of my braid, and she hums a little as she sets to work redoing the plait. My eyes flutter close at the gentle caress. "Your sister here will be the Matriarch of the Orchard Clan one day. It's a good thing she understands how important the Blackwoods are. A necessary evil, as the humans would say."

I bite my tongue on the question I'm keen to ask. If they so special, why didn't she invoke the Reunion of Kin and bind us back to the Coven? But I keep my mouth shut and let her work on. She's got to have a reason.

Mama's hands keep at they work on my hair. "Now, it appears you've given up on lessons. Kylie, Lillian, recite the sister clans, then go on to the bedroom and fit the sheets. They're folded on the chair."

Both my sisters grumble and speak together. Well, mostly together. Lillian gulps down the mint and keeps a sharp eye on Kylie's lips, a near echo to the middle child. They name them all: Blackwoods, Everglades, Springwell, Hammerbrew, Mangroves, Orchard, Pineshift, Saplings, Marshheld, Braesland, and Vineside.

Mama grins a soft pleasure, then the duo retreats. Smug heat curls in my gut at being kept behind. It hangs there like dew drops on rose petals, light and crisp. Silence stretches between us, her hands at my hair, and the cadence sends my eyes to close after a few minutes. Mama works quick, and she tugs the end when she's done, just like she did when I was a child. "You read Grannie's passage today."

The braid gets set over my shoulder. I pick it up and eye the blond strands. "Yes'm. 'Bout the Bloodbud curse. Been a bit since I seen that in the grimoire."

When Mama don't respond, I turn to her. There's a darkness in her gaze, one brought on by troublesome thoughts. Worry creeps its way through the self-satisfied glow in my belly. I think I see a hint of gray within the willow moss and kindling there, but it's gone quick. My stomach churns all the same. She's had three daughters, the gift stretched thin—an easy target for a powerful spirit to possess. That's why we've been taking precautions.

Every two weeks we gather for the Poultice of Protection from the Beyond. It's complicated, and Mama hates asking me to do it, but I wouldn't stop even if she begged. Sometimes, I don't tell her I'm making a new batch, my chest tight at the guilt etched on her face. I'll simply set a flask of the potion on her nightstand.

"Mama, you need more medicine?"

The question brings her from her stupor, and she gives a rough shake of her head. "What? No, Ellie, I've got plenty left."

I'm not convinced, my hand at my wrist where the silvery line works its way 'cross from the dozens of cuts I've placed over the same spot. It's my job as a first-born daughter. The poultice requires my blood.

Mama's hand covers my own and pulls it 'way from the pinched flesh I pick at. She frowns, then rubs her own thumb over the raised wound. Her right arm bears the same mark from where she'd made the poultice for Grannie, a scar I've seen many times. And it worked. Grannie passed from age, a peaceful descent into the Beyond to join our Ancestors. Nothing like them Requiems so many of us witches face, a ritual only the Blackwoods can perform. I purse my lips, and my gut churns. What if Mama do get sick?

"Go on and ask, Eleanor." Her brows raise at the red indents of my lip.

The gift swirls, uprooted by the churning in my gut. Shouldn't question her—Mama's always done what's best for the Orchard—but my mouth opens anyways. "Why didn't you do it? When you was the same age as Great Grannie Miriam and you was meant to call for the Reunion of Kin?"

She sighs, then her fingers tighten on my arm. A glaze passes her sight, followed by a glimmer of gray, then the willow moss and kindling sharpens 'gain. "The Blackwoods be the head of the Coven, but it don't mean we need to be part of the body. I like to think of us as the soul. One can exist without the other, but they shouldn't be too far apart. If we rejoined, well, I fear our soul would be lost." She pierces me with a hard focus. "But, there will come a day when a Reunion of Kin is necessary, and a Hallivard will be the one to bring the Orchard back into the fold."

My nose furrows. That don't make no sense. She makes it sound like we a dead clan, left to flit 'round with nothing solid to hold us together. But I don't get the chance to question her. Mama pats my scarred arm, then folds my hand between hers. It's a gesture she did when I was young, one to let me know she was 'bout to tell me something important. My shoulders tense, and I try to catch her eye, but she's lost in her own thoughts, gaze fixed over my shoulder. A dash of pink darts out to wet her lips. "Ellie, you need to watch your sisters. Keep Kylie on house duties, and don't leave Lillian alone." Her hand grips my wrist, and the skin blooms whiter where her fingers wrap clean 'round.

Babysitting duty? I want to rebuke her, tell her I'm too old at eighteen, more useful down in the Orchard taking care of the trees in bloom and nurturing those that have yet to bear fruit. My time is best spent with the people I'll be charged with, the ones I'll need to keep safe when she passes the title of Matriarch to me. She could ask one of the younger neighbors to watch them, or let Kylie take care of Lillian herself. She's old enough.

But, the hold Mama has me in makes the rebuttals catch. I wait. It takes her a moment to continue. "The hundred years has passed. I saw them today, those Bloodbuds, poking out of the wounds of a dead townsman that wandered into our woods. He was by the myrtles, right where our Ancestors met the Blackwoods for the Requiem that started all of this."

Mama hesitates, and her nails bite into my skin. My ears lose they focus, and a shrill ring starts up in them. It cain't have been a hundred years already, could it? A chill taps down my spine, then rushes the sides of my neck. The magic in my belly unfurls, a soft flutter that sends ice into my flesh. I push it 'way to focus on my constricting throat.

Her jaw works itself, then she sucks in a breath and lets it go in a long exhale. "He got cut up by a boar, I think. We're not sure how he got all the way back there. Probably knew he was trespassing on our land. You know how the townsfolk can be with us, 'fraid of things they don't quite understand, though our apples and harvest keep them from starving some winters when game is scarce. Your Papa burned the body while I watched to make sure we got them all. But they'll come back. The ground brings the fruition of the curse, and the Forsaken shall spread its seeds. Least, that's what the Ancestors foretold." She releases her grip on my hand, and I bite down on my lip, hard. "Ellie?"

My throat's still tight, too much so to speak, but I nod. If any of us—Mama, myself, or my sisters—touch the Bloodbud, we'll complete the ritual.

Mama's lips purse, brows creased together. There's a crash, then a squeal that can only be Lillian. I crane my neck past the threshold when Kylie hollers something to my sister, but they don't come into view. Weight pools in my gut. How am I supposed to keep the two of them maintained? I turn back to Mama, question at the tip of my tongue, then swallow the words.

Her eyes blur when we lock gazes, something gray and unfamiliar in her willow moss and kindling, then it's gone. My stomach sinks further, and I hold my hand to the silvered thread on my skin. Mama don't mention nothing, so neither do I. She'll find 'nother flask on her nightstand by tomorrow evening, and neither of us will speak 'bout it. "So, I got to watch Kylie and Lillian."

Mama nods, her face worn and lips drawn. "Just until this year's cycle passes. If we make it to then, the curse won't return for another hundred years."

I close my eyes. An *entire* year. They have to be corralled, kept from danger: Kylie with her haughty temper and Lillian with her incessant need to grab what have her. The gift spins 'round in my chest, a flurry of movement that brings my frets to new heights.

It's the blessing and curse of us witches: an ability to see hallucinations and shapes that don't exist, frightful messages in the shadows between worlds. The deranged manner of hearing voices that ain't there, soft hisses that warn 'gainst enemies, prompt toward magnified creation, lull happily in the presence of familiar magic. And the veined touch of the nonexistent. The chills that crawl up my spine when in danger, and the warmth that furls through my chest when I'm near William.

We don't have five senses; we have eight. And all of mine are locked rigid with fear.

Just as my breaths tighten and catch in my chest, Mama's hand is at my hair 'gain. Her palm makes a smooth journey over it in continuous strokes 'til I can breathe once more.

"A year," I say and meet Mama's gaze.

Our willow moss and kindling greets one 'nother. I think on Grannie's writing, of the warning I've read to Kylie and Lillian a dozen times over, but didn't quite get to today.

If a Hallivard sees a Bloodbud, with petals gray like thunder, leaves red as the setting sun, run. Always, always run.

2

FLASH OF A FROG'S TONGUE

Ellie Hallivard

"LILLIAN," I growl, the wind a harsh bite 'gainst my face as it sprinkles dirt along my lashes and hair as we make our way to the pond.

My sister don't give up her chase. Just feet 'head, the gray bunny bounds beneath a bush. Its twined branches give a great shudder at the impact, but Lillian's flash of auburn don't slow.

She's not ...

Lillian launches herself after the animal with a squeal. Her shoulder ends up 'gainst the brush, skinny arm thrashing under its branches in her futile search. I'm unsurprised when her hand returns without a prize. Suits her right, the way she's now ruined her dress. It's yellow and bright, with flowers sewn in the hem by my own hand. Mother's cain't quite hold the needles right no more.

I fiddle with the fresh bandage over my wrist, then wince. The cut's still tender, even with the healing gauze I smoothed over it this morning. Mama's medicine will be firm and ready to bottle by tomorrow evening, though she wasn't happy when she spotted my bound arm earlier.

Lillian helped my bitter mood lessen, telling me how she likes my needlework, all delicate and pretty. I cain't help the blossom of pride that swelled in my chest 'cause Grannie used to be great at her needlework and told me I got the hands for it. Lillian smiled, all bright teeth, cheeks plumped up as she traced her fingers over the threaded petals. It's a smile I cain't see right now 'cause she's plunged herself waist deep in the foliage after her hand came up empty. As I watch, she wiggles her way deeper.

"Lillian!" My teeth snap together, and she stills, then scampers up onto her knees to peer down into the bush, like the creature hasn't already scurried far off. My arms are as cross as I am. "Lillian Hallivard, you leave that bunny alone now, you hear me? It done got 'way already.

I huff when her lips pucker out, all pink and glistening. Babysit my sisters, Mama told me, like it's easy to keep them under control. I should be in the Orchard with the other witches my age, picking the harvest and singing beneath Ol' Molly, her ancient limbs hung low like they sagged in age. Today's a good day, too, with the breeze and all. But Lillian had taken off at first chance, and I was left to chase her. She's bent on seeing what she calls "her lily pad pond." I done told her it ain't named after her, but she's stubborn, this one. She skips 'head of me, a flurry of soft hums and giggles.

I keep a sharp eye on the flaming locks of red that curl past her shoulders, then set my gaze to check the area 'round us as we walk. There's a phantom weight to my wrist, like Mama still got 'hold of it, and my ears sting with that fearful tremor in her voice as she spoke of the curse. The gift spins in my chest, but don't give out no warnings that something might be wrong, and the tension in my shoulders eases.

At least Kylie's happy to follow Papa along his routes out in the fields. She'd make a better rancher than a witch, but it don't matter much. Most likely, she just wants Papa's approval, stuck to him the way I'm stuck to Mama. But I sometimes wonder if there's a boy out by the pastures, and that's why she heads off at dawn when she's able.

I bite my lip, thoughts drifting to William: his green-grass eyes that crinkle in the corners, warm smile that lifts bowed lips, sweet aroma of pine dust and sweat and cider and, on occasion, strawberries. But he ain't of the Orchard so he don't know 'bout the witches. He's a townsperson, and his daddy don't like me no how. Still, he's mine to cherish, the man I want to keep by my side. The gift fans out in my chest and leaves warm trails in its place at the notion of William. My magic sure like him, too.

"Sissy." Lillian stomps the ground in front of me. I shake my mind to clear the musings. My sister's got her lips pursed and brows furrowed. "You gon' come on, or do I gots to wait on you all day?"

With a roll of my eyes, I lift my skirts and pick up the pace toward the pond. Lillian's a whole 'nother story, Ancestors guide her. Even at eight, she's got a spirit like none other I know. A neighboring boy, Timothy, calls her *rabid* when they play leaps and frogs 'cause Lillian's always jumping *high* instead of *long*. Just this morning, Mrs. Broussard had called after us as we made our way to the edge of the woods and beyond, a glint in her eyes and laughter at her lips when she deemed Lillian a spinster heart. And she is, an uncontrollable force that cain't be yanked inside a house and domesticated.

So, I follow her with a nervous flutter to my chest as we break out from the forest and into the acreage that hosts the pond. Part of me wants to yank her up and keep her inside 'til this year's over. The other part knows that ain't a way to live— life cloaked in fear of what might come. It's why I gave Mama a grim smile as we left the house this morning for the pond.

My gaze catches skyward. *Lillian's* pond. Though she ain't

got claim to it. A chuckle bubbles in my throat, but I push it down as we reach our destination.

It's a large clearing, though the way it's enclosed by the trees makes it cozy still, like a big blanket. The sun peppers out over the water to cast shades of green and gold on the surface. Lily pads litter the top of the smooth body, and Lillian runs straight to them. My spine snaps taunt, and I search the shadowed edges for a hint of red or gray. There ain't nothing, just overgrown shrubs, thick vines, and trees competing 'gainst one 'nother for light.

"Sissy, hold me up," Lillian shouts, her eyes agleam as she turns back to make sure I'm behind her.

The dress has a splatter of dirt down her left side, and I bite my lip to hold back a howl of frustration. "Why I gonna play with you when you gone and messed up your dress? I've just got more laundry to do."

Lillian's eyes draw wide, on the verge of a shine that touts a tantrum. But I hold firm. She needs to grow up a bit, especially with Mama in her condition. If she breaks down in sobs, I won't coddle her—she can wail all she wants.

She don't. There's a shift in the grass to her right, and her eyes flash to the movement. "Lizard!"

I flinch at the squeal, then she's off in her own little world, different as it may be, to chase down the reptile that's caught her attention. Her curls bounce and dance as she sprints, a coil of red over the sunshine of her dress. The flowers I sowed in the hem drag on the ground, and I hold back a groan, then make my way in a loop 'round the edges of the clearing. Lillian's tucked inside where I can keep an eye on her.

Even as I glance into the shadows and pull brambles back to peer into the forest beyond, eye out for flashes of red and gray, I ain't too concerned. The gift's curled up in a slumber like it ain't got a care, so it ain't sensed something I should worry 'bout. After 'nother pass, I plop down near an oak, frowning at the way Lillian hovers near the water's edge, her hands a frantic reach-drag, reach-drag as she tries to grasp a lily pad just out of reach. Her brows furrow, and the slim pink of her tongue pokes out between slender lips. It's times like these that I wonder how I came out level-headed 'cause my sisters sure got some funny little antics.

Mama could get Lillian to behave, but she's losing focus more and more. A lone glint of light hits my eye, and I squint upward. The canopy overhead weaves out a thicket that blocks most of the sun. I wish I could block out the spirits that threaten us in the same way, crisscrossed limbs formed from strength and grace and impunity.

Mama's got more gray in her eyes every day, but she refuses to acknowledge the spirit that's settled on in. She mutters to herself now. I can hear her at night, talking 'bout the ice in her mind, how it's all cold. That's what she'll tell Papa over and over 'gain while I sit just outside the door and listen. Cold. So *cold*. There's always the rustle of fabric as Papa tries to tuck her in tighter, give her a warmth that I don't think she can feel no more.

If we weren't exiled, we'd call on the Blackwoods for a Requiem. They could try to dispel the spirit from Mama's mind. But she refused the Reunion of Kin when time came for her to contact the Blackwoods.

My gut churns, and the gift kicks up from its slumber. I push it 'way. What's been done is past, we've got the now and the present. My hand clenches, and I rip up a patch of grass, the dirt cool where it falls from they ends to crumble in my palm. A breeze rustles through, and I glance 'round for my sister, but she's nowhere I can see.

She cain't be far. Probably chased that lizard up a tree. I lean back and wait for her to sneak behind me. She does that—likes to scare Kylie and myself when she can. Crickets chirp all 'round, the wind gentler here under the copse of the forest, as opposed to our trek out in the open. 'Nother few minutes go by while I watch a frog on a lily pad, mouth ajar, patient in its wait for a water bug to crawl just the tiniest bit closer. All at once, its tongue erupts out from its gaping maws and whips out over the water. Just like that, the bug was there, now it's gone. A blink and I wouldn't have seen a thing.

I glance 'round for Lillian, certain she'll pounce at any moment to tell me 'bout the scene. She loves her lily pads, after all. I know she was watching.

But she don't.

"Lillian?" My voice carries in the clearing with no response. Under my hand, I twist more blades of grass and swallow 'gainst the slender ice in my chest. "Lillian?" Still, no response. Stomach clenched tight, I scramble to my feet and whip my head 'bout to scan the full circle of the clearing. "Lillian Hallivard, you get yourself over here right now! Right now, I says, unless you don't want to play."

My voice wavers, a sick harmony of anger and fear. I'm supposed to keep an eye on her. She ain't to be left alone. Mama's stern face and wide, worried eyes flash in front of me. It had been a moment in my mind, thinking 'bout her affliction with the spirits. There's no way it's been longer than that.

Movement catches my eye, the frog from before. It flicks its tongue out at 'nother unsuspecting insect, the pink little more than a dash. Then, it leaps and submerges beneath the surface, the same place Lillian was leaned out over, trying to touch them lily pads. My gut drops and flips.

The pond.

Lillian's pond.

I'm at the water's edge in an instant, staring into its surface like the algae hue will grow crystal clear just for me. If only I could cast spells, like them highest of the high in the Coven, like them Blackwoods do. My thoughts take a quick leap to the grimoire Mama got tucked under a false bottom in her cupboard, filled with spells of black magic. Maybe I could speak a few words of the Old Tongue and turn the water opaque to search for Lillian. But I cain't. Instead, my hands pass over it in a frenzy, before dipping in to paw at it like our hounds when they swim.

I wrench at the surface and screech out my sister's name. Under my knees, the dirt turns to mud, my dress ruined, but it don't matter. Not when Lillian's gone. The gift lunges forward from where I'd pushed it 'way. It twists a white-hot brand of fear in my throat.

"Lillian," I shriek, voice broken and raw from that single word I scream 'gain and 'gain. "Lillian! Lillian!"

Only the wind answers. The willows flutter in its grasp, all soft and calm, like they taunting me. There's no use in this. I cain't find her by thrashing 'round like a fool. My hand gives a final, desperate scrape, the water threading between my fingers like wearisome birdsong on dewy spring mornings. I stumble to my feet and spin 'bout, ready to sprint home and find Papa. Someone. Anyone who can come here and help me. Or hold me.

Then the gift stills and sinks, hardens and comes forth in a slow stretch, like it's uncertain. The magic unfurls to cast shadows over my vision. Shapes extend out from it, images of ghastly canines that still my blood, followed by collapsed figures and burning torches. Black silhouettes with clawed hands that cut to a marrow-deep place where the magic rests, sending a bout of fear stronger than any spirit's ever invoked.

Smoke clogs up in my throat, even though the day is clear as fresh-blown glass. I choke 'gainst the soot and taste of iron, the feel of winter's air on my teeth and fire in my heart. The visage gags me, but I fight it 'til I can think clear 'cause Lillian needs me to be strong, to leave here now and find a witch that can help.

Then the voices burst forth in a lamentation that wrecks my mind and drops me to my knees.

Curse. Empty. Death.

I think I wail. It feels like it, the way my throat clenches up and my chest burns. My mind wrenches, and I drop my head to my hands like that will keep the voices from shattering it to pieces.

Forsaken. Forespoken. Infected.

Mama's frail hands and frantic face sifts to my mind's eye. Charcoal grips my throat. *Ancestors, guide me.*

Lillian ain't in the pond.

Opus lex Baeroot - Protection from the Beyond

Ingredients to be gathered the night of an absent moon or a full moon.

Poultice protects daughter-bearing witch from the spirits. It creates wards around the mind that provide stability to sanity and further strengthen the bond between the body and the gift to slow degeneration of thoughts.

- Bark of oak, aged 102 years
- Left femur feline, black of coat
- Sage
- Hawthorn
- Robin's egg, fresh lain
- Blood of daughter, first-born, from source
- Moss of willow
- Spirit ash
- Groot worm, live
- Beak of crow, whole

To be mixed before sunrise.

Light sage and allow smoke to envelope oak bark until rot has firmed. Place in cauldron.

Crush left femur of feline until it is of a fine powder. Place in bowl. Strip hawthorn and mince, then add to bowl. Burn moss of willow until it is ash, add to bowl, then mix all contents until blended.

Pour mix into cauldron. Stir in blood from first-born daughter, then place cauldron on hearth and bring to simmer. Set until last bird song of morning.

After last bird song, add yolk of Robin egg. Repeat name of daughter(s) thrice. Bring to boil. Slowly stir in ash of spirit while chanting the Last Lamentation. Upon the final word, stop addition of the ingredient.

Add groot worm and mix until disintegrated. Drop in beak of crow. Beak of crow may be worn around neck for added protection. Bottle brew. Take one spoonful of poultice every night. If symptoms of spirit possession occur, begin taking a spoonful of poultice in the morning and at night. Poultice does not guarantee protection from spirit possession, but aides in warding.

3

OUR LITTLE LILLIAN

Ellie Hallivard

LILLIAN'S alight in her own brimstone of joy, the way she bounces at the balls of her feet next to the pond like this ain't the worst day of my life. *Our* lives. Mine and hers and our family's and this Clan's and all the Coven's. She's still got that splash of mud down the length of her dress, but there's 'nother stain, too. Darker. Deeper. Spread out on her breast and over her skirt at her knees. Right in the places where, if she knelt and fanned out her dress, the fabric would sweep the ground.

"Sissy," she says, continuing to hop from one foot to 'nother in her fervor, the water's surface murky beside her. It warps her reflection, distorts the chubby flesh of her cheeks to something jagged and dark. "You gots to come see this. It all pretty and delicate, just like them flowers you done sewn in my hem."

Then, soundless in a way she ain't never been with her squeals and clambered steps, Lillian bounds into the woods. Her auburn curls disappear into the foliage like a fox tail. But I cain't move to follow. If it weren't for the harsh gusts of my own heaving chest, I'd half-believe I wasn't breathing. The voices shriek at me. *Flee. Run. Predator.* Down in my legs, the gift wrenches itself to pieces, a demand to escape the threat it's sensed. All 'round, the foliage moves, shifts. It warps itself to scenes of fangs and clenched hands that be more like claws. There's a threat here, a monster.

It's Lillian. Little Lillian.

Lillian, with her hair a wild ring 'bout her head, palms made to grasp what she shouldn't, eyes frenzied in they need to explore and pursue. My sister, who makes my jaw twitch when she shirks her chores and who causes Kylie's voice to rise in ire at her childish antics. Sweet Lillian.

I haven't moved. Here by the pond, I can pretend nothing has happened and it's all the same. Like we've just arrived at the water's edge, and she's up a tree after that lizard, just as I'd thought. That this clearing's safe, just as I'd thought. I'd made my rounds, checked the shadows and the forest beyond. Maybe I'm asleep, and this is nothing but a nightmare made to haunt my dreams. Just Kylie pulling pranks and slipping night terror into my morning tea. She's done it before.

But the gift ...

That image shatters when Lillian bursts back into the clearing, eyes wide and lit in something that flashes and sparks. "Sissy! You gots to come on, now."

Her voice wavers in excitement, drawn out like the clicks of crickets as they slide them legs over one 'nother. Any other time, I'd roll my eyes at her and trudge on after the blighted path she made between the trees. Now, I gasp a stuttered breath. My limbs shake under the magic that begs them to escape the predator it senses.

Lillian waits on me, her head tilted forward, and 'gainst the will of the voices that scream she's a monster, a beast, a killer, I move to follow. 'Cause *this still Lillian.* She's right here in front of me, almost the same. There's only a phantom thing of change. My sister's answering beam sends the gift to brambles, the screams heightened 'til my head might burst. But it's my heart that stutters. It's such a Lillian smile, full of excitement with a sugar crisp of mischief. Goose prickles rise along my arms, and the pond shifts to illusions of snapped bones, all while the voices keep they chants.

Forsaken. Killer. Predator.

Despite the violent pull of the gift, a part of me brightens and coos at her gleeful expression, happy to please her, happy to follow and do as she bids. It's a backhand of a contrast, the fury of the voices 'gainst the gut-rolled desire to submit to Lillian's whims. My mind throbs, woozy.

Lillian stays feet 'head of me this time, rather than scrambling off so far that I cain't see where she left to like she's grown to do in recent years. The wood's quiet as we walk. There's no trill of birds or deafening rattles of cicadas. All along my skin, gooseprickles of unease spread.

Unnatural, the voices mewl. *Forespoken. Infected.*

I shake my head as though I can dispel the sandpaper grate of they words. When Lillian pulls up to a stop, I don't notice 'til I'm right on her. She smells … different, like winter air before a harsh rain. There's 'nother flash of disquiet in my chest, a wrongness that clenches my throat, but I cain't place it. Her nostrils flare, eyes a quick spark of kindling and silver. Just the way Mama's eyes flash with the shadow of the spirit in her, only I flinch at this glint. It's sharp, a needle-prick to draw blood. The gift moans, but I slam it down as best I can.

I'm 'bout to insist we turn 'round, head back home to Mama and Papa 'cause surely they'll know how to fix this. Then, Lillian spins to me. "You see them, Sissy? Ain't they pretty?"

My brows furrow, and I glance left and right. See what? It's all vines and brush and trees and Lillian's body wound tight and set to quiver in her anticipation. She moves 'gain when I don't answer, 'round a rotted trunk that reaches over my head and extends longer than my arms. The coiled nausea in my gut twists, but I walk past the dead tree anyways—follow Lillian though a blackened part of my soul *knows* I shouldn't. When I step into the little inlet of grass, the gift *howls*.

I shriek at the onslaught of the voices and grasp my head in my hands, but they don't let loose. My mind rings with they wails, immobilized, and tears well in my eyes as I bite back a sob for the pain they cause me. They need to *let me go*; they need to break they hold on my bones so I can see what's causing them to scream, or so I can finally flee the way they been begging me to.

It's been seconds at most.

It seems an eternity.

Finally, the voices slacken enough that I can blink bleary eyes into the scene 'head of me. My hands cover my mouth as it drops in dread.

A lady's set up 'gainst a cedar, her dress torn and face ashen.

Dead.

At once, I reach to grab Lillian, but she's too far 'way, tiptoeing to the corpse like I didn't just have a fit. My stomach churns, and I take a step back. The body must've been here at least a day. It's all pale whites and blues and creams—even the brown of her hair's been dulled to a somber hue. That's when I see it, poking up from the woman's bloodied palm like she's holding it for safe-keeping. Its blooms stand out, stark gray, just as Mama and Grannie said they would be, and its leaves burn red as the setting sun.

Bloodbud.

'Nother bloom shies out from her shoulder, this one smaller, and a final flower creeps between the swollen flesh of her shredded knee. As though pushed by a breeze I cain't feel, Lillian nudges forward. She kneels all graceful—too much so— and her knees rest in a rusty puddle 'round the body. I choke in a breath as the tacky substance soaks into her dress.

Blood.

The stain is *blood*. My hands tremble, and I take 'nother step back. Twigs crunch under my foot, and the voices crescendo, a litany of pleas and warnings and belligerent wails, but I cain't tear my gaze from my sister kneeling in a thicket of the corpse's remains.

Don't matter how hard anyone scrubs, that stain will never come out. Not ever.

She's a painting of red and yellow and cream, backdropped with the foliage and shadows 'round us. Iron hits my tongue, and I release my bottom lip from my teeth. The flesh burns from where I've bitten through, but it don't matter as Lillian shuffles 'round on the ground.

My sister brushes the lady's hair back all ginger like, as though the corpse is just sleeping and she don't want to disturb her. The lady's eyes stare out, already the glossy blue of the deceased, and Lillian passes a finger over the petal sticking up from a pale shoulder. It shifts; brushes back, I think, the way it lifts to the hand that pets it, straining to rub gray buds 'gainst her open palm.

My gut drops. This ain't happening. It cain't be. It must be a night terror, and I'm lain out by the pond. There is no Blood-bud, no body, no oil in my stomach that threatens to fill my throat and suffocate me. No aching voices or gooseprickles.

I can almost believe it, if I close my eyes. But they wide open, just like the lifeless blue ones of the dead woman in front of me.

Lillian looks up. Her gaze silver like lightning in the midst of a storm. They have the flash of whips and shift like serpents.

The voices scream.

I do, too.

'Cause this is real, and even if I close my eyes, I'll still see Lillian's. A wounded whimper rips past my lips. It's a lamentation that breaks my magic as much as my heart. Those silvered eyes widen. Already, the edges start to glisten, the way they do when she's on the verge of unleashing a sob.

"Sissy," she gargles.

It's a wet sound, and I almost imagine she's my Lillian. Little Lillian. But she's not. She's lost her willow moss and kindling.

This is the curse Grannie warned us 'bout; the ritual Mama told me to keep my sisters safe from. *Grace of the Coven, bless me.* I've failed us all.

But it's too late now. Lillian's gone. So, I do the only thing I can, the action ingrained in me through bedtime stories and Clan lessons and the bracing instinct of the gift—I run.

Over the shrill screeches of the voices, I can hear Lillian. She screams my name over and over and over 'til it's a wind-song, ready to haunt me no matter where I go. That winter's air I smelled on her wraps 'round my chest and fills it with a numbed stream of fear.

I can run from the Bloodbud, but I cain't run from my sister. She'll follow me in my nightmares, my guilt, locked in corners of my body I dare not touch lest magic and regret singe a hole right through me. She's not a witch no more, but no one knows what to expect when the curse comes to full fruition. Not Mama nor Grannie nor Miriam Hallivard.

Trees slash by me, branches breaking 'gainst my face and snagging in my hair. My foot hits the ground wrong, then turns, a slice of pain lancing up my shin. But I don't slow down. 'Cause of the few things I do know, one is to run.

I've brought destruction down on the Coven, if the prophecy of the Forsaken is true—the creature brought forth by the Bloodbud. I know Mama will never look me in the eye 'gain, nor Kylie. My throat tightens, and my breaths lock up. They stagger out in harsh chords, and my chest burns from the strain. The forest blurs when I cain't tamp down the terror and grief that's amassed in my stomach, and it tumbles out in tears. I know a good many things, terrible things, but the worst of them stings deeper, to a spot in my heart that bleeds.

My sister's a creature that ain't witch nor human. The Ancestors warned us of the Forsaken to come of the Bloodbud, an evil being, a predator more vicious than the spirits.

But they didn't know it'd be our Little Lillian.

4

A CURRENT THAT ACHES

Lillian Hallivard

IT HURTS, the way my tooths slice through gum and flesh, pricking my tongue to draw blood. Why do they throb so? Like they alive and begging me to do something with them. It's a constant thrum that crosses my eyes and makes my lips twitch, the world nothing more than a mad landscape grating 'gainst my skin. I want Sissy. She makes things better. She'd know what to do. She's good at healing pain.

But she ran from me.

My lips quiver, and I stroke my Bloodbud. The blooms lift they petals to my fingers, all smooth and velvety, and a wet hiccup leap out my throat. There's a rattle o' pebbles in my belly where it sit all unsteady and such 'cause I gots to go home, but I also know what this flower be. It a bad thing. Sissy told us 'nough 'bout the Bloodbuds from Grannie's journal, so I know it a curse, and I know I Infected.

I lift my hand, but it don't look no different from where I been petting that pretty flower. Hesitant fingers prod my cheek, then slip in to touch my new tooths. They all sharp and sleek, like them canines our mutts got. A furrow draws down my brow, and I take a slow stand from where I been plopped down by the lady with her hazy blue eyes. Ain't nothing different 'bout my legs, neither.

It just be my sharp, new tooths.

This ain't bad at all—sure ain't a reason for Sissy to have run or for me to not go home. A grin slips 'cross my face, all wide and loony. That's what Sissy always say when I smile real big, that I look loony. She ain't never told me what it mean, but I'm pretty sure it's got something to do with being happy.

My tooths throb 'gain, a pounding that shoot up to my temple like that lit gunpowder the humans got and that Papa hate so. It pull a groan from my throat, and I huddle over. Maybe this the evil thing, a pain that worse than the voices when they get to they warbled hums and hisses. It make sense now, why we shouldn't touch them.

Even as I think it, my eyes flick up to the blooms that be sticking out that girl. The ones with they petals gray as thunder and they leaves as red as a setting sun. My fingers twitch as a static flows through me, an impulse to lean forward and touch, to pluck that flower right up out the body and keep it cradled close.

A rustle sounds on my right, and I prop my ears to it. A bunny, maybe? My shoulders perk up, and I turn to watch the shadowed edge o' the trees, with they snaking vines and gnarled branches. There's 'nother rustle, then a shape catches on the inner fringes o' the pines and oaks. A large shape.

My nose sniff him out 'fore I get a good look. There's a wafting scent o' tobacco and cornmeal mixed with iron. I wrinkle my nose up—it ain't nothing like Kylie's honey and hydrangea or Mama's vanilla and beeswax mixed with a hint o' mint. It definitely ain't Sissy's leather and sage.

My lips tremor even as the human step into view. He got broad shoulders, similar to Papa, but he squat like a boulder 'stead o' tall like a bloomed pine. Soon as he out from the shadows, the voices *scream*.

That gunpowder that move from my tooths to my mind blow, a bright pain that light me on fire and flame me out. I cain't scream, cain't move; I'm stuck still while I burn up inside. The voices wail at me to *rip, tear, shred, feast, kill, rise.* This be it. They trying to *kill* me, to gobble me up 'cause I touched the Bloodbud and they angry.

I blink bleary eyes up at the man as he come closer. There an odd smile on his lips, something that remind me o' the slime that build on the bank o' my lily pad pond. He got a stain on his shirt, like the one all 'round that girl, the one that's on my knees from kneeling in it. It's sprinkled on his pants, too, and drips down the dagger he got clutched in hand.

He say something to me, an off-beat coo, and I know I should turn and run, follow out the way Sissy did, but the voices break a crescendo. and I look up, up, up to his jaw and them veins that flutter out under it.

They blue, like the lady's eyes. And they beat, kind o' like my tooths. There's a large one that run up his temple toward his hairline, and a flurry o' them thread they way 'cross his forearms.

So many o' them little blue streams be under his skin, and my tooths snap forward. The voices scream and hiss at me to *rip* and *tear* and *shred,* but I stay right where I is 'cause I cain't do that. We don't kill, us Orchard witches. Mama told us that even as we learnt o' the Coven history and the way it doused in blood.

The man say something else, take 'nother step forward, then his gaze slip to the lady. There a change in him, a slack-jawed shift, and he stills as he stares on. The dagger dangles in his hand, then drops to the ground as he look toward the body. We wait, a pause in the air, 'til his fingers twitch, sight locked on the bloom that popping out her shoulder, 'nother caressed in her hand while the last one pokes up from a shredded knee. He takes one step forward.

And a snarl tremble out my throat even as my lips pull back to show my tooths.

It's *my* Bloodbud.

I fling myself on him, and though he a boulder and I a lone weed, he crumple to the ground when I collide with him. His eyes bug wide, lips furling back like he 'bout to roar, but all I care 'bout is that blue vein in his temple that's set to a rapid pulse, those little streams in his forearms that bulge when he curl his hands to fist, that line in his throat that expands when he opens his mouth to yell. The voices shriek as I yank his head back and sink my tooths in deep where that vein be in his neck.

Then there be blood. It spurts out to flood down my chin, and I can feel it all over my yellow dress that Sissy was huffed up 'bout cleaning, but it don't matter. Everything taste o' stinging tobacco and dry cornmeal and warm, wet iron and daisies. The man shouts, tries to pound at me with those fists o' his, but they don't move me no how. Growls rumble out my chest, and I tug his head back further as warmth spreads through my body like hot cider on a winter morning.

Don't take long 'til he ain't moving no more, but I keep my tooths in and feast 'cause that's what the voices be chanting. *Rip, tear, shred, feast, kill, rise.* And I does, all the way 'til there nothing but a trickle dripping from his throat. When that warmth stops, I grip one forearm tight and plunge my tooths in. Then, I do the other. I feast and feast and feast 'til there ain't nothing left and my belly 'bout to burst from how much o' the man I got in me.

Don't know how long it's been when I pull back. The man got a look o' carnage to him, and the blood turn over in my belly. Carnage what Papa always said be left when vultures plucked 'part dead animals. I know this bad, but everything feels so good, a summer sun over our harvest. Mama said we don't kill. Never kill. Not us Orchard witches.

A whine slips out my throat, and I wring my hands in my dress. Mama gon' make this right. She gots to.

Legs all wobbly, I stand up. There blood on my hands and dripping down my face. I cain't go back home like this, so I stumble to the stream Kylie and I found not too long ago while we was here. It run a little ways up from my lily pad pond, and it's always got silver fish lazing in it, so I like to go look when we nearby.

There's a soft bubbling sound to the stream when I get there, with little fins darting 'round under the surface. If my belly weren't all filled with pebbles, I'd try to snatch them up. 'Stead, my mouth tug down and tears blur my eyes as I set to work rubbing my hands and mouth in the water.

The blood ain't easy to wash off, but it does. The stream blushes with it, clear to pink to russet, then back to clear 'gain. I splash some water up on my dress, the yellow darkened from the wet and the stains, and scrub. My hands scrub and scrub and scrub, but it just make things worse, the stains fanning out like a cloud that's grown to blot out the sky. My lips pull back as I work, the pads o' my fingers sandpaper raw.

No wonder Sissy'd get so mad when I came home with dirt and muck 'bout my clothes. Blunt tooths dig into my cheek as I think on Sissy and her sure fingers. She'd take my dirty clothes and make them all clean and good 'gain, like she done magic on them, but I know there wasn't none o' that involved in everything getting all nice and pretty. Sissy just good like that. I growl and drop the skirts all balled up in my fists.

Maybe Sissy can fix this, too. All o' it. My chest lighten, and the pebbles in my belly start to crumble 'way. We family. We gots to be together. We the Orchard, rooted deep. Mind made up, I leave the stream and make my way towards home, past my lily pad pond and beyond, 'til I'm at the forest's edge.

My skin's all tight under the sharp glint o' the sun. It pokes my flesh, leaves little pricks o' discomfort along my nape and arms as I pass from 'neath the thick canopy o' the trees and out near the Orchard's herb garden. A soft, comforting scent o' damp soil makes my nose twitch as I cast my gaze to the drops o' water that laze on them mint leaves. Mint like Mama. I inhale deep, let it fill my chest and swirl 'round in there like the gift did just hours ago. But my mind catches on the tender flesh o' my mouth where my new tooths stick out. What Mama gon' think 'bout them?

My palm blocks the worst o' the sun from my gaze as I squint out over the thyme and rosemary plants, straight 'cross to where our house be, past the little hill. If I could fling a rock a mile far, I bet I'd hit it. Smack Kylie's window right there on the front, with its shutter that always bang hard and loud during thunderstorms. My hands wring up in my damp dress, Sissy's flowers lifted over my ankle where they been set all delicate and pretty by her stitches.

She was just scared 'cause that body. Always did shriek when I flung bugs and such at her. I catch my lip 'tween my tooths— the flat ones, not the pointy ones—and chew.

But she didn't take me with her; she left me behind like I was a stray cat she wanted rid o' or a rattler she needed to flee from.

I keep walking through the herb garden and over the hill. There ain't no one out. Not a witch nor a human, and the tightness o' my skin raise up in gooseprickles. Everything all odd. A heavy scent o' rose blossom and honeysuckle hangs in the air, but it tinged with a jarring undertone o' rotted rind. I ain't never caught a smell so fierce as I do since I touched that bloom. Just like Sissy's leather and sage that wafted 'round the shadowed tree trunks and coiled vines when she disappeared into the thick o' the woods.

Despite her leaving, a warmth swells in my belly, and my tooths slide out as I grin. My Bloodbud, with its leaves gray as thunder, petals red as the setting sun.

When I crest the hill, our house sit all crooked-like. It's taller on the left, with a wrap 'round porch and stocky windows that give it a loony smile, kind o' like mine. Kylie say it broken and need to be fixed. Mama say it has character. I just think it look like me. Home.

Even from here, Mama's vanilla and Kylie's honey flutter to my nose. It smell o' family and comfort, Sissy's sage a bridge for Papa's cedar. As I get to the bottom o' the hill, the voices slither up to swirl in my mind. They get to they hissing, a drum-roll o' noise, and I growl at them. I probably wacky, growling at something that ain't there in the open, but that okay with the witches. They know 'bout this stuff that cain't be seen or heard or felt by just anyone.

The voices shriek once more, only to settle back with a warning trill. Then, the door bursts open. It slings wide, the spring a great creak as the wood smack the side o' the house and bullets back to the frame. I flinch 'way, the noise a gunshot from the strength that it hit our home. Papa stands in front o' the door, his cheeks and neck flushed a vivid red. My legs tremor, then I'm at a sprint to him, feet light on the ground. He gon' catch me and fling me up in his arms, call me his Little Lillian 'fore he swings me 'round. My face lights up as I reach the porch, mouth open and ready to squeal, but a boom cuts through my glee.

"Get back!" Papa's bass hits me in my breast, then knocks the air from my lungs.

He ain't never used that voice on me. That one saved for rowdy townsfolk and stubborn livestock. My eyes cow wide as I look up to him. His cedar's cloaked in sweat and something hot, a pepper like them ones Kylie dared me to eat. It was red and raw and brought with it a heat that scraped up my belly and throat like a caged squirrel.

"Papa ..." My voice tapers off when he grit his teeth.

There a vein in his neck that stand out when he mad. His jaw get all tense, and it pokes right up like a river under his skin. It's there now, a faint pulse to it, that current steady where his blood runs. The ache in my tooths comes back and *sears* me. I cry out and reach up to hold the pain back, but my hand hits the points o' my new tooths and cut through the skin. It don't hurt near as bad as my mouth do. There ain't much blood, neither, but Papa looking at me like he done seen a spirit in a witch's flesh.

The vein falls 'way with the tan hue o' his face, an ashen pallor spread over his lips. Why he acting like this? He being just as bad as Sissy was. There's a low hiss at the back o' my mind, a subtle tick for every time my tooths throb with they fire. My gaze go all hazy when I seek out that vein. I like the way it move, how it *smell*. The voice crescendo. *Blood, prey, weak, feast, rip, tear.*

"No," I whine out. 'Cause they want me to hurt my Papa, and I ain't gon' do that.

The porch creaks, and I whip my head up, try to hear 'round the voices and the roar in my ears, and prop my ear to him. His throat right there, so close, and he got a sweet, happy scent in that cedar, even if the pepper a smoky sting in it. I want to sink my tooths in and *taste*.

"Go," Papa yells 'gain, only this time he gots his body blocking the doorway to the house. Where's Mama? Or Sissy? Or Kylie? Why ain't they here to help Papa 'cause there gots to be something wrong with him.

I'm shaken from the thought when he yells 'gain, only this time, he towering over me, arms curled to fists, flush a steady rise back to his neck. And as it rises, so do that sweet, sweet cedar that make my mouth water and my tooths throb. "Get 'way from here! You-you ain't my little girl no more. Ain't my Little Lillian. Get out o' here, beast!"

His voice thunders over me, and the voices shriek. They scream for me to break him, rip him 'part, take that cedar and sweat and make the ache stop. I stumble backwards. My heel catches on the bottom o' my dress, and I crash to the ground, my head snapped back to hit the hardened dirt, but it don't ring like it would have once. Papa takes 'nother step down from the porch. His gaze darkened from they hickory hue so they seem black. It's like he snatched a pair o' beetles from the dirt and plunged them in his eyes.

Then the door crash open 'gain, and Mama steps out. That warmth in my belly twists even as I whimper. Her eyes be rimmed in red, the willow moss and kindling bright, even from here, and that auburn hair that burns like mine is pulled back in a tight bun with a smooth coil in the back. Vanilla and beeswax with a hint o' mint fill my nose, and I suck in. There ain't a flurry o' veins to her like there is to Papa, but she still make my tooths throb.

"Mama," I choke out.

Her hand trembles where she's got it placed over her breast. I wait a moment while she stare at me, mouth agape, eyes the size o' ripe apples. Papa strides to her with wild movements. "Anne, get back inside. Now. Back with Eleanor and Kylie."

The sharp sting o' that pepper takes over everything now. Sissy and Kylie inside, too? Why ain't they out here to help me? I sit forward, ready to pull myself back up to my feet. "Mama!" My voice lurches out, shrill as that waxwing bird that sometime sit in the cove o' trees near my pond. "Mama, help me! Sissy—"

"Lillian, go," Mama says, voice made o' gravel.

Her gaze sits on the stains that be all over my dress. I bunch it up in my fist 'gain. She don't mean that. Cain't mean it. "Mama, you do—"

"Now," she shrieks. I flinch back, then burst to sobs. They

47

ain't never treated me like this, and my heart beats a rapid tempo in my chest. Mama pushes Papa 'way from her, and, for a moment, I think she gon' come to me, wrap me up in her arms. I stand and stumble forward, but then she's wailing at me. "Go, Lillian. You cain't be here, cain't come home. The Orchard … the Coven, they'll hurt you if they find you. Kill you. O-or you'll kill them."

Her words cut off on a gargle cry, and she sways into the balcony, her hair flashing red in the sunlight as she grips the railing tight. She don't mean it. She cain't mean it. They ain't—

"Leave!" Papa roars, then bats his chest with his fists. Mama's cries punch the air 'round us. Then, Papa launches himself down the porch at me, madness in his gaze, eyes glossed over in a wetness that ain't never been there 'fore. "Go, cursed thing. 'Way from my family. Don't you never come back!"

I scramble back and whirl 'round.

Papa swings his fist through the air as he howls. "Stay 'way from the Orchard, 'way from our land! If I catch you near here, I'll shoot you myself, don't care how much it hurts." His words gargle out at the end, like his throat closed up on him, and Mama's wails ring higher. I should leave, but I cain't move, frozen when normally I cain't keep still.

My feet shuffle, and I glance back to him and Mama. Papa's eyes is pink and puffy, too, and that vein be back in vibrant form on the side o' his neck. "Papa, it's me. It's Lillian."

"Go!" he screams one final time, a Merlin to my waxwing, then he picks up a cauldron that been set out to dry and flings it at me.

It clatters somewhere, but I don't look to see as I take off. My boots slip on gravel as Papa yells, his voice a background beat to the thuds o' each footfall as I run. The Orchard road turns, and the howls fade, but I don't stop. I cain't. Not with the way he looked at me, the things he called me. Not with Mama's cries in my skull. My heart hammers off rhythm to my sprint while the pebbles in my belly tumble and roll. But it's my tooths that push me on, lead me out, the miles easier than I thought they'd be. And when I reach the final curve toward town, my nose twitches on a sweet scent o' iron and daisies. A scent that calls out to me and sears my tooths.

Blood.

5

THE COLD THAT TRESPASSES

Ellie Hallivard

WILLIAM'S HOME'S always a mix of fine sawdust and the sharp scent of linseed oil. My nose wrinkles as I round to the shed he and his daddy got in town, they craftsmanship settled out on a well-furnished porch in the front of the shop. I cain't stay at the house with Mama and Papa. Cain't look into they eyes with them knowing what I've done, what I let happen. Cain't be there when Kylie returns from her day mourning beneath Ol' Molly.

My throat clenches as I swallow the solid hive of dread that pricks my throat, the guilt dammed up in my gut, never to break through. It'll build and build and build 'til I burst. The cotton of my dress is rough in my hands as I pick at it, a startling contrast to the satin ribbon wrapped 'round my wrist. A subtle tremor wracks my lips, and I clear my throat, then swallow 'gain like it'll change anything.

Our Little Lillian's gone. And it's all my fault. I let loose a beast that—

"Ellie?"

William's baritone rumbles to my left, and the gift flairs a sudden warmth, pushing out to my fingertips so it can touch him. A comfort. A safety. He steps further into the shop, backlit by the sun that filters in through the open door. It casts a soft glow 'round him and the log he's got hoisted up over his shoulder, the veins of his forearms strained like they might burst.

A giggle slips past my lips, then 'nother, and I double over at the harsh way they wrack my frame. It seems my Poultice of Strength and Prosperity works a little too well. Kylie'd have fits if she were here. And Lillian'd run to William, ask him for sweets, pop them in her mouth, then grin wide and loony in that way she does.

Did.

At once, the giggles crack and shatter, morphing to hitched sobs. And I cain't breathe. My arm flings out, vision blackening. William's voice rumbles 'round me 'gain, but it's distant and muddled, like he's in a different room with the door shut. Something warm clasps my hand, then slides up to settle 'cross my shoulders like a bar. The gift leaps, then tumbles up to that warmth and settles itself 'gainst my skin as though it can seep clean through. Content, the magic curls close, but my chest throbs 'cause I still cain't—

"Breathe, Ellie." William's voice worms its way to me, crisper this time.

I shake my head with palm at my breast. "C-cain't. Cain't breathe, William. C-cain't."

"Yah you can. Come on now, just breathe with me." That warmth wraps 'round my wrist and pulls it to something solid, something that moves. "Breathe with me. There yah go."

My palm follows the rise and fall of William's chest, but it cain't fix how my throat closes, mocks me and my pain. I scrunch my eyes tight and listen to William's low, "In ... out, in ... out, that's my Ellie." We stand there while I pant and gasp.

The clouded blackness of my gaze recedes with every new breath I take 'til light filters back in. William keeps his litany of praise and guidance. As he speaks, I sag into him, and he bares my weight with ease. That sweet aroma of cider and pine dust drapes over my neck and fills the aching chasm of my chest.

Eventually, the panic subsides, though I don't move from William. He keeps his arms wrapped tight 'round me as his hand traces soothing circles and lines up and down my back.

"What happened, Ellie?" William's breath gusts over my crown, a warm puff. His chest rolls in time with his low timbre.

I bite my lip and look up. His eyes are emerald in the sun that glints off them, a tiny hint of honey in they depths. They shimmer and spark a letter of concern, like everything William dares not to say just yet lies written in they hues. There's a tremor to my jaw, but I cain't cry 'gain. I've already shed so many tears.

"Lillian's dead." The whisper catches in my throat and makes its way forth in a husk.

William's hands still, his body rigid, then he pulls me 'way from where I'm cradled into him. Why's he separating us? The linen tunic in my hands crunches up as I ball my fingers to fists, unwilling to let go of him. He cain't leave me, too. I cain't lose my William.

That familiar clench forms in my throat, then a hand slips under my chin and lifts my face up. William's brows crinkle together 'til I cain't tell where one ends and the other starts. It wrinkles his nose and makes the soft line of his lips pull tighter. "Ellie, what you mean, Lillian's dead?"

Those green-grass eyes disappear as he blinks. Once. Twice. Like each time they reopen a new piece of my revelation settles into place. The longer he watches me, the brighter they grow, 'til his shock filters 'way. His gaze slides to the left, and I follow it. Then choke on a new sob.

Sitting on the chair Mama asked him to fix is a pile of

sweets. Chewy and tough, with raspberry extract woven into a cream taffy—just the kind Lillian liked. William tugs me in, wraps me up in his arms and squeezes. It crushes my bones, makes it difficult to breathe, but this time it's a good restriction, a comfort. I'd never take 'nother breath if I could stay right here in his arms.

The gift unfurls out to him and basks in the way he surrounds me. Cider and pine dust fills every inhale I take. *Home. Safe. Fortitude.*

"Oh, Ellie. I … what …" He trails 'way, unable to voice the emotions.

I know. It's impossible to put despair into words. Guilt. Shame. To feel this, mourn for yourself, then try to comfort 'nother.

But we've a story ready—Mama, Papa, Kylie, and myself. Mama said no one can know the truth. At least, not 'til we understand the gravity of what's happened 'cause the Forsaken may be a monster but it *looks* like Lillian. And it speaks like her. Enough so that I followed it to the Bloodbud and was compelled to touch the bloom myself. The gift shudders, then slithers up my spine like that'll dissipate the memory.

I bite down on my tongue, let the tiny tinge of metal ground me as I lie to the one person I wish I could speak the truth to. "We went to the pond." Lillian's pond; her lily pad one that she loved so much. "It was just her and I, and when she went off to chase the lizards, I fell asleep. She—" I stop and suck in hard, my nose twisted up in William's shirt, my forehead resting on his shoulder. "She fell in. When I woke up, she was face down in the water and …"

The words taper off, story caught in the pained tendons of my heart. There's a pit in my gut that won't never close 'gain. And in it I see that frog, vivid as the wiry brush of William's beard on my cheek as he hushes my broken sentence. I can picture its wide black eyes and the slimy green sheen of its skin.

Can practically touch the sticky pad of its tongue and catch the flash of its pink existence in the open. Just a moment. A dash.

"What can I do?" William asks.

I burrow my face further into him. "Just be here with me. That's all."

So, we stand, clutched 'gainst one 'nother. For a time, I don't feel shattered to pieces, like a mirror that's been beat and hammered to powder. It's almost enough.

William starts at the clang of metal and wood. The noise pulls us apart to spot Kylie, her face flushed and hair wrapped high atop her head. Her hip swings near one of William's many work spaces, nails and stains scattered on the table, and while she feigns accident, I know she ran into it on purpose. Her shoulder bobs up and down, head tilted slightly to the right, and her gaze locks on mine before flitting 'way. William furthers the distance between us, and a cold trespasses into the empty space. Almost as upset as myself by the loss, the gift swirls and frets.

William's hand reaches to tug at his beard, eyes hesitant as he opens his mouth then snaps it shut. I swallow hard and place my hand on his arm. What can he say to her? How can he ease our pain?

Kylie talks first. "It's best not to speak of it right now." Her voice waivers, but, otherwise, her composure remains together. Shoulders back, chin tilted up, the same as Papa when he's assessing the Orchard gates. Stoic and reserved. "But ... I appreciate"—she sucks in a sharp breath, sight trained on the sweets in Mama's rocker, then breathes out—"everything."

William nods. "Of course. I'll help however I can."

I squeeze his arm, a parting gesture, and he sends over a slim, somber smile. Kylie's most certainly come to fetch me, and I've been gone long enough. William murmurs something 'bout bringing the chair tomorrow, then Kylie and I leave through the front door and descend the pristine porch steps.

The town's a mass of movement blurred out in browns and

reds and blacks and creams. A few men circle a wagon with a broken wheel, while children squeal nearby, chasing wooden hoops 'cross a lone patch of grass. Despite the noise, silence stretches between myself and my sister 'til I cain't take it no more.

"Kylie—"

"A man's missing. And two women. Some of the townsfolk was talking 'bout it at the saloon. I didn't ask nothing after it, but they was loud in they gossip." She cuts her eyes to me, then looks 'head. "Do you think it's Lillian?"

There's a soft roar in my head as my blood rushes then fades. I count my breaths while I think on it. "Kylie, Lillian's dead. The thing that's now her, well, it ain't her. Like a witch with a spirit in them."

"So, she's possessed?" Kylie swings her head to me, body open and hope in her raised brows. "We can call for a Requiem. The Blackwoods, they'd have to come! They as much a part of this curse as we is."

I hush her and glance 'round. No one pays us any mind, and though I'm bathed in guilt and shame, I glare at Kylie 'til she tucks her chin down and thins out her lips.

"Didn't mean to speak so loud 'bout the Coven," she mutters.

No, but things we don't mean to do tend to harm us the most. A horsefly whizzes past, and I duck out the way. Kylie swings at it and knocks the pest to the ground. It gives an angry buzz, sets at us 'gain, then disappears high overhead, a black speck in a cauldron of blue sky.

I take a moment to collect my thoughts. "She's not possessed. It's not—we cain't fix this with a Requiem. It cain't be fixed at all." The chasm in my gut yawns wide, then cackles at my misery. It makes my stomach rumble with nausea. "She's gone, Kylie, and the thing that's left is a monster. The Forsaken. Nothing else."

She dips her head, and we keep walking. The town passes by

slow, then we're on the road that leads the four miles to the Orchard. Sweat starts a steady gate down my back while the flush on Kylie's face deepens. "And the man? The women?"

People disappear all the time. Boys and girls run 'way to the growth of cities. Wives flee they husbands and leave they children behind. Husbands abandon they wives and forget they have children.

But I know the Coven. Blood brews the strongest poultices. Sacrifice crafts formidable spells. It's mainly the Blackwoods that follow those archaic rituals these days, but our kind have been behind many a disappearance. There's no reason this curse shouldn't lead to some. "It's possible."

The hustle of town dies 'way, leaving the steady rhythm of our footfalls and soft whisper of our breaths for company. Even the birds have quieted in the trees that lie scattered 'bout, though the cicadas keep to they song. My vision loses focus and catches on the path we follow, crafting mirages that shimmer and fade. I'm lost in a space of emptiness, kept going by lack of thoughts and a hazy sight, when Kylie startles me by speaking.

"I don't think I can forgive you. Don't think I ever will. But I don't hate you, neither. Cain't. You're the only sister I got left."

My eyes blur over. These tears must never end, a waterfall that wells deep in my body and replenishes as fast as blood bubbles forth from a cut. I bite my lip and keep my gaze forward. It's more than I could ask for, but I'm selfish when it comes to family, and I need more.

When I'm sure I can talk without losing control of my voice, I clear my throat. "I'm still to be Matriarch of the Orchard. Cain't change that I'm the first-born daughter. Someday, you'll have to forgive me." I pause to look at her, but she keeps her eyes forward, the honey wheat of her hair blinding under the sun. "And someday, I hope I'll have earned it."

Opus lex Baeroot - Blessing of Strength and Prosperity

Ingredients to be gathered during sunrise. For most potent blessing, create during waning moon. Do not mix in the occurrence of an eclipse— consumers have been known to suffer infertility in these cases.

Poultice heightens chances of consumer finding prosperity in life while strengthening both the physical body and the mental wellbeing.

- Ripest apple from Ol' Molly in Orchard
- Two silver coins
- Canine mandible, 2 years of age
- Bark of oak, palm-sized
- Strands of the unheard
- Garden weed
- Wings of dragonfly

Boil apple in water until skin is soft and supple. Remove and puree. Return to boiling water. Melt coins over hearth and add to mixture. Stir until blended. Grind canine mandible until it is a fine powder. Add half of the powder to kettle and recite gratitude for affluence and health.

Lower to a simmer and whisk in strands of the unheard. Recite chosen name of consumer thrice whilst stirring clockwise. Recite name of consumer thrice whilst stirring counterclockwise. Allow to simmer for half a day.

Burn garden weed to ashes, then mix poultice until blended. Whisper wishes for prosperity and strength into dragonfly wings so they might carry words into brew. Crumple wings in hand and stir into poultice. Return to boil and pour in remaining powder from canine mandible.

Simmer through night. At first light of day, remove from hearth and allow to cool. Bottle brew.

Consume with care— no more than one ounce should be ingested per week.

6

IRON AND DAISIES

Lillian Hallivard

THERE ARE people out in town. Dust settles 'round boots as they stomp and kick, then flies up to cling on clothes the way flour do when Mama and I cook for the family. No one notice me at first. It's probably 'cause I so small and they all looking straight 'head rather than down. Might be why they don't see the dust the way I do.

My tooths throb a painful beat, and a groan builds up in my throat. I want Sissy back 'cause she good at healing my aches. There's a sharp twist in my belly, and I double up, but it ain't a hunger. This a different twinge, one that be sharper than my cry for Sissy. It 'bout them Bloodbuds that I left behind.

My Bloodbuds.

Grannie'd always babble on 'bout the curse and the Ancestors and the Bloodbuds. She'd just snap her mouth, all angry-like, and tell us they evil, same as the Blackwoods that curse the Orchard Clan with them. The voices told her the flower would bloom for us—it like our blood. And that what the gift shown me in the clouded blue eyes o' that dead girl 'fore I petted those blooms. Didn't do what Grannie said we should: run. If a Halli-vard witch touches them, the ritual done filled. It's a premonition.

My nose wrinkle, and I turn the word over in my mind. Prim-uh-ni-shun. Kylie said it like seeing in the future. Kind o' how we know when it gon' rain 'cause the air catch a scent o' damp grass and the sky go gray.

I think they all nice, them Bloodbuds, the way they leaves burn red like the setting sun, petals gray and lovely like thunder. If I'd been thinking straight, I'd have gone back to my lily pad pond with that lady and the blooms that been sticking out o' her, but Papa scared me sideways, yelling at me like I a crow in a field, ready gobble up his harvest. So, I ran up the gravel path, my feet a flurry, chest filled with a hail-storm heart that hit and pounded like ice was trying to break through and puncture me. And here I is, with my tooths on fire. My nose sniffed out these ambling folks the way hounds find ducks pebbled through they throats by bullets.

It's the blood. It calls.

This the town I never did get to come to when Sissy visited William and Kylie helped the Orchard sell apples and jams and ciders at the square. I squint over at a blue wagon with pink and white and yellow flowers bundled up in it. It gots to be the one Kylie'd always came home and coo 'bout 'cause she wanted to paint our wagon, too. Maybe Kylie's here? She could be just 'round the other side, then she can take me home to Mama and Sissy. She ain't yelled at me or ran from me.

I step forward, but someone 'cross the way hollers, and I stumble back. Everything's all wrong. The noises is so much louder than they need be, and my eyes focus on ruddy cheeks and bobbing necks from too many paces 'way. The sun's a blanket where it drapes over me, oh so nice, though it make my skin feel a size tighter than it should, and my nostrils burn, joyous with the scent surrounding them. It smell like iron and daisies. My tooths throb a hair harsher.

"Where's your family, child? It ain't good for you to be out all on your own."

I whip my head 'round to the voice. It's a man, his neck red from the day's heat, a crescent o' sweat along his hairline. He looks a little like Sissy's William, but not really. William all tall and strong and sure, while this one got a pudge to his belly and his arms jiggle when he swipe dust from his brow. He smell sour; grease mixed with apricot. My nose wrinkles, but there's a searing ache in my tooths that makes my belly grumble.

I cain't tell him my family don't want me no more. He cain't know how Sissy ran from me, her face twisted in fright, watching my eyes like they stung her. My stomach flop, tooths sinking down into tender gums. It's all new. They didn't use to move like this, my tooths. I sniffle and blink at him. The man put his hand on my shoulder like he 'fraid I might disappear if he let go. "Girl, you alright? Where's your family?" His gaze bug out, as wide as Opal's, Mama's mare, as he look at the stains on my dress. There's a twitch in his fingers where he grip me. "This ain't your blood, is it?" He eyes the russet, shakes his head, then gives me squeeze after a moment. "We gonna find your pa and ma right now, so there's no need for them tears you got building there. It all gonna be okay."

His eyes so kind, glittering brown and green and gold and black. They remind me o' the forest edge at day break, like home, and I whimper 'cause he smell something terrible, but it good, too, and I don't know how to tell him that my family sent me off, that they ain't any place 'round here for him to find.

All o' it makes my head hurt, and I'm sure I got a wood-pecker after my mind, the way it pricks so. Don't help that my tooths blaze and my gaze stalks his throat where blue veins wind down 'neath his shirt, same as the vines on those trees 'round that body where the flowers perched. Those ones with red leaves and gray petals.

I didn't want to leave them, but I had to.

Taking his rough hand in mine, I pull him 'way from the curious people o' the town. They let us go like they still ain't looked down to me, off minding they chores. The man follows my lead behind a building and past the wagons 'til we at the trees. It's odd, how the town all dusty, the roads gravel and stunted, but there's always woods 'round, the ground covered in pine needles and grass. His scent pushes me forward 'tween soundless trunks, the forest crackling 'neath our feet the deeper we go as sunlight drips through branches overhead. This a day for running in the fields and playing with the hens.

His big hand squeezes mine and tugs. "This cain't be where they at. Come now, we'll go back to the square and get you set up with Madam Roux. She can take care o' you 'til I find your parents."

I don't say nothing and stop 'stead, looking 'round. We ain't going nowhere. Not really. We was just getting 'way from the others 'cause the warped hiss o' the voices telling me that we gots to be alone. They all jumbled up there, not at all the way my mind used to talk to me 'fore I touched those pretty flowers. That's what gift the witches got. We see things that ain't there and hear things that don't make sound and feel things that cain't be touched.

But now, the whispers be all harsh and grating—they clench 'round my chest and make me think 'bout doing terrible things, things I need to do if I want to keep on. My thoughts flash to the man in the woods, with his scent o' tobacco and cornmeal, and the way his blood was oh so sweet in my throat.

I stare up into the kind eyes that furrow at me in concern. "Don't you want to stay with me?"

The man sway a bit, then lean forward. His eyes cloud over with a dusted haze and he tilts his head like he need to be closer to me. I wonder if he got a family, too. Do they love him, or would they leave him if he touched a Bloodbud, same as my kin? I can still see Sissy as she disappeared 'tween the pines and willows, deaf to the way I screamed her name. How Mama howled as Papa held her back and roared for me to leave, to abandon the Orchard.

The man smiles at me. "Of course, I want to stay, if that's what you want."

I nod, and the voices loose a crazed screech, a vile instruction. Kylie always said that really bad things be vile, like them Blackwoods is. My eyes land at his throat. I don't want to—I cain't. Not 'gain, like I did that stocky man near my lily pad pond. But then my tooths jut forward, all pointy and excited, and my nostrils twitch.

Everything in sight shine and dew over, and my belly's queasy, but the hunger means more than anything now. "Yes'ir, I want you to stay a bit longer. I want you to sit down."

He don't question me, gaze locked on mine, then he drops to his knees so my eyes leveled on his forehead. We the same height like this, with him on his knees, those warm eyes on mine; I bet he could see how dusty the town is if he stayed here.

Mama always said the humans gull'ble. She used that word a lot—gull-i-ble. It means something like easy to confuse, I think. But he don't seem confused. Nah, he just be willing, like saying no ain't possible. Maybe if I told him to leave, he would. I should do that, push him 'way and tell him to run, fast as he can, the way Grannie and Mama said we should flee from the Bloodbuds. The way Sissy ran from me even as I shrieked her name to the empty trees.

I don't. I do the vile thing them voices hiss in my mind.

It happens quick, his homey eyes widening 'fore my new tooths tear at his throat. I grip his shoulder with pale hands, stronger than him even though I'm just a tiny girl.

We tumble back. He screams.

There's blood everywhere, and I cain't think through the joyous shrieking o' the voices and the sweet, acrid smell o' grease and apricot and iron and daisies that grips me. It don't take long for his head to loll, body held close by my clasp on his hair and shoulder. My tooths rip and tear and shred at his skin. I'm fevered in my hunger and relief floods my belly and my aching tooths. I ain't never felt so good as I does now, not even when Sissy was there to brew me healing poultices or to fix my dresses all nice and delicate with flowers sewn in the hem.

My belly still coiled up, but it ain't prickling. Nah, this like lightning in the dawn.

7

IT'S WARM IN THIS BODY

Ellie Hallivard

"AGAIN," Mama croaks, voice hoarse. It cracks like our shutters do in the wind, when they snap all harsh and angry. "Tell me again."

Kylie stands straight by the porch rail, her hands a fierce twist as she mottles together mugroot and silkworm. Her work stays calm and focused, but her eyes find mine with a glint that speaks a truth her tongue never will.

Mama's worse. Lillian's gone.

I said I'd earn Kylie's forgiveness. This is as much my fault as it is the Ancestors. As it is Lillian's for touching that Bloodbud she *knew* not to touch. But now that we're home and trying to move forward with that weight of what's been unleashed on the Coven and the fear of Mama's condition, I cain't wrap my mind 'round how to keep trudging on without sinking right through the ground and into my own grave.

"Mama," I sigh, exhausted beyond sleep and bones. Today, I

was supposed to meet William under that copse of Wisteria that winds its way on up Madam Roux's saloon. Instead, I'd sent a note of absence with Pearl and Jericho when they'd left on the Orchard's market wagon, off to town to sell the Clan's wares. "I done told you so many times. It's finished. She's gone."

Mama's eyes flash, the thunderous gray evident in them. It's a sickness we've all come to accept. Even Papa. I don't know how much time she's got left, but it cain't be much. She mixes names up, has all but forgotten the horror of Lillian's coming home, and she tried to leave the house just yesterday in her slip alone. We've a rotation between myself and Kylie to keep her from harm. Or from harming others.

"Once, Eleanor. You've told me once what happened, and you will tell me again."

Even Kylie sighs, despite the blame she places on me. I've retold what happened near the pond so many times, I think my sister could state the events in my stead. She don't. So, I indulge Mama 'gain. Every detail, every miniscule part that she would want to break down and chew on. 'Cause Mama might be sick, but if there's a way to get our Lillian back, she'll know. Some days, that's what keeps me going.

When I'm done, we sit in a silence that's broken only by the grind of Kylie's work as she prepares the balm for Mama's neck. I told her it ain't gonna help, but she's making it anyhow. It's a recipe for clarity, and if Mama were losing her mind 'cause of age, it would be of aid. But this a spirit.

A breeze saunters through, and I lift my chin up. It's a cool day. That's why we out here, even though there's only one rocker. William's yet to bring the other back, allowing my parents they space to mourn. Kylie shifts to lean 'gainst the bannister, her arms swollen and strong as she twists her wrist, and I've perched myself on the top step, the rail a thin brace 'gainst my back with my legs stretched out in front of me. It's cloudy overhead. Every so often, a rumble rolls 'cross the darkened sky, just like those shadows that crawl in Mama's sight. A warning of what's to come.

Mama mumbles to herself, then stands and throws a fistful of dirt over the porch edge. "For the chickens," she explains. Neither Kylie nor myself tell her it ain't seed she had in her hand, nor that the chickens have been in the coop for the past year to keep them safe from the coyotes. She sits back down and continues to rock without 'nother word. My gut coils, and I swallow through the tightness there.

Kylie halts her hands to rub at her wrist. My own ache for her, knowing how the motions burn. Brewing and blending and mixing the poultices takes patience and, in many cases, sinewed muscle. My fingers flit over the ribbon on my arm, the ever-present scar hidden from view. Papa started to stare at the risen skin with an ashen face, hand tight 'round Mama like he gonna lose us both, so I've taken to wearing long-sleeved dresses. He's gone today, left to the pasture for care of the horses. Kylie'd be there, too, if it weren't for Mama's condition.

My sister huffs and swipes a palm 'cross her forehead. "What we gon' do? 'Bout the Requiem?" She don't look up, voice low so only I hear.

The wind picks up, a soft scent of honeysuckle 'long its trail, and I sigh. What 'bout it? Mama refused the Reunion of Kin with the Blackwoods, so we cain't hold one. I don't say so, lest Kylie brutalize me with them eyes that so keen and wrathful. "We could ask the Matron for summons. But you know she ain't gonna come. It's nothing but a waste of parchment to call on them outside the mandated generation."

My sister frowns, brows puckered the way they do when she's got a bad thought. "Could do it ourselves, I'd think. The Requiem."

Bad thoughts, indeed. Already, a tense drum starts up in my skull. "You got what ingredients we need? Virgin candles? Splice of the Beyond? No, didn't think so. I bet you don't know them words of the Old Language that have to be spoken, neither. Even if you did, we ain't got a chance of pronouncing them right." I think to the grimoire Mama's got hidden in her room and the black magic that lay within. Each enchantment's got a bit to be recited in the Old Language, words that we ain't got a hope of saying right. I fling my arm in the direction of Ol' Molly, out of sight where she towers within the namesake of our clan, teeth grit. "We'd choke on our tongues right there in the Orchard and leave Mama with no hope whatsoever."

The mortar shakes when Kylie brings her fist down on the bannister. It clatters hard and nearly topples off the other side. Her lips roll up, and she clicks her tongue at me. "Fine, then. What hope does Mama have? She gon' leave us if we don't do something." Her voice quiets to a barely-there gust. "She gon' leave us, certain as the spirits."

I glance to Mama, perched on that rocker William made two years past. She's scratching at a splintered piece of wood near the edge of the arm. When she looks up, her willow moss and kindling is shaded in gray. The gift recoils to hide behind my sternum, nervous at this proximity to a spirit that's grown powerful in its vessel, but I shake it down. Mama's still here —for now.

"We stay with her." I try to give my voice a soothing lilt, but it don't quite lull enough. A subtle vibrato makes it waver. "And when it's time to choose her over the spirit, we will."

"You mean slit her throat," Kylie hisses, her tone low so that I almost think the voices have spoken. A shiver slides along my shoulders and up to my temple. She thinks I'm that cruel?

"Of course not," I snap back, my own patience at its peak. My eyes flash to Mama as she jerks and mutters, then I hush my voice. Not all sections of the Matriarch's grimoire are meant to be shared, and this certainly be a secret. But Kylie needs peace. And I can give it to her. "There's a poultice in Grannie's grimoire. It's meant to put vessels like Mama to rest when the spirit done taken over."

At this, my sister sits back, eyes widened in surprise, a patch of shade on her cheek that slims her face to a hollow side of frail. "How come I didn't know 'bout this? You think I don't listen when you read, but I do, Ellie. Our history means as much to me as it do you."

A heat rises to my cheeks, and I glance down to pick at the loose threads of the ribbon 'bout my waist. "It's for the Matriarch to know and any heir apparent. Mama gave me some special passages since I'm to be the leader of the Orchard when she's gone." And only now, I realize why she'd shown me that particular passage three months back. She'd known. My chest tightens, makes it hard to breathe, and my eyes flutter shut for a moment. I'm such a fool.

"Oh," comes Kylie's soft reply. She's got her attention on Mama, who's slid down a little in the rocker, eyes shut. Them broken, huffed snores that myself and all my sisters got slip past her lips. It was never a question who we inherited them from. "Ellie, how did Lillian get 'way from you? You was always so good at all things you supposed to do. So how?"

It's sudden and abrupt, the question, a hint of proclivity in it. I know Kylie blames me even as she loves me. *I* blame me. But I never thought she'd point her finger and say the words. She's more like to glare and snarl than string together biting sentences. Minutes pass while I gather myself to answer. "I got lost in my thoughts. Didn't make much of it when I couldn't see her. I'd checked the clearing for them Bloodbuds, and the gift was settled right down without a worry or a care. You know," I catch myself, a slow, hard blink as I revise my words, "knew … you knew Lillian. She'd go off and shimmy up a tree and we wouldn't hear from her for hours. It was minutes. Couldn't have been more than a few. That's all it took."

Kylie nods as I speak, then fiddles with the mortar and

pestle. "I think you couldn't of stopped it, even if you tried. Think it was fate, the work of the curse for balance. One of us three was bound to turn. Such is the way of Coven magic, an endless circle that comes to fruition. Just … just wish it'd been me." My sister's head bows, her hair loose today to frame her face and roll down her shoulders. "Ain't right for me to have been this angry at you. I just didn't know what else to do, not with all these emotions. Being angry was easier, but it wasn't right."

I've half a mind to shake her, tell her she *should* be angry at me, blame me—not herself. My body sits heavy on these steps, bottom numb from its long perch. Mama's snores still ring 'round us.

"Hush now, you. Don't you say—"

"What?" Kylie growls. "You to be Matriarch. Couldn't have been you. And Lillian was, well, she was Lillian. Our sister would have done something great with that spark she had."

"Kylie Hallivard, if you weren't here to keep the peace of this household, we'd be nothing more than fallen apples without a hope, you hear me? Mama and I would fight nonstop, Lillian would've run rampant, and poor Papa wouldn't have had anyone to help him out in the fields, since we both know these hands ain't ever gonna hold a plow."

I lift my hands up to show her, calloused from time brewing poultices. It's a thin, sad safety layer of skin when compared to Kylie's rough and strong palms. Her lips tilt, the barest hint of a smile. It's not much, but for now, it's enough to bring a scattered warmth to my heart.

"Where do you think she is? Lillian?"

To my surprise, Mama answers, her voice still hoarse from her earlier lamentations, no doubt made worse from the little snores. "Lillian? Lillian Hallivard?"

"Yes'm," I answer. She squints, then examines her hands,

turning them one way, then 'nother, like she ain't never seen them before. A frown creases my brows. "You alright, Mama?"

I brace myself for her to have a spell of sickness. We haven't gone on a walk yet, today; she might enjoy a stroll near the pasture. We could see Papa, maybe even get her to feed Opal an apple.

"I'm mighty fine, little witchling. Oh, so fine. So *warm* here in this body. A bit weak. There was a spot on her lungs that took time to fix, but that's gone now."

A chill rushes over me. *No. It's too soon.* The mortar spills from Kylie's hands and clatters to the porch. Without thought, I release the gift from where I squashed it down earlier while tired of its cautions toward Mama. It rises in an instant, straight to my mind with phantom visages of a wide, yawning mouth lynched in threads of ice. The voices squall.

Spirit. Banish. Destroy.

I'm frozen on the step, just like them apple trees out in the Orchard that are rooted down into the ground, and the terror runs as deep. Kylie's pressed 'gainst the bannister, an attempt to get as far from the thing that wears Mama as she can. My stomach roils, mind a blur to that day by the pond and how Lillian was still Lillian, but *not.*

Ancestors, guide me—I cain't lose 'nother this way. Cain't see Mama here, and yet, not.

Then the spirit smiles, a sharp, twisted grin that warps Mama's face into something nasty. Dangerous. All brazen teeth and gray, thunderous eyes.

"Kylie," I say, shocked that the words waft forth smooth and steady, "there's a vial on my dresser. Smoky and blue. Grab it."

She's off, a rabbit with a coyote's jaws snapping at her hind legs, and disappears 'round the corner of our porch to the side door that leads into the washroom. Mama watches her. Or the spirit does, Mama's body wrapped tight 'round it like a twister encased in cobwebs. A fragile balance.

Her head whips back to me. "Look at you, Little Matriarch." Mama's neck shunts to the side, then back into place. Unnatural. "Little Matriarch, with your willow moss and kindling alight and your mouth sharp while it barks orders. All mutt-like. Sent that young one off to get a poison, I bet?"

I don't respond and rise from my spot. The spirit cackles, but don't remove itself from the chair. Instead, it rocks back and forth and runs its palms over the sanded wood.

"Shame," it sighs. My stomach twists, the gift in revolt of the calm I'm trying to maintain while Kylie gets the vial. Mama's face and hands and body move in a way she never would, all lax and spiteful. This ain't Mama no more.

The spirit grins, like it knows what thoughts be in my mind. "Could have answered that other one's question. With a price, though." Mama's tongue clicks. "Always a price. You witches taught us that."

My lips purse, and I wait for it to continue. But it don't. The sun's on its descent and overhead the sky grows darker already. A clap of thunder rolls 'cross as the storm creeps ever closer. A shudder rocks through me even as I stand steady in front of the porch stairs. The spirit's at a similar game—keep me busy 'til it can scamper 'way. It ain't strong enough to fight me off, yet. Not while it's getting used to being in the physical world, to being able to touch and speak and move within the confines of Mama.

My stomach pitches even as it jolts forward, only to slide back into the seat. But the movement spurs me on, words on my lips, 'cause I need to keep it here 'til Kylie returns. We need take care of Mama before this thing can overpower us both.

"What question?" I blurt out.

It grins, and Mama's pink tongue slinks out to graze along the fronts of her teeth.

"About that Lillian Hallivard and where she's been since she was Infected."

Lillian. I suck in hard enough to cough. It's a trick. Spirits be evil, and they'll do anything to remain in a fresh vessel. But even as I think the words, my heart aches out. *Little Lillian.* Is it possible she's okay? My cheeks pull tight in my distress. It's enough for the spirit to settle back. Mama's shoulders roll, and the spirit slides her hands down the arms of the rocking chair 'til thin, pale fingers clutch the end.

"What will it be, almost-Matriarch? Would you like to hear all about your sister? We of the Beyond talk much of the living. Present and past. All of your Ancestors are there with us, too. They *cluck-cluck-cluck* about things. Witch talk of all sorts, like enchantments and Seers and gates and curses long since cast. Curses that come back to destroy their kin here, now. Curses to continue into the future. How they oh-so wish they could stop it and the twisted blackness that's yet to break through. Oh, how they want to speak to you live witchlings."

The side door slams, a sure sign that Kylie's on her way back 'round the house. My chest constricts, though whether it's the gift or my own guilt, I cain't tell. But it don't matter. This spirit has heard the Ancestors. They've spoken of the curse. Perhaps, they've mentioned how to stop it.

I know the choices I've made. The ones that led us here to begin with. We've a moment before my sister rounds the corner. Just enough time to leave out the opposite way.

And I know Kylie—she'll run down the front steps when she sees we're gone, not 'cross the porch to the back. The spirit wobbles and stands when I motion it to follow, and we disappear 'round the nearby corner.

A thick oil settles in my joints, the world a daze 'bout me. But I have to know if I can fix this and save what family I got left.

Kylie calls out my name, her voice shrill. There's a clatter, then a bang that can only be her shoving the rocker out of the way so she can run down the steps of the porch. I count my breaths, shaky as they be, 'til I cain't hear her calling out for me no more. The spirit snickers, Mama's lips pursed, like it had a victory of some sort. But I ain't done with it yet, and there's a knife in a holster at my thigh that Papa insists I carry at all times. I pull it out and hold it to the jiggling throat.

The sight's all wrong, my hand at the crevice of Mama's jaw and neck with a weapon. I force back the nausea. How have we gotten here? There's a choked noise as I bite down a sob, my skin ice that burns, but I have to focus. The Ancestors and the curse and Lillian. They my priority right now, and if there's anything Mama would want from me, it's to fight for our family.

The spirit's eyes flash, her lips pulled back to show her teeth, but I don't flinch. I'm to be the next Matriarch, and that means I protect what's mine. So I will.

"Tell me everything you know of Lillian and the Bloodbud."

8

NEW TOOTHS, NEW HOME

Lillian Hallivard

I'M HUNGRY.

Short grasses prick the bottom o' my thighs where I sit on the ground. It's cold here, in the shade 'neath the trees, and there ain't no birds or bunnies or squirrels to chase. Animals don't come near me no more. It's like they got a sense 'gainst me now that my tooths all pointy and my nose sniff so good.

The voices hiss, annoyed at this loneliness, but more so at my helplessness. My shoulders roll forward and hunch over. I cain't just stop them thoughts, though. It ain't right, the way my family forced me 'way and turned they backs like I never done existed. I miss Sissy. I even miss Kylie, though she all judger-mental and such. That's what Sissy called her when she'd pester us 'bout the way we done our work. Judge-er-men-tal. Sissy told me it mean Kylie think she better than everyone else 'cause she Papa's favorite. I don't think that right, but I cain't know it wrong, neither.

My tooths ache in a fierce way, and a whine slip out my throat. I need the blood 'gain. It feel an eternity since warm stew and hot bread soothed this hunger. They all taste pale now, like bark. There's no flavor, no sustenance. Mother always said we needed that—sustenance. Witches got it from the gift and from the ground. Food and shelter. Comfort and protection. I don't have none o' that here in this clearing outside o' town that I dragged that man with the kind eyes to. Plus, I'm pretty sure I'm something else altogether.

A breeze blow through and ruffle the curled bits o' my hair that sticking out all over. That familiar thunder beats at my temple, and I groan low in my throat. The grasses crunch as I lift myself up and find the two little trees with pretty white flowers on they branches. That's the way out o' my new home to where all them people live. My feet track the familiar path I've made from the deep dark o' the forest into the slouched and dusty square. Don't take me long to get there 'cause I ain't in the woods too far.

It's a slow day. People cross from one building to 'nother, the red dye o' the ground mixed with gray gravel. It's kind o' pretty in a sad, worn out way. I stick to the shadows, looking for a lone person.

They'll bring my count to four.

Four throats ripped open. Four fleshy gardens for that pretty, delicate Bloodbud that peep oh so nice out they wounds. Four bodies pushed into the stream by my new home.

I think it bloom for me, that flower. It belong to me, and I belong to it.

No one can take that, at least.

My tongue slides over the points o' my tooths, slipping along they curves to outline every little bit o' them. I like how they always so smooth and sharp and shiny. I seen animals that got teeth jagged and nasty. They shake they heads back and forth when they kill, then rip and tear the prey in they mouth as they tackle it. Then, there them animals that leap out from holes to drag the dead back down or that pounce from above to land atop it. Sometimes, they stalk it for as long as they need 'til it an easy slaughter. Always so sneaky. Always so sly.

I ain't gotten sly, still all sloppy when I eat. I wonder what Mama would say. Bad things, I think. But Sissy'd be worse. She'd fuss over the russet stains on the collar o' my dress, the bosom, the place where my knees settle on the ground and the hem drag, its daisy yellow tinged in stiff rust, those delicate flowers all but hidden.

From up high, the sun drape over me, my skin tight and uncomfortable in its brutal touch. I don't move back to the shade, though. 'Stead, I wait. I watch. An older woman shuffles out from the ice house. This one's perfect. She hobbles, a cane in her left hand. No one pay her any mind save the dark young woman that follow a pace behind. That one's got her hair pulled back in a lovely blue bonnet. I bet Sissy could put nice embroidery on it, with some pink and white flowers that make the colors stand out, just the way she do on my dresses. Like that wagon Kylie always went on and on 'bout to Papa. The lady shout something and the girl scurries 'way. They far 'nough from me that I shouldn't be able to hear them. But I do.

Something wrong with me. That, I know. The slant o' silver in my eye tell me I different, no longer a witch, but if that weren't 'nough, the screams o' the voices in my head and the thirst for blood would have. Mama's stricken face haunts my mind, and I push back the image o' Papa dragging her 'way from me.

Now, I kill. My tooths tell me when I hungry, not my stomach. They tingle, then throb, then *ache* so fierce the pain beats my temple and down my neck to poke at my spine. It ain't like nothing I ever felt 'fore.

Hidden in the edge o' the trees, I stalk the woman, catch the twist o' her knee and wobble o' her hands. It don't take long for her to be 'way from all the others. She bat her head with a hand-kerchief. That's why she don't see me when I walk out to her, slow and graceful, my steps silent despite the crunchy dirt 'neath them. Already, the voices sing in they hollow and off-tune way. It's an effort to keep my tooths from sticking out. I clench my fists tight and tell the voices we need get home 'fore I feast, like that's the way to make my tooths stay tucked tight. They don't say nothing back. They never do.

"Oh," the woman says when she done patting her crown. Her lips draw slack and the loose skin o' her throat gives an appalled jiggle as she glances 'round. "You're worse than a hog, look at you! And all this blood, my goodness, child. What is this? Off with you. Off!"

Her voice warbles, thick and turkey-like. Each vibration makes her cheeks shake, the veins all blue and wispy where they thread under her skin. Every breath I suck in make my skin pull tighter, like the sun want to shrink me to nothing. It ain't hot, but it ain't comfy, neither. And the voices be all screeching. I'm so *hungry*. By now, I'm certain my tooths gon' slip out if I open my mouth, so I stare at her forehead real hard and try to focus on the sad, frail drips o' water that cling to her hairline.

Her lips dip lower and she hobble back. "Leave me, now!"

My tooths poke 'gainst the tender flesh o' my gums and I grimace to hold them in. My skin wrapped tighter than leather hide pinned to a chair, and I curl my hands to fists at my side. She be acting just like Papa did. I don't want to be here by myself, but I is 'cause I got to do what the voices say if I want to live. They tell me to *lunge*. To *rip* and *tear* and *shred* and *feast* and *kill* and *rise*.

My eyes close and a shudder ripples over my body. This lady smell like powder and mint mixed with maple syrup. It an odd combination, not like the outsider I snatched last week. He had a scent o' fresh pollen and strawberries; my mouth watered hard 'nough that I almost grabbed him right there off the road.

And they always got a bit o' iron and daisies mixed in, like that just a piece o' the blood in all people.

'Fore the voices ruin everything, I speak. "You want to come with me?" My tooths break resolve and snap down, and I wince at the pain on my tongue. Iron bubbles out.

"I ..." she pauses, a glaze I'm familiar with in her eyes, "I think I do, little one. Yea. I want to go with you."

A grin split my lips, and I turn. She ambles after me, the wild fear gone from her gaze, and an off-balance rock to her step. The sun heats my back and gnaws on my cheeks. If only a cloud would come and keep it off me a minute. But we're moving now, and I'll be under the cover o' branches and leaves soon.

The woman's cane creates little craters in the dirt as she moves, but I don't slow down. My tooths throb and pulse. I need her home. I need to taste that mint and syrup, have it fill my belly on up. As we walk, she talks to me, but I don't listen. Every once and 'gain, I'll look back and ask her to follow. Her gaze dims and loses focus each time. This a part o' what I am now, an unnatural thing, like the voices and the gift. But I like it. I'm a strong girl, like Mama told me I needed to be. Not as strong as Kylie, but that's okay for now 'cause I still got some growing to do.

Cain't stay little like this forever. One day I'll stand tall and proud like Sissy.

It takes longer to reach my clearing with the lady 'cause she old and struggles to clamber over thick roots and gnarled bush, but we reach it eventually. I got a stump here to sit on, the soft gurgle o' a stream to fill the silence, and patches o' moss I collected to comfort my sleep. There's pieces o' it in my hair—they hang heavy—but it's better than the uneven and harsh ground.

Normally, I let the people sit on the trunk. It's easier for me to reach they throat, since I all tiny and slim, but the voices know we alone. *And I'm hungry.* They screech at me to kill and to take. My vision swims with the image o' fangs and flowers, gooseprickles rippling over my pale flesh. I cain't wait no longer.

She don't see me, her head turned like she got her ear out to something in the distance. Maybe she hears the stream. It's for the best. She seems kind.

They always do. It never matters.

I'm rough when I grab her, and the shoulder bone gives a great crack without my meaning it to. She shrieks 'gainst the pain. This one frail and brittle, like her body lost the desire to keep on, but I don't want her to hurt, so I clamber even closer still to make this quick, gleeful when my tooths slide out from they place in my gums, ready to dig deep into her flesh. I bite down hard on the veins under her jaw.

Blood flows out in rivulets and a pleasured grumble rises in my throat. It tastes just as I thought, bitter and herbal with a touch o' sweet. Warmth floods my belly, and the beat that's been at my spine all day slinks off like a pleasured feline. I shift when the woman slouches in my arms, her weight on me, but I keep her upright. It's so good, the balminess in my throat, cool shade on my skin, and, at last, the calmed husk o' the voices. This what I made to do. I'm a predator, just like all them animals I so keen on.

Time passes. When the final drops o' blood slide over my chin and down my throat, I release the woman. She hits the ground with a soft thud, eyes open and glazed the way they get when the soul done fled. There's no other sound save the low creak o' crickets and gentle patter o' the stream. All the animals from the area left me to my dinner.

Wiping the blood from my face, I pull the lady to the edge o' my home, sure to sit her up where the light cain't get her. If I want to see the Bloodbud, she need be in the shade. My pretty, velvety bloom withers in the sun.

What if Sissy were to touch the flower, too? I think she'd be like me. Then, we could be together. I wouldn't be alone, scared to sleep 'neath booming thunderstorms. My throat tightens, raw despite the blood that just soothed it down, and my lips quiver.

Orchard witches ain't s'posed to take human life. That's what the bad clans do, like the Blackwoods and Hammerbrew and Braesland. Sissy and Mama and Kylie and Grannie taught me that. But if I don't eat, I'll die. And I've already fouled over on animals.

After Mama threw me out, I tried eating a rabbit I found, caught in a trap, its leg twisted in a way that made my belly roll. Funny, that I've killed people with little thought, but seeing that bunny with its bone popping out made me want to cry. I ate it anyways. It didn't go down well, kind o' like Sissy's squirrel broth. That always made me sick after, my chest heaving to get the taste back out.

That's when I knew my body needed people. And when my head started to pound and my spine crackled in fire, I went back to the village.

Even thinking 'bout a shy possibility o' stopping has the voices reared up in a clamber o' angry, broken words. I shove the thoughts down and crawl to my plot o' moss, then curl up on my side. Now that my belly all full and happy, everything slows down, my body ready to nap under the green leaves, all hidden from the day's watchful blaze. With a final glance at the lady, her mouth open and eyes wide, I slip into a nice slumber.

Something snaps, then the voices slam to the forefront o' my mind, guttural growls scattered to every inch o' my body. A person here. I sit upright, the patter o' my heart painful where it thumps in my chest, and catch sight o' the intruder at once.

It's that girl. The one with the pretty bonnet.

She's at the edge o' my clearing. My moss pad's laid all up in the shaded bramble o' the trees, so I doubt she seen me when she stumbled in. 'Stead, she's stock still, hand at her mouth and eyes wide as she stares at the body lounged 'gainst the tree. My breath stops, eyes wide; ain't no one come to the clearing without me telling them to. Yet here this girl be. She pays me no mind, unable to tear her gaze 'way from the lady.

That's when I see it.

My bloom, its leaves red like the setting sun, petals gray like thunder. Bloodbud. My fingers itch forward, so eager to touch that, for an instant, I forget there someone else here. But, the girl jolt.

She closer now, and I expect her to see me and scream, to run from this place, from the corpse, but she trudge forward, movements sluggish, like she in suckling mud 'stead o' crisp grass. One step. Two step. All the way to my bloom. A snarl builds in my throat when she reaches out to touch.

It belongs to *me*.

But the voices warn me off, so I wait. Her hands reach out to swipe the flower's petal. There a heartbeat, a moment o' stillness that hang 'bout us.

Then, the voices *wail*.

A wounded shriek rips its way out my throat. I lunge forward, intent on charging from the brambles to grab my flower, but my foot catches on the ground, and I trip. My elbows hit the dirt first, taking the brunt o' my fall. It has to stop. *They* need to stop, they chords scraping 'way at my mind. I clutch my hair and rip at it—doing anything at all to remove the voices and the way they chant *kin, kin, kin*—to make them stop 'fore my mind shatters like a spirit done gotten inside and drove me to madness.

It sounds like victory and fury. A battle cry and a rejoice-ment. Blood spurt from my mouth when my tooths snap down into my lip. But it don't matter. I think I might die. The voices will be the end o' me. I'm sure o' it, ready to crumble into the dirt and never move 'gain. But there's 'nother shift, and they stop.

The sudden silence shatters me more. I gasp out a moan,

terrified to move, the soul-deep burn unbearable even as the voices depart to they place deep down. I could stay here an eternity, but the girl calls out. "What—oh, there's a new feel."

What I wouldn't give for Sissy in this moment. But she's gone, so I push past the tightness o' my limbs and look up. The girl stands tall, though her hands shake something brutal, and the bonnet's fallen to the ground to reveal wavy black hair that sits stiff near her nape. She like the night in a body, oh so pretty, but not in a delicate way. She be bold.

I struggle to my feet and look her over. Only then does she notice me, eyes flicking up to meet my gaze. And the voices hum.

She got silver in her sight, just like I got. There's a pull, something like comfort. Like sustenance. And when she smiles at me, soft and predatory all at once, I see smooth tooths in her mouth. Shiny tooths. Sharp tooths.

The warmth in my belly start to simmer, and I grin back. What would Mama say? Probably something hushed and difficult, meant for me to figure out after a struggle. But I don't like them word games, so I say something else. "Yea, it different, but you'll get to like it. I'm Lillian. You can be my sister. And 'cause you my sister, I gon' teach you how to bite."

The girl's brows pull tight, her lips puffed up like a mushroom. So, I smile, bright and big the way Sissy said made me look loony. But the new girl sees what I showing her. Slow, hesitant, she let her lips spread 'til her teeth on display. Those ones that just like mine.

I'll make sure Sissy and Kylie get tooths like us, too. Then, I'll have all my sisters 'gain.

Opus Lex Baeroot - Ritual of Séance

Ingredients to be gathered any night. For most potent communion, breach the Beyond beneath an absent or full moon.

Poultice creates bridge between one of the Beyond and the host of the ritual. Beware accidental release or possession.

- Elder twig, carved to flute
- Fluffweed, whole
- Object of belonging from one to be summoned (for potency)
- Grave dirt, recent burial
- Chervil
- Bay Laurel
- Candles of virgin blood, for summoning
- Chalk, for summoning

To be mixed under any night. For most potent communion, breach the Beyond beneath an absent or full moon.

Play songs of summoning on elder twig flute. Refer to Opus Lex Vexan for best melody to attract the one from the Beyond depending on season and region that séance shall take place.

Beat fluffweed until it is a pulp consistency. Add fluffweed to cauldron. If an item of the deceased to be summoned is ascertained, set in cauldron and leave within the poultice for entirety of brewing.

Stir in grave dirt from a recent burial. Chop chervil and bay laurel, then sprinkle into cauldron. Speak the name of the one to be summoned thrice, then cool poultice to congealed state.

Host will draw summoning circle using chalk and candles of virgin blood.

Pour poultice into chalice and place within the middle of the summoning circle. Light poultice, then move outside the bounds of circle. Light candles of virgin blood. Recite "Summons of Thee" from Opus lex Vexan.

For image representations, summons incantations, and expulsion incantations, refer to Opus lex Arbaream.

Take care in crafting summoning circle, as spirits have been known to intercept communion and break free during séance to possess the host which has called upon them.

Possession cannot be undone.

Warning to Creators: this poultice is of black magic. It will tarnish the soul due to splinter that is offered to the Beyond. The creation of too many poultices invoking black magic will cause negative symptoms, such as lack of protection against possession, loss of emotion, inability to separate reality from falsities, and, in serious cases, an implosion of magic. These are only a few possibilities. Refer to Opus lex Vexan for full list of recorded symptoms and conditions related to black magic.

9

MONSTERS IN THE ORCHARD

Ellie Hallivard

THE SPIRIT WEARING Mama rolls its shoulders like they a tight fit. The gift shakes, but I keep a firm hold on it. For Lillian. I have to know how she is and if there's a way to reverse what's been done to her.

We've moved to a quiet place in the Orchard. With the sun in its descent, everyone's either inside or off to other chores. We're alone here for now, with its trees of plush leaves and weighted branches—some flowered, others an expanse of green. All of them are blotted in bulbs of the fruit. Ol' Molly rises in the center, a towering silhouette that blocks out part of the sky and watches through every crevice of bark and leaf and fruit and life. At any other time, I'd find peace here. Not now. And knowing Kylie, she's on her way to Papa, who will rouse the rest of the witches in search of Mama and myself. That's not to mention that the longer the spirit's in Mama, the stronger it grows.

I don't have much time.

Shadows cast themselves 'cross the ground and the spirit that wears Mama, her face half-hidden in the dark. Part of me wants to scream and thrash, to pull at the smile in front of me like I'll rip off a mask and Mama will be underneath. But that won't happen. It ain't the reality. My jaw clenches, and I tilt my chin up. "Tell me 'bout my sister or there ain't no use for you."

The spirit lifts her brows, high and poised, so different from the single arch Mama would raise when she 'bout to reprimand us. The ground seems to sway. Every time this spirit makes Mama's face do something it shouldn't, something she wouldn't, it's like I've been dropped into a new nightmare. My personal curse.

"Now, witchling, shall we familiarize ourselves first?"

I grit my teeth and tighten my grip on the dagger. "No. Tell me of Lillian. That's the only reason I've spared you, spirit. If you don't got anything to say, then I don't got a reason to keep you 'round. I'll give Mama the peace she deserves. So you best start talking."

The spirit hums, so close a note to the way Mama started off her lullabies that my head aches. "My information comes at a price. Or did you forget that?"

"Fine," I snap, "what is it?"

"I keep this body and go on my way once I've told you all I know about your littlest sister and that dastardly curse your kin created a century ago. Fair, if you ask me."

My spine straightens, and I shake my head in disbelief. This thing wants to bargain Mama's body? It means no burial rite, no words to soothe her passage to the Beyond. Heat and horror lick they way to the tip of my tongue. "There's no way, in any past or present or future, I would let you keep her body as your vessel."

The spirit's lips tug down, so similar to Lillian's when she would pout, and I'm struck by the familiarity between Mama and my sister. My heart tears further.

"And why not? The other witches give us bodies all the time in return for favors. Sometimes it's an ingredient from the Beyond, sometimes it's knowledge of the past that they can't quite reach the Ancestors for … really, a great many things can be traded."

Other witches? My lips furl down, and my brows pull into a line. The spirit must read my confusion.

"The Blackwoods, witchling. What did you think those Requiems were? They're a hagglers meeting. We offer them payment for the vessels we take."

It's a slap, and I cain't help but take a step back to ground myself. This … cain't be. Nah, we might be ostracized from them Blackwoods, but they don't perform false Requiems. They don't leave witches like Mama in the clutches of these banshee-like creatures for … for ingredients. The clans would have revolted by now. That's the main service the Blackwoods provide, to protect the Coven from the spirits, from the evils of the Beyond.

"Stop lying."

The spirit stretches Mama's lips to a grisly smile. "Lying gets me nowhere in this instance, witchling. I've promised to tell you what I know. And in exchange, I want what we spirits always ask for: a body."

My breaths grow shaky. I inhale, harsh, the air in my lungs slim compared to how deep I try to breathe. The gift don't help, with the way it slams from one part of my body to 'nother in an obvious plea for me to run. To get 'way from the spirit. But if this thing wants to lie, so can I. "Fine. You …" I suck in and close my eyes. Even the deception is too difficult to say aloud. But I must. "You can keep her." The last bit comes out lower than a whisper, but from the way the spirit slinks closer, a sway to her shoulders, I know it heard.

"You may be a leader, yet. Ask and I shall answer, witchling."

I disregard the comment and open my eyes. A cool breeze drifts through the Orchard and the tree limbs bob 'round us. They scent carries 'cross, crisp and delightful. I might choke on it.

Ol' Molly stands erect and dark in the distance, an ancient force that dips as far into the ground as she does into the sky. Her roots sit under me, here. And that's what we are, the Orchard Clan. Constant. *Rooted deep.* I inhale and try to draw strength from Ol' Molly. The spirit shifts ever closer, ready to answer and leave; I cain't let it slip 'way.

"What happened to Lillian when she got Infected?"

"Straight to the soul, I see." The spirit stops to make that hum 'gain, her eyes a quick switch back and forth, like she's in search of something in the air 'bove my crown. "The witchling was the last part of the ritual. She finalized the curse that, had it been done *right*, would have been rather horrid for my kind. As it is, she's been left as something between the living and the dead, as the original intent of your Ancestors' poultice was to create a bridge between here and the Beyond. It didn't go as they planned."

A bridge between the living and the dead? "We've got seances for such things. If you're gonna lie, then—"

"You don't have need of me. Yes, you've said as much. I didn't say communication. I said bridge. A physical thing. Similar to the path of a Seer, except the body would come *with* the witch that passes over, not the soul alone." Her grin turns nasty, lips pulled back to bare her teeth. "Of course, there are things worse than us in the Beyond, and they'd love to slither out. Souls splintered and burnt past repair."

Something worse than the thing that's twisted up Mama's face even as we speak? It's too incredible an image. Too terrifying. I exhale and gather my scattered thoughts. This spirit's left me with so many questions, but I need to think of Lillian. I need to get my sister back. So, I tuck every curiosity 'way and focus.

"Can the curse be reversed?"

"You mean, is there a cure?" The spirit clarifies. I think over the words, then nod. "No. Your sister will remain as she is for eternity."

"You mean, when she dies, she won't be an Ancestor?" My eyelids flutter, and my heart clenches. I'd suspected as much. She's not a witch no more. But to hear it aloud forces me to acknowledge the possibility.

"*If* she dies. She may outlive this world." My heart halts. Even the breeze stutters off, and the trees that surround us stop they rustle of leaves. I swear Ol' Molly leans closer, the tips of her branches curling toward us. If. *If.* "Lillian Hallivard is a new beast altogether. Forsaken. The first of her kind. At least, she was. Now, she's created another thing that is, what's a way to phrase this, undead? Yes, undead is good. Not alive. Nearly without a soul, and yet, not dead either. A creature that needs the blood and warmth of the living to remain strong. Your Ancestors created something terrible, they did."

The spirit laughs, its head thrown back, the length of its neck exposed. The Orchard's filled with the bright tinkles of Mama's laugh. One I only heard when she'd fallen into true joy. My jaw quivers, and my teeth grind together. I tighten my hand on the hilt of the knife.

"It's not true," I hiss.

"You're too blinded and naïve to see the truth." The spirit falls further into its laughter. "It's your kind that lie, witchling. If you're to be Matriarch, learn your lesson now. The witches are the monsters in this tale."

"No. No! You—"

A twig snaps in the distance, then 'nother. Voices shout, just discernible. I whip my head to the noise, eyes wide. My time's up. I have to take care of the spirit now. When I turn, it watches me through Mama's gray-tinted eyes, head tilted. It's unnerving, like I'm an animal and it's observing my moves with a detached curiosity. "So, what shall it be? Are you a liar, too?"

The knife hangs heavy in my hand. Papa sharpened it just this morning. The spirit swallows, the slightest tremor in its movements, and Mama's throat bobs, just like the apples that dance in the trees 'round us, just like Lillian's head when she would duck beneath the brambles and bushes in search of a new animal to chase, just like Kylie's wrist as she mottled the poultice for Mama earlier.

I hardly think before I move. My hand's quick, the knife sure when it hits the spirit's throat and pulls through. There's shock in those mis-colored eyes, then it laughs, a horrid cackling sound that turns into a gurgle. "Remember this, Matriarch-to-be, there's always a price to pay. I'll be back. And when I come, it shall be for your family alone. Such is the price of broken words. You've cursed them yet again. And Kylie will be my first, once her mind buckles and shatters. Got a taste of the Hallivard brood. She won't be hard to find." The body teeters back, grin on its face, *Mama's* face, before it slumps to the ground with a wretched thud. And I cain't breathe. Cain't see through the tears that clog my eyes. I drop to my knees next to Mama's body, the spirit's question a blade in my mind.

Am I a liar?

"Depends on who you ask," I choke out, just as Kylie darts into the Orchard. Her gaze lands on Mama then the knife I've got a white-knuckled grip on, and her face hardens to granite. I close my eyes to block it all out. "Depends on who you ask."

10

THE HAWK AND THE LIGHTNING

Lillian Hallivard

DOROTHEA FROWNS at me from our stump while I pick the flowers. I got to tug something fierce to get them out the bodies 'cause they roots dig deep under the skin. I think they might wrap 'round bone and tendon; Sissy used to complain 'bout those while she be cooking up animals, talking 'bout how they tough. Strong.

"Why you pick them, Miss Lillian. Just leav'm on there. They ain't gon' leave."

My fangs snap out, and I bare my tooths at her. At once, I grimace. "Sorry, Dorothea. Didn't mean to do that. It's rude."

I put the five Bloodbuds I've pulled out on the ground. They all bloody and torn at the ends where I got the stem to snap. A breeze wafts through, nice in this grungy heat, and the hair o' the lady in front o' me floats 'round 'til it covers her face. That ain't right. She got a nice face, all heart shaped, so I brush it back.

The flower in her wrist still don't want to come out. My lips pucker, a tightness at my throat as I push back the sob I want to let loose 'cause this maddening. When did picking flowers get so hard? I used to tug them right up from the ground, and when Mama and I was in the herb garden, she had them snippers that clipped them nice and clean.

My hand stops. Mama's snippers. I smile, so my tooths drop down further, then lean over the body and bite on the Bloodbud's stem. It take a few tries, but I get the angle right and slice right through. This bloom come 'way all nice and pretty, no blood and tears. A pleased squeal leaps out my mouth, and I turn to show Dorothea, but she lounged out 'cross her own moss, looking up at the trees that wave at us from overhead.

She don't get it. The Bloodbuds nice to her—ays-thet-i-cal, she'd said—but they *everything* to me. There a pull to them, the way my magic used to nudge at me in my belly when I was a witch. 'Cause there ain't no way I'm a witch no more. The gift scattered and broken, cold 'stead o' warm, and my body all different, too. I don't think I'm something worse, like human. Just something … different.

The voices liked the bloom oh so much when I was by my pond that day with Sissy. They lead me right to it. Dorothea ain't so inclined now, but I know that initial tug. It ain't easy to resist.

My tooths tug at my lip while I work with the blooms. I lean back for a moment to wriggle my nose and grab the blooms. Dorothea got her head cocked to the side, and I does the same. "What you thinking 'bout?" My Bloodbuds get arranged from biggest to smallest.

She tilts her head the other way while she watch me, brown eyes laced with a dash o' silver. It a bit like a lightning bug, lit at one moment, disappeared the next. "That woman saw us in town, yesterday. She pointed out 'cross her porch."

I pause, my hands hovered over the gray petals. "Yea, and she called you that word. That one—"

"Don't say it," Dorothea snarl. The growl cut off, and she sit up like a bolt, eyes wide and hands over parted lips. "Miss Lillian, I didn't mean it. No'm, sure didn't. I won't speak like that no more."

Speak like what? She didn't say anything near what Sissy and Kylie would say to me. My lips furl down, and I stand. There's dirt on my skirt, some from just now, bent in the mud, but most o' it from the weeks I've been out on my own. "You didn't say nothing. Least, I don't think you did. And I won't never say that word if you don't like it. Don't think I could 'member it, anyhow."

I do. It didn't sound bad. Not like the way Mrs. Broussard called me frog-legged, or how John would tell me I was a spinster-witch and there wasn't no doubt that I'd get boils on my nose when it grew a foot long. My fingers find it now, ginger-like, and feel 'round. It still seem like it a normal-sized nose. And Mama's nose never grew too big, so I doubt mine really will. Even Kylie and Sissy's noses all tuckered in.

But Dorothea my new sister, and she didn't like that word. Her shoulders hunched over, and her back tensed right up like a tree limb that done snapped in a storm. Even now, she scared, so I walk over and pat her hand. "It's okay. I ain't mad; I promise. And, if I ever say something you don't like, you just let me know. Sissy always tells me it's important to com-communicate. She'll be doing a lot o' that when she's Matriarch." Dorothea's brows pull together, but it don't matter if she's confused. She'll learn. I sit next to her. "Want me to braid your hair?"

"Oh," she say, and pat it down, "never had someone ask to braid *my* hair."

"Mama and Kylie always used to braid my hair. Sissy did the embroidery. See?" I pull my skirts from under my legs to show her, but there's so much dirt on the hem that we cain't see the delicate flowers there. A whimper slip out my throat. "Ain't never been this dirty 'fore."

It's barely a whisper. There's a gentle touch at my arm, then a tentative hand slip round my waist. I blink tear-streaked eyes to Dorothea. The tension in her face smooths the longer we huddle together. She hug me closer, then release her hold to stand.

"Come on, now. Let's go to the stream and bathe."

"Cain't bathe in a stream. It ain't hot 'nough if it didn't sit in the kettle. And anybody can walk up and see."

She huffs, then puts her hands on her hips, kind o' like Mama would. "There's no one here to see, and the water don't got to be hot to do its job. Com'n, Miss Lillian. I got a sharper sense o' smell now, and we're both rotten."

I furrow my nose and sniff my arm, but there ain't a whiff o' rot. Maybe Dorothea caught a scent o' old mushrooms. I ate one o' those once. Kylie yelled at me the whole time I was laid up over the side o' the bed with a bucket nearby. Still, Dorothea got that intent look on her face, the one where her lips puff out and her eyes squint, so I grasp her hand. We stop so I can put my Bloodbuds under the moss, that way the sun won't get to them, then she pull me to the stream.

"Strip," she says when we at the water's edge.

I glance 'round, waiting for Jericho and Pearl to pop out from the trees and make fun o' my trolled hair, but nothing happens, so I does as Dorothea says. She takes my dress and sets it 'cross a bush, then removes her own clothes. Her skin be dark even under her gown and slip. I frown at mine, the same color as the salamanders and geckos that I'd find 'round the porch at home. Hers more like the big birds up in the trees that I never could catch 'cause all they got to do is lift they wings and fly 'way.

A splash o' water makes me snap my gaze up from her belly.

She's got that frown on 'gain. "Miss Lillian, are you okay? I can go 'way."

'Way? I lurch forward at that and grab her hand. "No! Don't leave. I just thinking you be like those hawks I couldn't never catch, and I'm a gecko. Geckos ain't as fun."

She don't respond all at once, the gurgle o' the stream the only response. It makes me want to splash her or duck under the water. Then, a grin split her face, big 'nough that her fangs slide out. "Ain't nobody say I look like a hawk, Miss Lillian. I— I'd very much like to be a hawk, I think. They hunters, you know."

"Yea, I know." My own lips slide into a smile. "Well, now you is." I stomp to let her know I mean it. "Dorothea Hawk is your name, now.

"Dorothea Hawk," she murmurs. "And you'll be Lillian—"

"Hallivard," I say, "'cause that's my name."

"No, it's got to be an animal, just like mine."

I pull my lips up so tight I think they might snap, my nostrils flared out real big. "Not gecko. Don't want to be no gecko."

"Nah, you ain't got to be a gecko. A … hare?" I shake my head. Dorothea scratches her neck, then shrugs. "We'll think o' something. Don't have to happen today. Now, c'mere. I'm gon' have to scrub you all day to get the dirt off."

And she does. Dorothea brandishes the soap we stole from town and sets to work. Her hands be harsher than Sissy's, what with the callouses she got, and she put every inch o' them to use 'til my body's turned pink and stings like I been burned. Then, she starts in on my hair. I bite my lip hard 'nough that a taste o' iron slip out while she combs all the limbs and leaves from my curls. When she finally releases me, I dart to the safety o' the bank and crouch there, and all the while she laughs.

"Least you don't smell no more," Dorothea calls.

My fangs slide out as I growl at her. I don't feel no different, save that everything hurts. While I pout on the clay shallows,

Dorothea set to work on her own skin. It don't turn pink or change color at all, staying the same bold as always by the time she's done. Maybe I should be one o' those chameleon things Pearl used to talk 'bout. Said them creatures change they color however they like, so they real good in pig-a-mint poultices. I squint at my rawed out arms, then frown. Nah, that still don't sound right. Dorothea and I just gon' have to keep on thinking o' animals for my name.

"You sit there and keep drying, Miss Lillian. I'll go scrub and beat our garments so they clean, too. Maybe we can get some perfumes from town this afternoon?"

She hums at the end, like it's a question I need answer, so I nod my assent and wiggle 'round 'til I'm comfy. It's different here than it is at my pond. The one with my lily pads. Bugs and such don't laze on top the water 'cause it always moving and never still. There's no willow trees here, with they long, ancient limbs that drip with moss. It always looked like beards to me. Kind o' like William, if he grew his out real long. Sissy would frown and tell me it don't look like that at all—says it's just a tree with moss and that's all there is to it. I miss those trees. The stream got some that tall and skinny, like even I could wrap my arms 'round them, though I'm a slight girl.

I let my eyes slip shut as Dorothea gets to her chores. A lizard clambers down a pine to my left, but my body aches from the bath, so I throw a patch o' ripped up grass at it 'stead o' chasing it. It don't scurry 'way, just watches me from halfway up, its skin shifting from green to brown like it's waiting for something to happen. Nothing do. I fall asleep, eyes on that lizard.

When Dorothea shake me, the stream's in shadows and the lizard's gone. She's got her clothes on—bonnet, too—and my dress is in her hands. It's clean as the day I first put it on, just 'fore I went out with Sissy. The flowers stand out along the hem, all delicate and pretty, and I cain't help my squeal when I grab it from her hands. "Dorothea, I'm right glad the Bloodbud made you my sister. Look! It's like you got magic, too. Sissy would be happy to put you in our family, I think."

Dorothea looks down, the way Kylie do when she'd flush at the compliments Mama gave her. I take it as a good sign.

"Yes'm, I right glad I'm your sister. Don't know 'bout that magic, though."

I wave her off and take my stockings from her hand. They dry, no mud caked to them, and slip on far easier than I imagined they would. It used to take me lots o' pulls to get them on, but I yank them right on up to where they meant to be. "Yea, you ain't a witch, so you don't got magic. That's okay though. Means the voices don't bother you." I crinkle my nose as they bubble up with a screech, like they was waiting for me to make mention o' them. "They gotten worse since I touched my Bloodbud."

Dorothea hands me the yellow dress in her hands and I put it on, but she seem off. Her eyes all squinty. "Miss Lillian, this magic you talk 'bout. It ain't … real magic, right?"

What she mean by that? "'Course it real. What use is fake magic? Though, I don't got that no more since I ain't a witchling."

My mouth pulls down, a hollow ache in my chest. 'Nother breeze rustles through, but I don't pay it no mind, distracted by how my heart's in pain. I won't never be with the Orchard 'gain. There's no leap frog with Timothy or gathering with Anna. My lip quivers, and I sniffle. This my home now, a lone stream and patch o' dirt. The voices linger and hiss, though nothing come out in words. More like emotions and pulses. I ignore them as best I can.

Dorothea's eyes gone big and round, the brown murky, then she blinks and curls a lip back to touch her tooths. "What is we?"

"Infected," I say, though I ain't real sure what that mean. "It

… we like … strong. That's what we is. And independent. And we got good senses, better than 'fore." And cain't eat nothing but blood. My belly twist up.

She nods, slow, a tiny bob o' her head on her stork-like neck. "I think we better."

"Better?"

"Better," she repeat, then take a sharp nod, her chin striking downward. "Than 'fore, when you was a witch and I was a human. Miss Lillian, cain't no one tell us what to do no more. Not a person."

I tilt my head at the ferocity o' her pitch and the way the voices purr with it. Then, I grin 'cause she right. She a hawk, talons and all. And I'm lightning, a blast in a dark sky, fast and true and one with this nature all 'round me. We hunters, and sometimes hunters got to kill.

"Dorothea," I say, then pat her arm where it's rested over her belly, "I got this feeling that it only gon' get better."

11

BENEATH OL' MOLLY

Ellie Hallivard

I LIFT my gaze so Mrs. Broussard can rub them ashes 'cross my cheekbones. They smell of sage and flesh, of herbs and Mama. Tears swell, my throat tight and tongue heavy, but I hold it all in so I don't ruin the work of the Clan Elders. If I could, I'd scream. I'd beat my fists 'gainst the ground near Mama's burial plot 'til they ran bloody and soiled the dirt, turned it a rusted burgundy to match that stain on our Little Lillian's dress from the day I let her down, too. But I cain't.

The oldest witches of the Orchard Clan surround me on Mrs. Broussard's porch, preparing me to take my place as Matriarch, but my face sits all swollen from grief, and my stomach lies leaden. Even the gift has folded itself 'way like it's trying to escape the brunt of my misery. Loneliness shrouds me like a suckling spirit.

A firm hand takes hold of my chin and tilts it up. "We near

done, Eleanor. It's a slow process to ready you for the Matriarch ceremony, but we're close."

Relieved, I let my eyes flutter closed and lean into Mrs. Laurelyn's touch. They've been at it for near an hour, the Elders: all three of them with brushes in they hands, and a gown spread over the balcony for me to don when the poultices on my body dry. I'm in my slip, nothing more, but it don't turn heads in this quiet corner of the Orchard Clan. Most people be keen enough to avoid our rite, anyhow. This be sacred. Ritual. It's not meant for the eyes of all the witches, so they keep they distance in respect of our shared customs.

A scroll lies rolled out 'cross the porch with odd symbols on it: the Old Language, I'd been told. They don't know how I've spied it in secret all those times I peeked in the grimoire Mama keep hidden in our home. Three bowls sit at our feet, poultices in them. What the brews are, I'm not certain. It's for the Elders to know, a knowledge that comes with age, not blood or status. They potent, a scent of mint and clay and iron in the air. On my skin. Soon to be melded with my soul. My spine stiffens, and I shudder.

It's bright out, today, the sun high and clear, a ripe setting that would have had Lillian at my hip. She'd beg and plead to go to her pond, then throw herself to the ground in a fit when I said no 'cause she ain't fed the hens yet. Mama would be somewhere nearby, hand on her hip, grin peeking out the corner of her lips while she told Lillian to listen to me since I gon' be Matriarch one day.

And now, I'm here, but Lillian's gone and so is Mama.

"You're gon' make yourself bleed, Eleanor," Mrs. Childress chides, her eyes kind, the wrinkles in her face a deep-set, scarred bark. She leans on her cane with both hands, and I tense when it wobbles under her grip. But she stays upright, eyes lit like she heard my thoughts. Maybe she did—her family's had many a kin with psychic tendencies. It makes them a closer junction to the Beyond than most.

I release my lip when she tugs it from my teeth. "You know, I painted your Mama, too, when she took her place as Matriarch. And I was friends with Karen, your Grannie, when she got painted. You Hallivards do the Orchard Clan right. Your Mama's not with us, and the Ancestors grieve for it, but you ain't alone. You got us."

She sweeps her palm out. There's a quiver to it, as though she struggles to keep it held up, but the Elders smile back at me. It's grim. The motion don't make they gazes twinkle, don't light up they willow moss and kindling, but the tension held in my body loosens all the same. That breathless squeeze behind my sternum exhales for the first time since we burned Mama and sent her to the Beyond.

There's still an ache, a fear.

"Kylie hates me. How could she not? I was there when Lillian died, then I …" The words sputter off, like the breeze came by and swept them 'way. "I killed Mama."

Mrs. Childress stomps her cane, and the porch gives a hollow *thump*. I jump, and Mrs. Broussard swats at her, but she's waved off. "You did not kill your Mama. Do not put that burden on a chain and clasp it 'bout your wrists. We lost our Matriarch the moment that spirit took hold of her body and spoke through her mouth. You gave your Mama the chance for a burial rite and protection into the Beyond is what you did."

There's a stillness to the air as her words catch, then we recite the Coven farewell together. "Be well in the Beyond, Anne Hallivard. We'll see you 'gain."

Pinpricks start up in my eyes, but Mrs. Childress shimmies her shoulders and keeps on. "Kylie may not understand now. She's young, and she done lost a lot in a short time—same as you—but she will come to learn in future years. Now," she pats my cheek, then lays a gentle finger on the most recent poultice application and squints, "it seems you've dried up. Go in and put that gown on. There's a mirror in the sun room."

The ache in my chest don't ease, nor does the pit in my gut. Kylie don't blame me for Mama's death; she blames me for the way it happened. When I close my eyes, I see her arm cock back as she flings the poultice I'd made, hear her sharp cry and the bright soprano of glass as it shatters, the Orchard's ground anointed in a smoky liquid that would have put Mama peacefully into her final slumber.

My hands shake, and I press my fingertips together, half surprised when they ain't still slick with Mama's blood. With a nod, I gather the soft fabric into my arms and enter Mrs. Broussard's house. Cool air greets me, kept crisp with the help of its warm cedar bones and a balming spritz. It's not much different from our own home. Knickknacks and ingredients lie in haphazard piles, dried herbs hang from a wooden plank near the washroom, and unlit candles are scattered 'cross bookshelves and cluttered corners, just in case there's quick need of a practice. I can almost pretend the world is right if I linger here.

But it ain't my home. A place I'd have had to remove Kylie and Papa from should I have held the ceremony there. It's the smallest of comforts, letting them stay there while I readied myself here, but it's what I could give them.

The dried paint itches my legs and arms and neck and face, and the gown I cradle to my chest brushes 'gainst my knees. I wander to the sun room, where a floor length mirror glints at me, and slide into the dress. It's cream and see-through, unblemished, lighter than even my slip. If it weren't for the gentle caress of the tapered sleeves at my bare wrists, I could close my eyes and never know it's on. The weight in my chest builds 'gain, and I push it down.

I am to be Matriarch. I've always known that. It don't change 'cause Mama ain't here to guide me through.

A faint aroma of mulled apples fills the room, followed by

cherries and oranges. Most likely a jam to be sold in town. Something to keep the Orchard standing and my Clan safe. And, that's what all this 'bout, right? We need a Matriarch, and that task's been left to my family for centuries. This ritual, this role, it ain't for me: it's for Jericho, Pearl, and Kylie; for Mrs. Broussard and Mrs. Childress, for the families of the Orchard that lost the protection they needed when the Blackwoods turned they back on us, for the safety that comes with one soul being tied to the Ancestors.

It's for Mama, too.

I inhale that scent of home and apples, then turn to the mirror. The girl that looks back ain't someone I recognize. Her cheeks lie hollow, eyes surrounded by plum circles and lips chapped from the constant pull of teeth. But there's something more, written in the lines of the Old Language on her skin. The paints shimmer, like they cain't quite hold they form, brushed on in blue and red and orange and yellow, the gray of Mama's ash on my face stark and bold. If I close my eyes and wait, the power in them simmers on the surface, like it knows what will happen. Like it's waiting to burrow down beneath.

The weight rises from my chest, gone to wrap 'round my shoulders. It won't never leave, I'm sure of that, but I'm not afraid of suffocating no more. I lick my lips to calm the dryness, then make my way back out to the porch where the Elders wait. Mrs. Broussard rolls the parchment up while Mrs. Laurelyn piles the poultice bowls atop one 'nother.

My fingers find the sleeve of the gown in search of a loose thread to work at, the end of my now-removed ribbon to fiddle with, but I stop they idle wandering and let them fall to my sides instead. "What now?"

Mrs. Laurelyn nearly drops the bowls and cranes her neck to me. She's got a stern face with few laugh lines, her hair braided in long ropes round the crown of her head. But when her eyes flit over the gown and the paint, she smiles. It reaches all the way to her eyes and crinkles her forehead. "Now, we go to the Orchard and recite the words beneath Ol' Molly. Once that's done, the Ancestors set to work. For all the fuss, it won't take more than half the hour. Suppose us witches don't waste time, even in the Beyond."

The Elders chuckle, and my own lips quirk up. Mrs. Broussard pats her hands down on her dress, then motions for me to follow. Our small procession dallies 'cause Mrs. Childress needs her cane to keep up at the slowest of paces. I half-listen as them ladies chat 'bout the winter season that nips at our heels. I know the idle talk is to soothe my anxieties, seeing as winter is when our Orchard thrives. Still, the closer we get to Ol' Molly, the tighter my body coils.

What if I don't live up to the Hallivard Matriarchs before me? I've not done much to stand out in these years amongst my Clan. If it weren't for my lineage, my being the first-born daughter, there'd be nothing special 'bout me. I wring my hands in my dress, then clench them to fists at my side. I cain't let nobody else down. Not one person.

And yet, I'm lying to them all.

My breaths sharpen and stagger out, a vice-like grip on my diaphragm. I've made more mistakes than most in the past weeks. They cost my family. Perhaps, if the legends are true, the entire Coven.

Forsaken. Forespoken. Infected.

The gift returns from its cowardly refuge, and the voices scratch 'gainst my mind. My teeth dig deeper into my lip as I slam them down and 'way. I cain't lead the Orchard Clan. What was I thinking? Childish, yet 'gain. My mouth waivers, and I reach up to clutch at my chest. We're at the gate to the Orchard, and the Elders wave me through, but I cain't.

"Eleanor," Mrs. Broussard says, a frown curving her face as her brows furrow together, "are you alright, dear? You've got to come through."

My breaths suck in, short and stocky. "No. I cain't. You need to choose 'nother first-born. Please." I'm frantic, my eyes wide as I whip my sight from one shocked face to 'nother 'til I land on Mrs. Laurelyn. She got her lips set to a thread-thin line, her cheeks flattened out. I focus on her 'cause she look like the disappointment and doubt that burns bright in my gut. "I'm gonna hurt the Clan even more than I already has. What if— what if I cain't keep the trees at harvest in the summer, hm? That's part of the Matriarch's job, to brew the poultice that makes them bear fruit when they shouldn't. Or, or what if—"

"Eleanor," Mrs. Broussard places her hand on mine, which have bunched up the front of my dress in they clasp, "the first-born daughter of the Hallivard family is always the initial choice to become Matriarch. You're groomed as such. But," she pauses, a moment passes through the Elders, then she nods, "part of the ritual is to séance with the Ancestors and gather their blessing. We may be exiled from the Blackwoods, blacklisted by the Coven as a whole, but the Ancestors will not leave us. And they gave you their blessing."

A blessing from the Ancestors? I search they faces for a hint of deception, but the smooth lines and open gazes display concern and support, just as they'd promised. Even Mrs. Laurelyn's creviced lines have smoothed over somewhat. The gate creaks, blown further open by the breeze, and the cut blades of grass on the other side shimmer as they dance. I could almost imagine them waving me through.

"You can decline. To be Matriarch is a choice," Mrs. Laurelyn says.

I open my mouth to reject the position, to give it to Kylie or 'nother family line altogether. But Mama's voice shifts in me and blossoms out. This is our *duty*. The job we serve for the Orchard. So, I pant, hand to my chest, and force myself to be better. "Lillian's not dead."

The Elders still, they willow moss and kindling shocked

wide open. Mrs. Broussard places her palm on her stomach like she might faint. "Child, that's a miracle! Your Mama was so broken—"

"Stop." That grip that's become so familiar the past few weeks sneaks back in, snatches my throat tight and digs a harsh punch into my breast. "She not alive, neither. She's—" My voice chokes off, and I squeeze my eyes shut. Pinpricks of light dance on the backs of my lids, and I clutch for the ribbon on my wrist. Only, it's gone, my fingers flush 'gainst the risen, scarred skin. Of course, it's gone—Mama ain't here to feel guilt over it no more. I burnt it the morning we performed the burial rites. She's dead. Dead 'cause a spirit got hold of her. 'Cause the poultice *didn't work*. 'Cause none of it *ever* works. We ain't safe, and Kylie's right.

Our family never stood a chance. One of us Hallivards would have touched the Bloodbud, and it happened to be Lillian.

The weight lifts, like I've wrenched it from my body and flung it to the Beyond. The anxious hunch of my shoulders, the shamed rot in my mind. It all dissipates, and a calm settles deep into my marrow. I open my eyes to the confused gazes of the Elders.

"Lillian fulfilled the Curse of the Bloodbud. She didn't die, but she's not alive, neither. She's something new. An Infected."

Mrs. Laurelyn gasps while Mrs. Childress sways on her cane. Even the chirps of the crickets pause a moment, then return with renewed vigor.

Mrs. Broussard clears her throat, eyes glazed over. "So, the visions that some of us gotten from the gift, the fangs and the blood, those have been 'bout Lillian."

My own visions swim to the forefront of my memory, the shadows of smoke and claws and serpents in the foliage of the forest. "Yes. She's the Forsaken."

"You lied to us all." Mrs. Childress stomps her cane then furls back her lips in a snarl. "This a travesty, the destruction of the Coven, and you kept it hidden just like them Blackwoods would."

"No," I snap. "I've told you the truth. Mama wanted to keep it all quiet. We still lost Lillian, still needed to mourn her—" I suck in, then loose a low sigh and rub the bridge of my nose. This must be why Mama always had her temple aches. "We didn't know what to do. And I still don't. But Mama ain't here so all I got is you, the Elders. And I still don't think we tell the Orchard. Not 'til we have answers of some sort."

"We cain't continue," Mrs. Childress says, then snaps her teeth. Her lips quiver, and there's a wet sheen to her gaze. "You cain't be the Matriarch, not after this kind of betrayal. You was with Lillian, weren't you? How do we know you're not an Infected, too?"

"Helen, enough," Mrs. Laurelyn glares at the riled Elder. "We will continue, and Eleanor will face the trials. The Ancestors know of what's happened, and they still proclaimed her Matriarch. If they so choose, they will reject her."

My shoulders tense. Reject me? What do that mean? I thought the Ancestors already gave they blessing.

Mrs. Laurelyn don't pay my furrowed brows any mind. "And, if she was Infected, the gift would have warned us. Just like Mary said, we've had visions of the sister who isn't even here. The gift would have revolted with Eleanor so close."

No one speaks. Mrs. Childress's mouth twitches and jaw flexes while Mrs. Broussard stares off into the darkness of the Orchard. A gentle breeze picks up. The paint along my skin tingles with it, and the dress flits 'round me. In the air lies a crisp aroma of pine and sunlight. If it weren't for the battle between us, it would be a beautiful day filled with peace and happiness. I taper off the laugh that bubbles up at the absurdity.

Mrs. Childress huffs, and her neck bobs, then she turns

sharp eyes on me. "Let the Ancestors decide. They know more than we."

A trio of cardinals swoop low to our left, then glide over the Orchard fence, they wings a flash of red and black, brown and orange, then they twirl up high toward a nearby tree. The Elder's willow moss and kindling follows them, then she begins a slow hobble toward the center of the Orchard where Ol' Molly awaits us. Mrs. Laurelyn slides her sight over me, then nods and follows the other. I wait for Mrs. Broussard to continue after them, but she's still lost in her own thoughts. When I take a step to move past her, she whips her face to mine, then settles her expression to pliant cheeks and soft brows. "You will do well to confide in us, Eleanor. With what you've told us, your Matriarchy might well be the deadliest in our history. And our sister clans have abandoned us. You'll only pass the trial if you're strong enough to ensure the Orchard's survival."

'Nother mention of this trial I've never heard word of before. A shiver slips up my spine and coils 'round my neck. I reach in to touch the gift, and it nudges back. My family's in tatters. The Elders hate me. It's near certain the Ancestor's will reject me.

And yet, I feel strong for the first time since Lillian became Infected.

'Cause I always turn to Mama or William or the Clan or the Coven, but every time I been blinded, naïve as a child, and certain they could protect me. My fingers trace the scar at my wrist, the raised skin that's lost all color, a ghost of flesh embedded in my body. Ain't nothing out there to protect us, but we still got to try.

I nod, then follow her through the gate.

Our group trudges through the Orchard. Trees rustle as we pass, a soft flutter to them from the constant flow of wind. Ol' Molly rises up from the center, her trunk a bright memory of myself and my sisters and our friends gathered with clasped hands, connected in a circle 'til we reached all the way 'round her wide body. The older we got, the less people it took, though never so few as five. She stretches over us now, a monument to everything our Clan is, and all it holds dear.

My fingers twitch. They grow slick with sweat, but all I can think 'bout is blood. Mama's blood. A tremor slides through my palm with the phantom weight of that knife I pulled 'cross her throat as the spirit bled out from her, laughter a sharp sting in my ears. And yet, Ol' Molly keeps a watchful eye on all, and the Orchard remains. Rooted deep.

"You'll stand here." Mrs. Laurelyn pulls me to a point in front of Ol' Molly, at the middle of her thick branches. "Now, repeat after us. *Exactly* as we pronounce it. The Old Language be fickle. Misspeak and you'll choke on your tongue."

Swallowing, I nod and clutch tight at my dress, ears strained so as not to miss a single syllable. There are five phrases in all. I'm not certain what they mean, and the Elders don't translate for me. But Matriarch's have said them for centuries. My eyes lock with Mrs. Broussard's. And if we survive this, we'll say them for centuries more.

When the last word leaves my tongue, harsh and steep and husky, the paint on my skin ignites. My eyes go wide, and I search out Mrs. Broussard, but I cain't catch her eye before the symbols on my skin *sink in*, like they trying to rip it apart and nest with my tendons and bones. A scraped-off scream leaves my throat, my eyes blurred out by tears.

I should have said no, should have declined to be Matriarch and ran 'cause now they killing me. Perhaps it was a lie, one big manipulation to get rid of the girl that would lead the Orchard Clan into ruin. That's what the spirit said, after all, that we witches are the liars. My ears ring, and the telltale odor of iron hits me. I must be bleeding, somewhere. I cain't tell. Mama's ashes run down my face, wiped off by the tears that stream in rivulets.

Then, I hear them. A cacophony of voices that grate 'gainst my soul, further down than the gift, thousands of them bubbling up and over 'til they the only things left. They shift and quake and devour 'til, at last, one reaches out; the way it grinds together like beaten rocks tells me it's ancient. And, though it speaks in the Old Language, I understand.

"Eleanor Hallivard, will you defend the witches of the Orchard Clan until the last of your breaths and give your magic until its final chord to keep them safe?" Before I've answered, a yes down in my chest, the voice continues. "Will you tear down any and all who stand against the safety of the Orchard Clan, be it enemies or lovers?"

Once again, my nuptial is ripped 'way before I can speak the commitment.

"Very well then." The Ancestor dips in, a hand over my heart, then into my magic; a coil and snap that locks us in place, together. "Let us see if we are one, Eleanor Gwen Hallivard of the Orchard Clan."

12

GOT A BOLD MIRACLE

Lillian Hallivard

"NOT THAT ONE."

Dorothea falters, her palm stretched forth like she gon' snatch a skeeter from the air. My hand whip out and yank her back behind that wagon I done ducked behind.

She cross her arms, eyes narrowed in that way she do when there's something that don't sit right 'tween us. "Well, why not? He look big, good to feed us for days."

Rather than answer, I lie on my belly and wriggle 'neath the wagon. Dorothea mutter something 'bout "hungry" and "fangs" from where she left standing, but I don't answer.

My tooths ache. They prick the spot that run up my temple and down my spine. The voices gon' start in soon, I know it. But that's not what got me concerned, now. I dig my elbow into the gravel, an afterthought o' the dirt on my dress and how Sissy would yell if she saw me here. But she's why I stopped Dorothea, so no one would hurt Sissy's William.

My eyes squint. The sun's too bright at first, harsher 'cause the gravel red, and that make it livelier than the grass at my clearing, but it don't take long for the little fake ponds on the dirt to leave. There he is, elbows 'gainst the cart he must've lugged from the woods, stacked high with blocks o' cut trees.

He's different than last I saw, when he came to our house to get that broken rocker from Mama. His hair's long, tied at the nape, and his shoulders sit broad and bulged, like itty-bitty boulders. He seems taller, but I'm also belly-down on the ground like a rattler, so that might be wrong. Hard to tell. A bead o' sweat drip down my face, and I brush it 'way, my hair loose where it's stuck to my cheeks and neck. If Kylie saw me now, she'd go on and have a fit.

"Miss Lillian," Dorothea hiss.

I don't answer. If William here, maybe Sissy be here, too. My belly flip-flops, and I wiggle my toes. Would she take me back, let Mama fix me on up? Dorothea can stay in my room with me, since we sleep near one 'nother, anyhow. I bet Kylie will like Dorothea, since they both like to argue and do what Sissy calls "mens-chores." I think that might be part o' the Old Language: mens-chores.

"Miss Lillian, people is coming," Dorothea shrills.

The voices growl and hiss, and my tooths snap out when the low grumble o' talking reach my ears. They too close. I should have heard them sooner, but I be focused on William. Quick, like them rabbits I chase, I try to shimmy back out the way I came, but the people that be talking is here.

"What's this? Get 'way from my wares, filth." It's a man, from the low, gruff way he speaks. There's a scuffle and some gravel gets kicked up at me. A tickle starts in my nose from the dust, and I sneeze, but no one seems to hear. Dorothea whimpers out where I cain't see, and my tooths sink lower, my lips pulled back as I snarl. That man must be talking to her. "Trent, kick the burrows up a pace or two, then check we ain't been robbed. Gon' send you to the sheriff, you—"

The wagon jolts, then rolls forward, right toward the narrow part o' my leg, just 'bove the ankle. It gon' break the bone, then what I gon' do? A hard, heavy weight rack my chest, and I cry out just as the wheel hit my leg, roll back from it, then rock all the way over.

The weight near my heart turns into a pained cough when I suck in hard, the air dry and rough as it comes out my throat. My tooths pull back up, then a sob breaks loose 'cause that tiny pinch in my leg must mean I'm gon' have a gimp in my step. Daylight hits me all at once as the wagon rolls 'way. Dorothea yells to me, but now that I let one sob go, more fall, tears a salty flow down my lips and neck. The voices screech in anger and demand I *take, kill, hunt, defend, protect, rip, tear, shred*. It makes the panic worse, and a garbled wail slips out my mouth, fueled on by the fear that my leg's useless. Sissy and Mama ain't gon' take me back now. Not with a bad leg on top o' what I become.

A hand lights my shoulder, and I jolt, blinking through water-lined lashes to the man knelt in front o' me. "Trevor, get off the blasted wagon and find help! You ran over a little girl, dammit." He turns back to me, face shaded by the tilt o' the hat on his head. "Pardon my language, little lady. Didn't mean to curse in front o' yea. This one here yours?"

My tears have slowed, and the sobs is nothing more than sniffles, but the voices linger, they hushed growls a command that I gots to nestle down if I want to focus. He waves to Dorothea, her chin tucked into her throat, shoulders hunched and hands drawn down. She ain't like the bold Dorothea that I been with the past couple o' weeks. Look more like a chicken than a hawk.

"Yes'ir, that my sister," I answer, then sit up. He scoffs, and my jaw tightens. "Ain't nice to laugh, mister."

That gets him. His eyes widen, and he side-eyes me, the way Papa do when I say stuff he ain't fond o' but that amuse him still. He'd give me that look when I'd call Sissy a knicker, sometimes. Or when I told the boys they don't play leaps and frogs right. The man squat down next to me. "You're right, ain't no place o' mine to laugh. Just cute that you think that'n yea sister."

"Well, she is." I cross my arms, cheeks puffed out, but Dorothea shakes her head at me, and my shoulders drop. Is she 'shamed, too? Surely, she won't leave me 'cause I got a bum leg. It got an odd pressure to it 'bout now, but that all. Maybe I will be able to walk on it. "You don't want to be my sister?"

Her mouth drops open, hands falling to her sides, but she pass her gaze up over my head 'stead o' saying nothing. Fine, if she don't want to be my sister, she ain't got to. I chew my cheek and turn my head, tears piling up 'gain. Then, a shadow pass me, and a great bosom o' a lady kneels down by the man.

She got a riotous mop o' hair that look like thin wires sticking out all over the place. Her apron's all askew, lopsided 'round her waist, and there a flush to her face. From the way she pants, I bet she run here. My tooths *sear* me, down to the root, and I groan.

She'd be a good dinner for me and Dorothea.

"Marcus, what did you do?" The woman bats at the man beside her.

"Don't look at me, Madam Roux. Trevor's the one that moved the cart."

"You will not blame this on that boy. He's in my shop with a cold glass o' tea and near tears 'cause he thought he killed a girl."

They an odd pair. I tilt my head, watch the blue pulse o' they veins beat faster the more they talk. They sure is working theyselves up. And the more they do, the better they smell. She got a scent o' sugar and citrus, while he smell all thick, like tobacco and smog. My nose wrinkles, lips peeled back.

The lady leans forward, and her hands flutter over me. "Oh, sweetie, you're in pain. I can tell. Where does it hurt?"

I sniffle, then wipe my face with the back o' my hand. "My tooths. And my neck."

Marcus coughs, and Madam Roux turns to glare at him, face

red—though not as red as my Bloodbud—and her lips pull tight. "You'd best not tell me you ran over this girl's *head*."

Even I flinch back from the alto bark she lets out.

"No'm. Ran over my leg. Right here." My finger tap the place the wheel went over, my skin hidden 'neath the stockings Dorothea washed and beat.

"Okay, honey, if it hurts bad, you just squeeze Mr. Marcus's fingers. And you squeeze 'em real tight, yea? Like you gon' take them clean off his hand."

The man stuffs his hat back to show his face. It's ruddy and round with a couple licks o' sweat in the crevices. He pinches his lips together and squints at Madam Roux, but holds his hand out nonetheless. I set mine in it, cream 'gainst his tan, and wrap my tiny fingers 'round his.

Gentle nudges prod my leg, but it don't feel no different than any other time someone poked me there. She lifts her gaze, eyes on my face, then press down a bit harder. "How's that feel, honey?"

"Feels alright, I s'pose." The words mottle out.

"Okay, I'm gon' try and lift your leg. If the pain is too much, you remember to squeeze those fingers tight and let me know."

Marcus huffs. "The girl gets it. Take my fingers off if given the chance."

Them two glare at one 'nother, and I shift. My leg don't hurt, anyhow; it's my tooths that throb, the way they egg me to let them out and sink into the lady's neck that bobbles right there, closer every time she leans forward.

She set her hands on my leg. "Ready?"

I nod, eyes locked on the place she holds. Then lifts.

"Don't feel nothing," I huff, then cross my arms.

Madam Roux's throat bobs, her nose flaring out, and she sets a sharp sight on the man. "Good lord, Marcus, you've done paralyzed the child."

This lady don't know what she talking 'bout. Katherine, the

Clan Healer, would laugh if she heard this one prattle on. Probably slip something in her tea, too. I like Helen—she all tricky like. She's the one that told Sissy to put Strength and Prosperity poultices in William's cider. That way, she could still send him good fortune, though the witches ain't s'posed to do that with the townfolk.

I suck in hard. William.

Without a bother for the two in front o' me, I leap up and spin 'bout. The cart's gone. William ain't nowhere in sight. The weight in my chest drop down low to my belly. Was Sissy with him? Did I miss her?

I take a couple steps forward, but the lady grasps my shoulder. "You're okay? Thank goodness. Must've been scared from when the wagon moved, that's all. Ain't you lucky?"

The man say something back, then holler over at Dorothea. He say that word she don't like, the one she told me I couldn't use, and I glance over my shoulder to glare at him. "Don't call her that. She don't like it."

His face scrunches, the fatty bulbs o' his cheeks pulled tight. Behind his shoulder, Dorothea scuttle back a ways. I think she might run, for a moment, but she hold fast. "That's what she is. Don't you mind her, she ain't got a say in it."

William forgotten, I turn to face him, hands on my hips. But this ain't my place to say nothing. The word don't make no matter to me. I search out Dorothea, but she's hunkered down, kind o' the way Kylie did when the girls called her hands rough. Sissy put them straight. My eyes narrow, and I tilt my head. Guess I'll put this one straight, like Sissy would.

"You ain't gon' call her that no more. Hear me?"

Marcus's eyes go funny, glazed, like he's lost in thought. But they come back quick with a sheen on them. "Listen here, now. There's no manners in telling a man what to do. Got that? You're all healthy now, no harm done, so that mouth needs to tuck itself 'way. And I'll call her whatever it is I want to."

He slings an arm out at Dorothea, his sausage-like finger pointed at her face. Her demeanor slackens further. It's like she turned into a flour sack that been slashed, wilting more and more while the insides spill out. Heat swell up my neck, and saliva builds in my mouth as my tooths work to snap down. I crunch my hands to fists.

"No," I growl, then wait for him to look me in the eye 'cause Mama always said it important to see the whites o' a witch's eye when you want to get a point 'cross. He ain't a witch, but I bet it work the same. He puts his sight on mine. "No one gets to talk like that to my sister or 'bout my sister. You gon' apologize to Dorothea, then you ain't never gon' use that word 'gain."

His gaze go glassy, more so than 'fore, a film o' a haze 'cross them. It reminds me o' the mist that settle over the fields early in the morning. Then, he turns to Dorothea, face slack, mouth ajar. "Sorry, Ma'am. I'm not ever gon' use that word again."

Madam Roux steps forward, brows knit together as she worries her lower lip. "Marcus, you okay. You don't look right."

He blinks a few times, then tilts his head to her, the hat lopsided atop it. "Sure am. You said Trevor was inside, didn't you? I need a word with him."

There's no farewell for myself or Dorothea. He just turns on heel and leaves to Madam Roux's shop. The lady sputters, her apron a quick bounce as her belly jostles. She's all alone now, that sweet scent o' sugar and citrus on my tongue. If I open my mouth, I'll drool from the built-up saliva there.

"Miss Lillian," Dorothea call as I take a step forward, fingers curled to claws, "we best be on our way now."

I hesitate. But she wave me over, eyes a frantic switch from my face to that o' Madam Roux, who's still got her sight on Marcus as he treks inside her store. My mouth water, tooths *angry* that I ain't grabbed a meal yet, but I follow Dorothea. We hurry off to the edge o' the forest then slink in. Soon as we out o' sight, she drop to the ground on her knees, hand over her mouth.

I sit next to her and pull at the grass 'neath my hands, then shred it. "What is it? You okay?"

"Okay?" She don't move her hand from her mouth at first, her words a hoarse whisper. The slimy grip in my belly worsen. Then Dorothea hobble to face me on her knees, a shine to her eyes, grin spread out over her face to show her own tooths. "Miss Lillian, I think you a miracle sent to give me new hope."

I chew my cheek and look down to the torn blades in my palm. "Ain't no miracle, Dorothea. It a curse. I done *told* you that."

"No, Miss Lillian." She takes my hands in hers, bigger and rougher, but they shiny and bold. "You a miracle. Back there, that wagon *did* rock over your leg, but you just fine, like nothing happened. You're strong, you cain't be hurt, and you can *make people do what you say*. Ain't no one ever stood up for me 'fore. Not like you did back there."

Dorothea gather me into her arms and tug me close. I stiffen. Sissy was the last to hug me, to embrace me and make me feel cozy and safe. It's different like this, the grip tight, awkward from our being here on the ground. But ... I like it. My body sags into her, and I tuck my head under her chin.

"You gots to stand up for yourself, too."

She squeezes me closer. "You know what, Miss Lillian? I just might. I'm a hawk, after all. Best that I act like one."

Opus lex Baeroot - Enactment of Discovery

Ingredients to be gathered at any time of year. For most potent enactment, create at sunrise.

Poultice tracks location of the one to be discovered. It is important to note that, once location is pinpointed, the poultice does not continue to follow the one to be discovered. Target can move, at which point a new poultice will be required.

- Bark of birch
- Fangs of viper
- Cow's milk, pregnant
- Soil of fertilized harvest
- A piece of the one(s) to be discovered, from source
- A piece of the one(s) to be discovered's kin (if above is not available)
- Map of foreseeable discovery area

To be mixed at any time of year or day. For most potent blessing, create at sunrise.

Strip bark of birch and crush to paste. Place in cauldron. Beat fangs of viper to powder, then add to paste. Settle over hearth. Stir in cow's milk. Continue to mix until bark, fangs, and milk are blended. Set to simmer.

In separate bowl, place soil. Add piece of the one(s) to be discovered. (If not on hand, add piece of kin. Do not add both—this will not increase potency, but will diminish effects of poultice.) Repeat name of the one to be discovered thrice, then set soil and piece aflame. Add mixture to cauldron and blend until poultice froths. Allow poultice to cool.

Pour poultice over map whilst reciting the "Ode to Find." Keep a slow tilt to the wrist and do not stop chants or flow of poultice until location circle is formed and poultice solidifies on map.

13

LIES AND BOULDERS

Ellie Hallivard

THERE'S SOMETHING INSIDE ME. My head pounds, ears caught in a roar that dissipates, then returns with a vengeance to block all sound. And there's a grip next to the gift, a dense place, like pebbles got hollowed out then settled there, but it's more, a thing that *writhes* and *shudders*.

Nausea rises in my gut without warning. I roll to my stomach and release the bile that's swept up my throat. It burns, and the thing quakes. Blades of grass twist up in my splayed hands, the ground cool and soft beneath me. It hurts to move, but I grit my teeth and push up to pant on my hands and knees. The landscape blurs, and my forehead furrows as I clench my eyes shut and try to place where I'm at. It's a haze, but it comes back. And the more I remember, the more I fight not to curl in on myself.

The Elders. The Orchard. The ritual beneath Ol' Molly.

My gaze snaps open and I gasp. The pain, the Ancestors, the voice—it swarms my memories and sends 'nother rattle through my body. Did it work? Desperate to get my bearings, I push the heels of my palms into my eyes 'til light sprinkles the backs of my lids, then clamber to my feet. They quiver and ache. I must look like a newborn colt, the way I stagger to stay upright as my knees wobble and threaten to give out. But I won't let them.

Ol' Molly rises up before me, a dark silhouette to cast shadows over my lone form. Red heat flashes up my spine. Those liars. They hadn't prepared me for this. To share my body with an Ancestor like it's a vindictive spirit in and of itself. My gut rolls 'gain, but I clamp down the sensation and shove it back. Overhead, the sky has bled out to plum and the soft shades of pink and orange that signal sunset have gone. A fresh scent of dawn and apple crisp coats my skin while the ritual dress ripples in the weak breeze. It's colder than it has been the last few nights, a chill that slinks through my flesh, and I wrap my arms 'round myself, a vain attempt at warmth.

Through the shear material of the gown, my skin seems translucent, a sickened pallor, save the bold color of the paints. I look 'cross the Orchard, but it's empty. They left me here, alone. A tremble starts, then tightens my cheeks while my nose flares. How dare they? I've lost Mama and Lillian, did they think to abandon me, too? Blood slips onto my tongue, and I release my teeth from they grip on my lower lip. I need to get 'way from here—return home and gather myself before I seek them out.

The being next to my magic rumbles. It spreads through my core and reaches the tips of my fingers like a vibrato. My eyes fly wide just before the voices start to hiss. Not the Ancestors, with they sandpaper bark, but the subtle rasp of the gift.

Predator. Flee. Death.

I whip my head 'round, eyes squinted to find what they've warned me 'bout.

Forsaken. Infected. Blood.

My feet stay rooted to they spot, but my heart thrums a staccato race. Forsaken? Infected? They've fallen into nonsense and left me here to die, just as the Elders did. I'll meet my fate in the

Orchard, which is fitting, since this is the place where I took my knife through Mama's throat. My chest clamps down on a lump.

I suck in and force my legs to move. They trudge a step forward, but it's like I'm stuck in a bog rather than standing on the green grasses of the Orchard. My vision swims, images of hands curled to fists and fangs that drip with saliva and something darker. Thicker. A flash of red hits the edge of my sight, and I spin to it. Then stop altogether.

"Lillian," I breathe.

I'm surprised she can hear me with how fragile her name comes out, but she tilts her head a tick, curls tossed over a shoulder, ear out to listen for more. She's just as I last saw her, a subtle shuffle to her stance. There's the same scattering of dirt and muck on the yellow dress she likes so much, but my flowers that are sewn in the hem lie hidden beneath a patch of what looks to be rust.

I know better. I was there. It's a feral stain of blood.

"Lillian," I choke out 'gain, garbled and wet with grief.

The way my breast constricts, I wonder if I'll be able to breathe right ever 'gain. She don't move closer, two stretched strides 'way from me, but she smiles when she hears her name. The left corner of her mouth crooks up, then that wideset grin I always tell her makes her look loony splits out. And there they sit, the fangs I've seen 'cause the gift. Those ones coated in death. I flinch back. Her smile falters at once.

"Sissy?" Lillian steps forward, then stops. Her hands wring together in a way I haven't seen before. Lillian never gets nervous. Not like this. I lose sight of her gaze when she glances down, her lashes a flutter of movement before she's back. And I see it—the silver that streaks 'cross her willow moss and kindling. Not gray, like the spirits, but something that crackles and sparks. "Sissy, why you gon' stare at me like that? Don't want you looking at me like you all frightened."

The being inside me shifts, heavy and rumbling. My throat bobs as I swallow. "I ain't afraid, Lillian."

Her shoulders sway, those keen eyes sharp when she moves forward 'til we're feet apart and facing one 'nother. I can almost smell that ever-present scent of honey and dew on her, a mixture of the sweets she'd sneak from the cupboard and earthen mess that'd stick to her skin from climbing trees and rolling in the fields. But there's an underlying smell. It's cold, like an empty bird's nest caught in a fog. Behind her, the rows of apple trees grow black in the shuttered sky. Like skeletons. Or spirits. The voices continue a steady hiss, they pleas a litany I cain't quite tune out.

"I done brought you a gift. Kept it all this time 'cause I know you gon' want to stay with me," Lillian say.

Her smile's back, those sharp teeth dropped down to touch her lower lip. I bite down on my own. Lillian's gifts are made up of lizards and unearthed plants and tricks that tend to leave Kylie soaked to the bone. I doubt this will be the same, and my knees start to wobble. My sister's left me unbalanced in a whole new way than from when I woke up after the Matriarch ceremony. I'm gutted, fleshed out with a carving knife. And I am a liar 'cause my nerves are lit in a fear so bright hot that it's like blades of ice.

She reaches behind her dress and fiddles, then pulls her hand back out to where I can see.

"No," I say, and stumble back, but she advances, a naïve light in her gaze, anticipation written on the dimples of her cheeks and outstretched reach of her hand.

There, she holds a Bloodbud. It glints in the low light of the waning moon overhead, a toxin in the form of a flower. The petals are gray, just as I remember them. Gray like thunder. The leaves shift and ebb, red as the setting sun. I try to move, to run, just as I know I should, but that infernal bog that ain't really here laps at my legs and holds me in place. Even when I look down, frantic in my attempts to lift my feet and stomp on the grass beneath me, they don't budge.

Lillian's head tilts the opposite way, her footsteps halted. Her hand falls to her side, the mottled yellow of her dress a backdrop to the Bloodbud's form, her curls all angry, a flaming halo 'bout her head. "You ain't gon' leave me 'gain, is you, Sissy? I can bring you and Kylie and Papa and all the Orchard with me. Every last one. We can stay together, always. You the Matriarch, now. All you gots to do is touch it. And it's all pretty and delicate, too, ain't it?"

I drop my gaze to the Bloodbud. There's a draw, an impulsive desire to touch. The petals lift on they own, a gentle sigh like they want to caress the tips of my fingers. They look all soft and velvety, and I bet they'd be warm to touch. My lips part, and I sway forward.

But the gift shreds at my chest, a stark contrast to the Ancestor that sits and waits and rumbles as it watches. My hand wrenches back from where it'd stolen toward the Bloodbud. No. I cain't do it. I won't do it.

"Lillian," I gasp out, "go. Leave the Orchard Clan and never come back. I'm begging you, please, find some new home far 'way from here."

If she'll just leave, I can protect her. She won't be a threat, though she'll remain a monster—an undead creature, as the spirit had said, its cackle a toll in my ears through the guise of Mama's voice. There won't be no need to go after Lillian if she disappears.

But my sister purses her lips and examines the bloom in her hand. Her silvered eyes flash. "I can't just go. Not like that, Eleanor. I'm the Forsaken, exiled in existence, and I can run a hundred, thousand miles away, but I'll still haunt you and the Orchard Clan and the Coven and the Matron until all of you are dead. I have an eternity to do so."

When she catches my eye, the stark truth of it all falls into place. My breath sucks in sharp through my lips to sting the back of my throat. A cold, smooth touch fills my hand, sudden in its appearance. I don't question it. Not this familiar grip, the handle a perfect fit for my palm. Just the way Papa made it. I clench the dagger tighter.

This ain't my sister, ain't my Lillian, just as that spirit wasn't Mama.

They curses.

The grumble in my gut strengthens, my hand a reflexive twist 'round the blade in my palm.

Lillian takes 'nother step forward. "Touch it, then we'll infect all the Orchard. A family for an unending lifetime."

She's so similar—the hair, the brashness, the sincerity—but that pale scent wafts under her honey and dew, the glint in her gaze that mares the willow moss and kindling a vicious taunt. 'Nother voice gathers, one separate from the gift, from my thoughts.

One that chords like beaten rocks. One that echoes a question I've answered yes to for years and solidified in my oaths as Matriarch.

"I love you, Lillian." The words bleed soft, and her face loses its sneer, the creases smoothed out to remind me of her innocence while at slumber. My heart shatters, and my hand shakes. "But you're a monster."

The rumble crescendos, and Lillian's eyes widen in shock, then her lip pulls back to reveal fangs as an inhuman snarl wrenches itself from the depths of her throat. She drops the Bloodbud and lunges, but I'm quicker. The Old Language singes my body where the paint's been drawn, and I sink the knife into her neck. The world burns white, that roar back in my ears, but Lillian don't do more than stumble back before she's at me again, her fangs aimed at my throat.

She's broken my heart.

So, I swing at hers.

It's over in an instant. Blood runs down my wrist and slides to my elbow; iron fills the air. I gasp, a stutter of breath, then I'm screaming as I fall to my knees beside her. My sister, with her open, dull gaze and slack mouth. Little Lillian, her yellow dress fanned out 'round her and that ring of red hair no less bright for the lack of life in her body. I hit the dirt and wail, begging the Ancestors to bring her back to me, to take my life for hers 'cause *it's too much*. I've lost her twice, and both times, I was the cause.

"Please," I shriek into the empty dense of the Orchard. Ol' Molly looks down on me, branches spread as though to protect us from the cruelty of the world. She's done as poor a job as I. "Please, bring her back. Take me instead!"

Only the rustle of the wind answers. Then, the ground rumbles. Lillian's corpse shakes with it, followed by the trees that surround us in the night. They here. They've answered. I choke on a sob, my spine alight in a dread and relief that sweeps out to my toes and my temple.

Then it stops. I startle, taken aback by the sudden shift, before the Old Language painted on my body comes to life. It slithers on my skin, burning ropes of blue and red and orange and yellow, the gray of Mama's ash like tracks of fire on my face. Pain and fury strip my voice as my mouth's left open in a silent scream. The Orchard shimmers, then drowns 'way, Lillian's body snatched from beneath my hands, and I swallow 'round the nausea as the reality I sit on shifts. Blackness creeps in, like the slow descent of sleep on an exhausted subconscious. I fight its hold, claw into the few blades of grass left under my hands and tense my jaw 'til I think my teeth will crack. But it's no use. The dark swallows me.

When I draw back to wakefulness, there's a quiet lull of chatter to my right. I try to open my eyes, but they won't move. My fingers twitch, then fall slack. And everything *aches*. When I swallow, my throat scrapes 'gainst itself, like I've eaten cayenne and nothing else.

"Shh, Mary, look," someone says, then fingers light my face. They cold, and I groan. "She's awake. The water basin. Now. She'll be thirsty and disillusioned. *Hurry*, Mary."

There's a rustle, then the welcome slosh of water. I work harder to peel my gaze open at the temptation of something to ease my barren throat. Someone wraps an arm 'round my shoulders and hoists me to a seated position. I blink as a mug touches my lips, then snatch it from the person's grip and lean my head back to take it all in.

"More," I rasp.

The mug returns in an instant, filled to the top. Silence settles, save the desperate slurps I make as I drink. The arm don't leave even as it shakes to support me, and after a time, my vision loses the hazy film that had settled over it.

Mrs. Broussard kneels before me, eyes wary. When she meets my gaze, she attempts a grin. It's grim, and I shiver.

"How do you feel, Eleanor?" She takes the empty cup and refills it, but I shake my head.

If I drink any more, I might upend it. My gut roils, arms shaky and legs a terrifying shade of numb. Mrs. Laurelyn and Mrs. Childress stand near. There's a thrum to the air. It tastes of bitter anticipation, like squirrel stew day.

"I feel …" My words catch, dry and sore, and I clear my throat, "drained. Like a fire swept through every crevice and burned me from inside."

She nods. "Yes, the Old Language will do that when it carves itself into your bones."

My eyes widen, and I search out my arms, visible through the gown. The paint is gone—every design—as though it was never there to begin with.

Mrs. Childress hobbles forward, her gaze locked on my right hand, curled tight into a fist. "Do you remember what you saw?"

My mind races and a ripple flows through me, just under the skin. A wave of horror and pain, tinged with the roar of ground boulders and scent of sodden sugar. Taken with the sensation, I fold forward, hand over my breast. A sudden desire to curl in on myself awakens, but there's something in my gut, the trickle of a rumble, that keeps me from toppling forward. I shake my head.

Yet 'nother lie.

Mrs. Childress gnaws her cheeks. "Some remember, some don't. We've never understood why the memories are fickle."

My chest constricts. What did the other Matriarchs see to make them lie? Things terrible enough to hide? My lips part to suck in a breath of nighttime air. "Did it work?" There's still a weight in my palm, wrist heavy from the blade I plunged into Lillian's chest. What if I'd failed yet again? Had the Ancestors rejected me?

Mrs. Broussard smiles, then pats my leg. "The Old Language took, dear girl."

Mrs. Laurelyn squeezes my shoulder where she keeps me upright, her face shrunken and drooped with lines of age. "The Ancestors are with you. Eleanor Gwen Hallivard, you're the Matriarch of the Orchard Clan."

14

HONEYSUCKLE, STEEL, AND MARROW

Lillian Hallivard

MY BLOODBUDS IS all poised and pretty where they laid out in a row, petals gray 'gainst the grass by the stream. It gurgles and frets while little fish dart 'tween pebbles and wayward sticks. I don't like it as much as my pond, with the lily pads strewn 'bout so frogs can jump along them. There's a constant *flap-smack*, *flap-smack* from Dorothea, her arms sinew as she beats our clothes 'gainst them boulders to my right.

"Hey, Dorothea, 'member how you said I'm strong and such?"

Her chin tilt my way, even as she keeps up the rhythm o' our laundry. "Yes'm. Sure do. Why, what you thinking 'bout?"

My cheek gets caught 'tween my tooths, the blunt ones, not the sharp ones, and I worry the flesh there with furrowed brows. "Think I can lift that boulder there that you working at? Looks heavy."

This time, Dorothea's pace falters. She peers at the rock 'neath her sodden slip. "Don't know, this a mighty sturdy one, here. You might hurt yourself."

"Didn't hurt when that wagon rolled right on over me." I huff and pull pruned fingers through the tangles atop my head. It ain't that big, the boulder, up to Dorothea's hip where she kneel next to it, just large 'nough that I cain't wrap my arms 'round it. "Bet I can, though."

She just shakes her head and shifts back to work. My belly grip tight, then a rumble start in my chest. She acting just like Sissy would when she didn't believe me no how. The Bloodbuds glint next to me, they leaves ruffled in the wind like they want me to do something. I bare my tooths out and a snarl rolls from my mouth.

Dorothea startle, one corner o' the gown slipping from her hands, and her eyes widen when she whips her head my way. But she don't cower. 'Stead, her own tooths slide down and a growl rumbles out her chest. The voices build, hoarse and angry. *Defend. Attack. Tear.*

I launch myself at her just as her haunches tighten to stand, laundry forgotten. She hits the ground on her side, leaves and pine needles crunched 'neath us, then she's shoved me off. Her eyes light in brown and silver—the original hue and the new one. But her silver ain't harsh like mine—ain't deadly and crackling, like lightning.

Her lips pull back 'til they show pink gums. There's dirt in her hair and under the nails that curl into claws, but it's the scent that catch my attention. My nostrils flare with it, a mix o' honeysuckle and steel and marrow and something empty, something like a frosted winter morning. It alights on the breeze and wraps 'round me: a threat. Like she's marking territory. The trees and stream go fuzzy, then white heat licks at the back o' my neck. In my mind, the voices shrill.

I shriek at Dorothea, then I'm on her 'gain. Just a bound o' my feet. The attack catch her by surprise, by the way she take a step back, mouth open like them fish in the stream, eyes bugged.

But it don't matter 'cause my tooths at her throat, then they sink in.

Her blood rush out and she struggle, but I clamp down on her shoulders and dig my knees into her belly. All at once, she drop and still, though her heavy pants hit my throat and flutter my hair more than the breeze did. I wrinkle my nose at the taste o' her but don't let go. It's not like the honeysuckle and steel and marrow o' her scent. Nah, it's more a muck, and it's cool. A congealed jelly that's a river's breadth o' difference from the warm syrup o' the humans. It's all wrong, but I don't gag. My stomach pitch then settle, and there's a tingle at the root o' my tooths. When she fall completely lax below me, I let them slide back in and release my grip.

Dorothea stay still when I scramble off, my own breaths no more than quick, whistling gusts. Her eyelashes flutter over glazed eyes, and a sludge settles in my stomach as I crouch next to my new sister.

"Dorothea, you alright?" My arms wrap 'round my legs, and I settle my weight on my heels. "You fine. Ain't nothing wrong. Why don't you sit up?"

She don't answer, just fidgets her arms. They twitch then flop. I shudder 'gainst the frosty touch that taps its way on down my spine. Tears well up, and my throat tightens. Did I kill my new sister? The voices have calmed theyselves, though my tooths still tingle. Every breath I take, my chest jumps and burns. A whimper slips out, but Dorothea still don't move.

She's dead.

I break out into a low moan and struggle to my feet. She's sprawled next to the boulder, our laundry strewn all 'bout the ground, and there's a trickle down the side o' her throat where my tooths sank in and held tight. Words paint theyselves every-where. In my skin, on the bank, through the rustle o' the trees, spelled out by them fish in the stream.

Death. Infected. Forsaken.

This be a cruel curse.

My hands ball up, and the screams I let loose burn in the way I think water might if I drank it down while it boiled. They rip from me, every wailed burst, and I cain't stop once I start. I let every shriek fill me up, then I let it carry over this space by the stream 'til I cain't make them come out no more.

Sissy's gone. Mama's gone. Kylie's gone. Dorothea's gone.

Fear settles in my chest and taps at my ribs. I'm all alone.

'Cept...

I tear my sight from Dorothea and pin it on the Bloodbuds. My bloom, set all nice and pretty and delicate on the ground, biggest to smallest, like a family o' they own. I swear, they still waving at me, them leaves lifted and happy. I don't need to be alone—I can make more.

The voices hiss a tune o' praise when I pluck one o' the blooms from the ground. It's heavy in my hand. A weight o' comfort. Overhead, the barest hint o' sunlight sprinkles through the canopy, though most o' it hits the stream and makes it sparkle. The rays ain't no threat to my Bloodbud here in the shade, but they will be later in the day while I'm in town. My bottom lip quivers, so I bite on it to stop from crying 'cause letting more sobs out won't do no good. Not right now.

Dorothea's blue bonnet lies to her side, fallen when she dropped the laundry in her hands and knocked her dressings over. I cain't look at her—not when she lying still, eyes half-open—so I scramble to the cloth, grip it tight, then throw myself 'way. My chest heaves, an oily clasp in it, but it don't matter now. I need to get out o' here. Gone from my Dorothea.

It takes a moment to cover all the Bloodbuds save the one in my hand with moss. Then, I wrap the big, weighty one in Dorothea's bonnet. Without 'nother glance to my sister, her body limp and vacant, I trudge back to the clearing, lip caught 'tween my flat tooths.

If I'm gon' make 'nother Infected, I gots to go where the

people is. It's mid-afternoon, a busy time for town, but I clamber through the forest to that graveled place anyhow. Dorothea'd tell me to wait a little longer, let dusk settle so we had cover, but my stomach burns from the loneliness—twists in guilt and shame. My nose sniffles, but I gots to do something. Cain't be on my own, not 'gain.

It's calm 'tween the dusty red o' the buildings. They sag, and I know they deflated, too, 'cause that what Kylie always say the town look like when she come back from selling Orchard wares. De-flate-ed. Means all limp-like. I cradle the bonnet in my arms. Maybe William will be here. My chest blooms and a grin spreads 'cross my face. If I infect William, then surely Sissy will come live with me, too. Me and William and Sissy. Maybe Kylie'd want to be with us. And Mama, with a soft smile sharpened by new tooths, her hands able to brush all gentle through my hair.

But she'd yelled at me. I clench my eyes, and a whimper slither out. I cain't see Mama now, not after having hurt my new sister. A rod shoves itself in my throat, and I choke on the thickness. Mama don't want me no how.

But William … Sissy … Kylie … maybe she'd come so she could be with us all. And I can show them how great it is to be Infected. A giggle bubbles up from my throat at the thought, and I scamper through town, searching here and there for any sign o' William, but he ain't nowhere I look. The bristling joy dampens.

He ain't here. And now that I spent time trying to find him, the town's cleared out o' people; probably 'cause it a bright burn out and they slipped into the shops or ambled off to Madam Roux's ice house. The simple happiness barrels 'way and leaves a hollow placket in its place. I twist the bonnet in my hands, careful to keep it folded 'round the Bloodbud that's shadowed inside.

I'm gon' be alone tonight, no Dorothea at my side to talk

with. Just the moon overhead, the stray crack o' a stick when an animal sneaks close, then gets a whiff o' me and tucks tail in a new direction. I chew my cheek, heart heavy. It ain't fair. Not the way I've been left to myself like this, cold and desperate.

"Hi."

I jolt and the bonnet almost tumbles from my hands. A boy stands behind me, head cocked to the side. He's got to be Kylie's age, or just, and he look familiar. His hair's straight and shiny— something Sissy would call sleek—with a gaze like hazelnut.

I squint at him. "What you want?"

He blinks, eyes bulged for a moment, then his feet shuffle. "Want'd to 'pologize. Ran over you with my wagon the other day. Well, ain't *my* wagon. It's my Paw's. Still ..."

So, this the boy that ran me over. Now that he let it out, I recognize his voice, just a shade harder than bells. Kind o' like the *clank-clank-clank* o' wooden chimes. He got a good scent, too, no smog. It's copper with a hint o' lemongrass and rose. I cain't help the smile that leap out, broad 'nough that I gots to take care and keep my tooths tucked in.

"Don't you worry 'bout that. I cain't break, so it didn't hurt none when you ran me over."

He make a strangled sound high in his throat. "I thought I didn't *actually* run you over? That's what Paw and Madam Roux said."

"Naw." I wave him off, bonnet clutched tight in my hand. "You rolled 'cross right here"—I tap my ankle—"but like I said, didn't hurt. What's your name?"

"Trevor." He blinks, then shuffles a bit more. The veins in his neck flutter. "Trevor Williams. You?"

"Lillain Hallivard." Even though my family left me, I think I still able to call myself a Hallivard. Be a shame to not have a name.

Never knew Dorothea's family name. Just Hawk 'cause she swift and clever, though she let her neck flag that time in town with Trevor's Paw. Even hawks can get hurt. My chest thrums, heart a flutter o' fear and pain, even as the voices hiss. It's like they mad at the weakness. The ache o' Dorothea being gone. And we never did find an animal name for me. Gecko didn't work, and I ain't no hare. I gots my tooths, so it should probably be a creature that has some as well.

My gaze snaps back to Trevor as he purses his lips, nose wrinkled, then nods. "And what's that you got in your hand?"

My fingers furl 'round the bonnet, a sly desire to keep his eyes off the thing that be Dorothea's. Besides, there's something much better to show him. The voices start they hissing, a sway o' a beat, and my lashes lift when I glance up to him. I meet the whites o' his eyes just the way I done to his Paw.

"You want to see?" His jaw slackens, and his eyes grow a haze, one that tell me this thing that I can do working, the one Dorothea was in delighted fits over. A thrill flits its way down my nape. "Come on, you gots to follow me, then."

I know I cain't infect him here, out in the open. It's an instinct that light the back o' my arms. We turn to leave when a voice breaks out 'cross the way.

"Trevor! There you are with that girl. You come back here to this shop before your Paw get after me."

A growl starts in my chest when I recognize Madam Roux's voice. She ain't gon' take him. I already claimed Trevor as my new family. Ain't never had a brother 'fore, and now, I can. We can play leaps and frogs in the clearing and splash 'round in the stream, then build miniature plats with the pebbles we find 'round on the ground. A fierce warmth unfolds in my belly. Trevor be *mine*.

He stills, the haze clearing, but I grip his arm and find his whites 'gain. "Trevor, you gon' come with me back to the clearing, then I'm gon' show you what I got in this here bonnet. Let's go."

Madam Roux watches from the balcony o' her shop, the *v*

'tween her brows deepening the longer Trevor don't say nothing nor make a move to go back to her. My heart pounds. I should let him go. She done seen us, done called out to him, and once he with me he cain't go back. Dorothea'd make us leave, tell me we gots to go so we stay safe.

But if I let him leave, I'll be alone. All alone. The thought makes my belly sink, a pebble in the stream, then it rolls as if the current swept it 'way. We've gots to go. Now.

"Lillian?"

My body pull taunt and the tension in my back snap. Sissy? My breaths shunt out while Trevor stands next to me, his lips twisting as the haze fades 'gain. Why ain't it lasting as long this time? I fumble the bonnet in my grasp, then turn.

There she is, farther back than Madam Roux, though I see her clear.

She skeleton-like, not plumped out the way she was by that body with the Bloodbuds. Her hair's pulled back in a plait, the caramel blond dulled. But her willow moss and kindling shines. The color jumps out as her eyes widen, mouth agape and hands clenched at her sides. She's looking at me like I'm a spirit. A monster. A parasite. If my throat weren't raw from earlier, I'd wail.

Madam Roux glances 'tween us, then settles on Sissy. "You know this girl?"

Sissy don't answer, just stares at me. I cain't tear my eyes 'way, neither. The woman repeats the question twice more 'fore Sissy breaks her sight on me.

"Sister." She chokes on the word, then clears her throat. "Was. She—" Her words taper off.

My belly drop, like when Jericho kicked me on accident while we was playing in the Orchard one day. *Was.* Like I ain't her sister no more. Trevor shifts beside me, backs 'way, and I whip my hand out to keep him near. There ain't no time left.

His cooper and lemongrass and rose wafts over me. I meet his whites once more.

"Follow me. Don't slow down and don't fall behind."

I don't wait for the haze to settle back in, just turn and run. Sissy and Madam Roux holler out behind me, but I'm a streak to the forest, then beyond. The light footfalls o' someone follow me—Trevor. We race 'cross the trail I, then Dorothea, made from the many times we walked to and from town. Our own deer path. I don't let up 'til we reach the clearing.

Soon as I stop, he do, too, and though I'm hardly winded, he bends at the waist and heaves, his legs trembling. The bonnet's clutched tight in my hand. I need to make him Infected, and I gots to do it quick. My eyes is a constant flicker to the entrance o' the clearing as I rip open Dorothea's bonnet, then groan.

Ashes filter out and to the ground. I must've let it open at some point 'tween seeing Sissy and running. Trevor's upright 'gain; his breaths is shallow, and his legs jiggle in place.

"Come on, just a little more. We gots to go to the stream where the other Bloodbuds be."

Trevor's knees warble, lips and brows fallen to a pained expression, but we cain't dally. He follow when I move, and I go easy on him, keeping a skip-jog pace to the stream. Once he's Infected, it won't hurt so. The gargle o' the water sounds long 'fore I see it, and we make it to the embankment while he still got that film in his gaze.

I pull the moss covering back and my tooths snap down, a scream built up in my chest.

The Bloodbuds is gone.

My body tremors as I stare at the place I left them, lined up biggest to smallest on the ground. It's empty, nothing but grass and dirt. Despite the raw sores in my throat, I wail, then lash out at the spot like my hands turned to claws, my tooths dropped down as a snarl rips forth. There's a crack behind me and the voices rise up. *Kin. Blood. Infected.*

I whip 'bout, ready to face Sissy, 'cause she's my kin, but honeysuckle, steel, and marrow greets me 'stead, my Bloodbuds cradled in a bold hand attached to a body standing tall. The snarl turns to a whimper.

"Dorothea?"

15

SPLICES OF GOLDEN SUN

Ellie Hallivard

"ARE YOU SURE?" William's hand rubs 'gainst my back, a point of contact to keep me grounded as we walk past the pasture. I might turn tail and run despite it.

She'd been there, right in the middle of town: Lillian. Her eyes were bright, open wide with such hope I'd almost believed she was *our* Little Lillian.

She wasn't.

That new rumble that's linked to the gift had turned to a growl, a coyote ready to pounce and grip her neck between its teeth, then end this curse with a hard wrench of its jaws and snap of her neck. I shiver. William presses tighter 'gainst me.

He's been in the shop today, a smooth scent of pine dust and sweat on him, and his callouses catch the fabric of my dress. But I lean into him, then nod. I'm sure, and he needs to know. I cain't keep this secret from him no more, especially since I'm the Matriarch now. My fingers tremble 'gainst the vial in my coat. I wonder how many times my heart can shatter 'fore there ain't pieces left to stitch back together, just shards that cut and dust that blows 'way to never be seen 'gain.

William follows as I continue our trek. Mama loved the pasture; her favorite pastime was riding. Opal, her old gelding, looks up at me as we pass, more interested in our figures than the short blades of grass his grayed muzzle munches on. His head bobs, and he canters toward the sloped fences, a few of the colts lifting they heads to check his progress. No doubt, he expects an apple. I don't have one, but Mama surely would have, and my chest tightens. I cain't even care for him in the proper way, and he's lost her, too.

"Are you okay, Ellie?" William's voice breaks me from my reverie. I startle to realize I've stopped before the horse, eyes boring into his.

"As well as can be," I mutter, then turn from Opal. His haunches twitch, the gray of them bright 'gainst the ruddy hue of his coat. "We should keep walking."

To the pond. Lillian's pond. It's the only place that feels right to take him, with what all I've got to say. My fingers twist in the cotton of my gown. We're to hold a meeting with the

Clan. The Elders and I had discussed long into the dawn that night when I passed the trials, and we agreed. My sister cain't be a secret. I shake my head and correct myself. The thing that once was my sister. The Forsaken. We need to come together if there's to be a hope of ending this curse.

It will mean destroying her.

I swallow, saliva thick in my throat. Every night I dream of the Orchard and my dagger in Lillian's heart, of the way she'd bared her fangs at me and lunged to kill. My hands shake, and I clench them to fists. The curse of the Bloodbud only ends one way for the Forsaken.

William stands by Opal a moment longer; there's no crunch of following footsteps. Then, he murmurs something low enough that I cain't hear and continues after me. I let go of a breath I'd held, of the tinge of fear that he would turn 'round and leave. He wouldn't. I know my William, a loyal man, protective, and that's what makes my stomach clench. 'Cause he'll have to choose me or his family. The Orchard or the humans.

Tears blight my eyes, but I rub them 'fore he catches sight of them. The vial weighs in my pocket like a dozen bushels of apples, too much to carry alone. We continue in silence, William's heat at my side. It don't take long. The pond ain't that far inside the woods. That's the only reason Kylie and I found it when we was young, before Lillian was born, the two of us after a mutt that Papa brought back from town. It disappeared into the brush, and we never saw it 'gain, but we found the little copse of trees, willows swung low and wide, they moss dipped into the water's surface.

When we brought Lillian, she dubbed it hers and latched her fingers onto the lily pads that coat the murky depths in brilliant shades of green, desperate to pull some up so she could take them home. The same pond I lost her at. The same pond I'm near certain I'll lose William at. My gut plummets, and I wring my hands in front of me, shoulders tight. When we come to the break in the woods, I glance back to William, my bottom lip caught between my teeth, brows pinched together.

He's somber in the low light that scatters through the canopy above us, his green-grass gaze soft, crinkles everpresent at the edges 'cause he smiles so nice with his eyes. Even when he ain't smiling, they there. Like now, his sight set on mine, lips turned down, head cocked to the left. But he don't ask me a question—just wait. A patient man. The lump in my throat grows. My hands grasp themselves 'til they turn white, the bones ready to crack and give way should I hold any harder.

I scan the ground, then find a spot that's more grass than dirt and muck. I settle onto the lone patch, my skirts draped out in a blanket, and William copies my movements with crossed legs. The vial clinks 'gainst the ground, and I wince.

Silence spreads between us. I cain't make the words come out, so I look to my lap instead and pick at the pads of my fingers. It's a calm day with no breeze to ripple the water or shake the willow moss so it waves at us. My skin tingles, little pricks, and it's hard to breathe. How am I gonna be able to talk? There's a rustle in front of me, and I lift my gaze to watch William.

He spreads his legs out and crosses them at the ankles, then leans back to bear the brunt of his weight on his elbows. There's a peace to him, in the way his chest moves in steady pulses, his eyes closed and chin lifted up like he's listening to a whisper. I cain't help the smile that flits 'cross my mouth or the way my hands lose they tremor.

One last, deep inhale, then I clear my throat.

"William?"

He hums, eyes still closed, a soft lilt to his lips. A sign that I've got his attention.

I fiddle with a twig on the ground. "I've got to tell you something"—I close my eyes, breathe in a second time, then focus on the serenity of his expression—"and after I've done told you everything, if you don't want nothing to do with me no more, I'll understand. I just need you to be set in truth with me if that's the case."

His eyes snap open, head turned to me. "Ellie, I ain't never gon' leave you. I want you to know that."

William's voice stands firm in its conviction. A frown dips his face 'gain, and I want to smooth it out with my fingertips. But there's a distance between us, a chasm that cain't be crossed lest it tear farther open and drop us in its depths. The gift yawns open in a plea to keep him near. Tendrils of magic shift within me so they can curl as close to him as possible. It nearly breaks my resolve.

I give him a grim smile. If he stays with me after I tell him of the Orchard and the Coven and Lillian, it'll be a miracle.

My hand extends out, as though to grasp his, but I spin my fingers back in on theyselves and place my clenched fist in my lap.

"Maybe not me, but you might walk 'way from everything else. From my duty and my family and my history, and that's okay, William. I-it's not what I want, but I'll understand. You're human, after all." From the furrow in his brows, I know the wording ain't lost on him. There's nothing to do save speak, and I don't lessen the blow of my words. Won't do no good, anyhow. "I'm a witch. Same as Kylie, and Mama, and all the women of the Orchard. We the Orchard Clan, and we got sister clans. Like the Everglades and the Pineshift. We part of the Coven ... well, in a way. That's 'nother story to itself."

I pause, suck in a shattered breath. The rumble that sits in my stomach has grown, though it don't seem angry. Just ... invested. Like it's ready to jump forth should it need to. My link to the Ancestors. It's powerful, just a small lash 'way from tearing me apart from the inside. I wish Mama were here to tell me how she managed with that kernel of fire in her core. It's overwhelming. And if it don't like what I'm doing here, I don't doubt it could singe me from within.

Even if it did, I'd tell William. He's a right to know 'cause I want to be with him. Forever. My soul tied to his.

William's gaze is still on mine, the green darkened to match that pond at our right, its surface smooth, like if I tapped it with my finger I'd find it to be solid. He don't move, not a twitch, then he nod his chin. An inclination to continue.

I snap the twig in my hands on accident and examine the broken parts. There's a shred of wood, stronger than the rest, that keeps the two pieces tied together. My thumb strokes over it. "Each clan has a leader. That person's called the Matriarch. Mama was the leader for the Orchard Clan, as was Grannie, before her, but now that Mama's done passed ..."

I hesitate, the words caught in my throat. What's he gonna

think? That I'm loony, most like. That I've born too much grief in the past few weeks and it's left my mind weak.

"You. You're the Matriarch," William says.

My hands tremble on the twig and the grumble rises. It shakes in my chest, a warning, but I push it down. He's to be my other half, if he wants to after this. I won't tie myself to William without giving him the option to leave. He ain't just binding himself to me; he's binding himself to this life.

The grumbles soften, then curl up, like the Ancestor's in acceptance of my reasons.

"Ellie," William begins 'gain, those crinkled eyes still on mine, "am I right?"

I nod. But I don't speak. Not much else to say if he's ready to leave. I slide my fingers down the outside of my dress to trace the vial.

William hums. His chest continues to rise and fall in that steady way, deep and powerful. "Well, ain't that a hoot, Madam Roux's been right all this time." A smile graces his face, this one with teeth, and my eyes widen. The thuds 'gainst my ribs shift so they come from my own hopeful heart, not the rumble of the Ancestor. William reaches over, right 'cross that chasm, to take my hand in his, the twig long forgotten. "Do I got to call you Matriarch now, or is Ellie alright?"

He squeezes my hand, but I don't return the gesture. My lips curl down. "This ain't a joke. I'm not lying. And if ... if you're gonna say yes to me today, I need you to know what you're getting yourself into. There's dangers in being a witch. Spirits a-and ..."

Lillian. I bite my lip and turn my attention to the pond. Her pond. I always said she was wrong, that she cain't claim it just 'cause of the lily pads, but now I cain't think on it any other way. The pond is hers. It will *always* be hers.

William's grip tightens on mine. "Ellie, look at me." I swallow 'round the lump in my throat and tear my gaze from the water's surface, still solid and flat. His mouth lies in a line, eyes on mine. "I believe you. And I ain't mocking you. I always knew there was something different 'bout the Orchard, all the towns-folk do, but there was more. All those ciders you brought me? I'd go to chop wood for the next week and pull double my haul." His brows raise, and I duck my head, cheeks flamed. "That was you, wasn't it?"

I lace my fingers through his, the skin rough from his work in the woodshop. "Never could get that just right, always made it too strong," I grumble. "Poultice of Strength and Prosperity."

William's grip tightens, and I glance up to eyes that shine in the low filter of sunlight. "That what it's called?"

I nod, then follow as William wraps an arm 'bout my waist and pulls me to his side. He's solid. The gift unfurls from its spot in my gut and moves to lean on him, too. A warmth like mulled wine sinks into my marrow. He tucks me in 'gainst him, and I lean my head on his shoulder. William's always been safe and soft and firm. A place of comfort. Somewhere I felt no shame in being who I am.

"Tell me more. I know that's not all." The words are gentle. His breath flutters the wisps of hair at my forehead to tickle my cheeks.

I close my eyes and breathe him in, a welcome scent of pine dust and sweat and cider. "You'll not like what you hear."

There's a pleasant pressure on my temple: William's cheek lain on my hair. "Makes it the more real, I s'pose. Life ain't always a good story."

So, I tell him. The sun sinks, and we shift every so often, but he never pulls 'way from me. I move to the rise and fall of his chest, grasp his hands when mine start to twist blades of grass from the ground. He stills when I tell him of Lillian, tells me he needs a moment when I explain spirits and they way of burrowing into a witch's mind, of possessing humans and the Clan alike, asks me to speak of the curse 'gain, nose wrinkled, lips drawn tight, after I've gone over it once, and tugs me closer still when I get to Mama, the Orchard. I don't tell him what I did—cain't, with the sobs that rack my body, curled in on myself. But I've told him enough, and the weight of the vial in my pocket hangs all the heavier for it.

In a sudden fit, I rub the tears 'way, angry that I done fallen apart like this in front of him. Why am I still choked up in this way? I have to be stronger—there are too many people's lives in my hands now—and I can mourn Mama and Lillian on my lonesome rather than out in the open like this. William don't seem to mind, though, and his hands come up to rub my shoulders as a few final shudders rack through me.

"Sorry," I whisper.

He grasps my chin and tilts it to him, brows creased in such concern I want to both slam my barriers up and burn them down all at once. The gift rushes to meet his touch, like its only desire is to leave my body and fill his.

"Ain't a damn thing to be sorry 'bout, Ellie. Not a one."

The swear breaks a huff of a laugh from my parted lips, and William graces me with a smile that's full of teeth, that dimples his left cheek. He always did have a good smile. A kind smile. It reaches up to his crinkled eyes and ruffles his nose. I sigh and dip my forehead to his. He meets me, cups the back of my neck, but I cain't settle yet. We're not done here. With laden arms, I pull back and push him 'til we can look at one 'nother, a foot apart. He leans 'way, gaze flitting over my face, then sits straighter, like he knows the air's shifted.

I palm the vial in my dress, but reach into 'nother pocket and pull out a flask, first. It's filled with a clear liquid, almost to be mistaken for water if not for the bubbles within. William eyes it, wary, brow creased.

"It's a Poultice of Lost Remembrance," I say when he licks his lips, a sure sign he's 'bout to ask a question. "If you don't ... I mean ... if this is too much and you'd rather forget it all, you can drink this. It will take your memories from the last six hours 'way."

William reaches out and grasps the flask. He stares at it, fit into the curve of his palm, then closes his fingers 'round the bottle 'til it cain't be seen. I swallow, my gut roiled, but meet his gaze when he looks to me. Without glancing 'way, William brings the flask to his chest and flings it. I jolt, then swing 'bout as the poultice *plonks* into the pond, gone from sight in an instant.

"Oh." My gut rises then flops, chest lighter. "That ... we could have kept the poultice for later use with the townsfolk, but—" I pause, then find his forearm and grasp on like letting go means losing him forever. "I love you, William."

His gaze softens, and the backs of his knuckles brush my cheek. My eyes flutter, and I slip my hand into my pocket to grasp the vial. My throat clamps shut, and I panic for a moment, terrified I won't be able to breathe. But air makes its way in even as I bring the vial into view with a trembling hand.

The poultice floats, a cream that glimmers and shifts like I've captured sunlight in its depths. William sucks in a breath and reaches for it, but I jerk my hand back. He halts, frozen between us, and waits on me. The green-grass of his eyes shimmers, a bright beacon that I don't ever want to lose. I bite my lip, fiddle with the cork on the vial, then straighten my shoulders.

"William Johansen, I love you. More than the harvest the sun brings or the prowess and power of the moon. I want to spend my life with you, and beyond that as well." The words catch, and I have to stop. My nails dig into his forearm, but I cain't bring myself to loosen the grip. He don't pull 'way, just leans closer. His chest has lost its steady rhythm, and each breath brushes my face in a heady pant. "When humans pass, they move to the Beyond, but don't go to the Ancestors. This," I squeeze the vial, then hold it out. He takes it in gentle fingers, as though afraid the slightest pressure will break the glass, "ties our souls in death. It means you'll join me. We'll both be with the Ancestors."

I gasp when the rumble in my chest breaks out into a frenzy, a cacophony that stings my flesh and bruises my ribcage. I tense my shoulders and grit my jaw, though William don't notice, he's got his gaze on the vial, lips tucked between his teeth as he thinks.

My molars grind together as I fight 'gainst the Ancestor that seethes and tries to rip up to my sternum. This is *my* choice, a poultice *I* found in the grimoire hidden in Mama's room. And I've made the decision. My body strengthens 'gainst the plundering in my gut.

William's eyes close, his breaths steady, and I take the moment to grapple the Ancestor back.

The gift rears up and, to my shock, bears down on the Ancestor, fighting to keep William with me—with *us*. It gives me the reprieve I need to focus. I summon the magic in the gift, furl it into a wall, and slam the Ancestor down past my chest to my gut, hold it there even as it shreds at me. An inferno builds, embers caught to flames that rival the pain of the Old Language when it imprinted on my bones. But this is *William*, and if he so chooses, I want him bound to my soul.

The Ancestor roars, but I take a ragged breath and stay steady. William lifts the vial and thumbs the cork. It flies off with a *pop* and the air between us fills with the potent aroma of pine dust and cider, of leather and sage. His throat bobs on a thick swallow. "If I drink this, all of it, you'll be mine for an eternity? And I'll be yours?"

I nod, unable to speak over the magic that rages within me, all of my strength on the task of remaining calm to William's eye. His hand shakes, and the vial slips just a hair too far at one point, but William catches the overflow with a finger. He meets my gaze, open and hopeful. Then, he tips the vial back, the poultice down his throat quicker than I'd expected, and pops the small drop on his finger between his lips.

There's a beat, then a spark races down my spine, 'cross my shoulders, and into my magic. It settles into the gift then simmers, almost imperceptible. William shudders, eyes wide and mouth gaped. He trembles once more, then brings his hands to the ground to support himself. The bellows of the Ancestor silence, then it curl down in my gut the way a stray cat crawls under the porch steps to hide. I let it go.

William's face lights, his smile spread wide, eyes crinkled, cheeks dimpled, and he sways forward to grasp me at my nape and pull me to him. I suck in hard, ready for our lips to crash together, then gasp at the chaste peck he plants 'gainst them. The gift all but *sings*.

He pulls 'way, then sets 'nother soft caress at the edge of my lips, then one on my cheek, 'nother at my brow, 'til he settles at the top on my head, his lips lingering there while he holds me tight. My heart quiets and shatters, a powder of stark joy, sharp relief, and a golden lining of something ethereal.

"S'pose we should get married, then." William plants the words next to my ear, his breath a warm gust there.

I huff, then laugh aloud for the pond and the willows and the lizards to hear. My palms find William's back and I draw him in, wrap my arms 'bout him in a tight embrace. This poultice done much more than the physical bond of marriage. He reciprocates and holds me close, like he ain't ever gonna let me go.

"Suppose we should," I sigh, then lean into him and prop my chin on his shoulder, "but that's an event for 'nother day."

The pond glints then ripples. A frog hops from the bank to a lily pad, its mouth open and pink tongue curled, the water bugs unaware. I close my eyes and tuck my nose into William's chest and breath him in. We've got forever.

Opus lex Baeroot - Enactment of Lost Remembrance

Ingredients to be gathered in the night. For most potent casting, create under a cloudless sky.

Poultice removes memories of the consumer (time lost depends upon potency of the brew, and amount of time that's passed between creation of the brew and the consumption).

led

- Leaves of mint
- Elder berry, whole
- Cardinal lungs, rotted
- Butterfly wings
- Dogwood bark
- Dried lavender and rosemary
- Forgotten Memory, bott

To be mixed at sundown. For most potent casting, create under a cloudless sky.

In bowl, puree and blend together leaves of the mint and elder berry. In cauldron, boil rotted cardinal lungs with water until softened. Stir in puree. Whilst boiling, whisper intent of lost remembrance to butterfly wings, then add to mixture.

Stir thrice clockwise and remove from hearth. In new bowl, light dogwood so that it is smoking, then allow incense to infuse brew for one to two hours. Puree dried lavender and rosemary and add to poultice. Allow to simmer in hearth. Mix brew continuously and remove from hearth.

Add bottled forgotten memory to brew. Be careful to ensure substance does not slip away before it reaches mixture. The longer the memory, the more potent the poultice.

Bottle brew.

Consumer must drink entire mixture for loss of remembrance to take place. Longer effect will be maintained if drunk by creator and cast with enchantment.

Poultice can be stored for three months in cool place.

16

COYOTES IN THE NIGHT

Lillian Hallivard

A FROG SITS on the bank o' our stream, his throat a clear balloon that fill, fill, fill 'til he gots to tilt his head back, then deflates swift so his body all slim 'gain. He's green and slimy with little balls for toes. My fingers twitch—I want to lunge after him, grab him right out the clay—but I stay near Dorothea.

My sister that still alive. I peek at her where she paces, then flash my tooths in a wide grin. She show hers right back, eyes crinkled, and I can *feel* the contentment that spark off o' her. It's like we linked now, all 'cause I sunk my tooths in her throat.

I spin patterns in the dirt 'neath my hand. "What got you all happy and anxious, hm?"

"There another one o' us. I guess I didn't never think 'bout having more, but now ... why, Miss Lillian, we could make a difference. Could find people like you and me that been abandoned or mistreated and give 'em a home."

Dorothea's cheeks glow in her fervor, tooths slipped out like she cain't control them. The voices hiss and slither up my spine. She make it sound nice, but I don't want just anybody in my family. My fingers twist and drag through the loops I made in the clay. On the other side o' the bank, the frog croaks, his throat swollen, then falls silent as it goes lax 'gain.

"No, we cain't do that, Dorothea. Family gots to mean something."

She stills, then cocks her head to me. "You don't think that'd mean something?"

There's a shift o' something 'tween us, like she let out a challenge. It twist in my belly, and the voices bare they fangs, ready to strike out. A snarl trembles on my lips, and Dorothea's eyes grow wide.

Just as soon as it started, the challenge fades, that tingle under my skin gone. I lean back, ready to keep talking even as Dorothea pants in front o' me. My brows furrow. "You alright?"

There's a clench in my stomach. Cain't lose my sister 'gain. I dig my nails into the clay and lean forward, eyes on Dorothea's chest to make sure she don't start her convulsing like she did when I bit her. But she relax 'stead, her breaths easier.

"I think," she gasps, then suck in hard, "that my body get upset when you mad at me."

That don't make sense. My nose wrinkle as I frown up at her. "What you mean?"

She plunks down next to me, her legs wobbly like that o' a newborn colt, which be odd 'cause we don't get tired that easy. Us Infected. The frog croaks one more time, then leaps into the stream and disappears. My lips tucker down. I didn't get the chance to chase it.

Dorothea flicks a bug from where it landed on her leg. "I mean, you got mad just then, and my chest locked on up, same as my bones." She run a palm over her breast. "Think you changed me when you bit me. Like when you feel something real strong, I feel it to."

My fingers toy with the hem o' my dress, running the soft pads o' them over the embroidered flowers there. I can sense

Dorothea, too, kind o' like talking underwater and in a different language. A silent one. I ain't get locked up when she upset at me, though. 'Cause she was real upset when I came back with Trevor. Hissterical. That's what Mama would have said. Hiss-ter-i-cal. Like she couldn't quite get her words right 'cause her emotions was all over the place, a bottle cap that'd been twisted off, the jug spilt over. It made my mind hurt, the voices in a tizzy 'cause they got jumbled up in my chest, too, but there wasn't nothing physical 'bout it. Not like how Dorothea acting.

I pat the dirt 'til it crunched together and smooth with no patterns left. "You mad at me?"

She stiffens, then glance over. Her lips push out the way they do when she thinking hard. "No. Not mad. Just anxious, like you said. But I feel good, too. Strong." She grins, tooths out.

I smile back, then leap up. "Come on, we gots to go see what he's up to."

Dorothea nod 'cause she knows what I mean. The path to the clearing's dark and twisted in the shadows. The sun is just now peeping up, but the foliage lies too thick to let little trickles through. My teeth dig into my lip, and I glance up. When we enter the clearing, he's there on the edge by the Bloodbuds.

Trevor pets the bloom in his hand just the way I showed him how, just the way he did when he snuck 'round Dorothea to the place she'd moved them to keep them safe, his hand a gentle caress on the petal, that way he won't send it to dust with too fast a movement.

He ain't put it down since he first touched it. There was that same shudder as Dorothea, like a spirit slid up his spine, then his tooths had pushed down to his bottom lip, the skin puckered 'neath them. If he bites a little bit more, there'll be blood. But he don't, just rolls his mouth a bit like he ain't yet used to the feel.

I drag my gaze 'way, back to Dorothea, the three o' us in the clearing. She squints at Trevor, then locks her sight on mine.

"Miss Lillian, they gon' come after us. That there boy had a father, and Madam Roux and your Sissy saw you take him."

My lips pucker out, and my tooths nibble my cheek. "I gots a Papa, too, but he hasn't searched once for me. Sent me off is what he did." Screamed at me, called me a monster. The voices hiss as I flinch back from the memory. "What make you think Trevor's Paw gon' try and find him? He ain't special."

I tuck my chin in and cast a side eye to the boy. He's smaller than Jericho, even though he older, and his flesh all frail and sallow. It's like looking at a shed cicada skin—there's still a dash o' color, but it's see-through. Dorothea don't budge from her spot near me, legs tucked under her body on my sleeping pad o' moss. My legs swing out from my own perch on the stump, and I kick my heels back at it.

"I think," Dorothea start, then shift a bit so her eyes hidden 'neath her bonnet, "that you too special. Your family ain't no good, leaving you like they did. Don't deserve you, I says. But that don't mean Trevor ain't one o' us, now. You know that."

I does. He's got that fever pitch that make my hair stand on end and my nostrils flare. My mind tags him a predator, but my tooths and the voices hiss and spark in that way like when I'd nod to Mrs. Broussard in the mornings on our way to the Orchard. One o' us. Still, it's different from Dorothea, now that I bit her.

We got a connection—a tingle. It clamps down on my mind the way prongs do and feeds her closeness to me. I could close my eyes and know she at my side, know her gaze lingers on my back. It gots to be magic. Ain't no other way to claim it 'cept magic. Like Dorothea a part o' the gift, or a new kind o' spirit, and I get ripples o' her emotions when they strong.

My heels thud 'gainst the stump, and I squint up at a bird in the trees, its caws shrill. "Where we gon' go? You gots a home?"

She shakes her head, eyes on the same bird.

I hum. "Well, cain't go to Trevor's home." The boy flicks his eyes our way, a split moment 'fore they back on the Bloodbud. He turns this way, then that way. I still catch that flash o' silver in his blue gaze. "Sissy won't let me home. Don't think I'm her sister no more, anyhow."

My throat tightens, but I swallow down the lump. Ain't a time to cry. Sissy always used to tell me to grow up—said I was too old to throw tantrums. I cross my arms tight over my chest and huff a great gust through my nose. Ain't a tantrum if it's true. A beetle sprints over the grass 'tween Dorothea and myself. I don't got a feel to chase it. Not when I think on Sissy and how she'd said *was* to Madam Roux.

We cain't go home, but what if we went close to home?

I perk up on the stump and spin to face Dorothea. She's got some woven pine needles in her hands, and I tilt my head to the side, curls heavy over my shoulder. Her hands always at work with something. It's as though she cain't stand for them to be still. There's a thump to the side that I assume be Trevor sitting down at last. Dorothea finish her careful wind o' the current pine needle, then set what look like a mini basket aside. "Yes'm? You got a twinkle 'bout your eye, you does."

A grin slips 'cross my lips, tooths out in this place where I ain't got to tuck them in. "What if we went to my lily pad pond? It belong to me, after all, so cain't no one take us from it. It'll be our new home."

Excitement blooms in my chest, followed by a cascading warmth that makes the voices snarl and shriek. I growl right back at them. Trevor jumps, then cries out when he almost drops the Bloodbud. He's already getting on my nerves, and I frown at him. He ain't bold like Dorothea or strong like William or brash like Kylie or solid like Sissy or caring like Mama.

Mama.

My smile widens. "And I bet Mama be okay with us living there. She always been more p-pru … more prudent than Sissy. That the right one, Dorothea? P-prudent?"

Her eyes sparkle, and she grin back, then shake her head. "Not sure, Miss Lillian, but it does sound nice. You really think we can stay at your pond?"

My curls bounce as I nod, the red a flash 'gainst the yellow o' my dress, all clean from Dorothea. The flowers that Sissy sewn pretty and delicate in the hem is still there, just like the day she first pulled it on me and held the skirts up so I could see.

"Just you wait. Mama was angry when I came back, told me I couldn't stay at the Orchard no more, that people would try to hurt me or I'd hurt them. But, this ain't the Orchard, it just close. And we can still come to town to eat. We won't feast on none o' the witches or they family. Mama gon' like you, I know it. Kylie, too. Maybe if we stay by the pond and don't leave but to hunt, they'll come visit us."

I can see it, Dorothea and I stretched out on strewn moss with the lily pads along the water's surface like it's got its own skirts to cover it. Mama could come sit with us and watch the frogs and the lizards, especially on sunny days when it gets all warm, the water bright and glistening.

"Come on." I hop off the stump and grip her hand, rough and calloused like Kylie's. They can do they mens-chores together.

Trevor blinks up from his spot on the ground, Bloodbud clutched to his chest. "Where we going?"

"To Miss Lillian's pond. That to be our new home, Mister Trevor."

My nose scrunch at the way she call him that. It don't sound right. Not like how she say *Miss Lillian*, all fun and proper in a way no one at the Orchard ever did call me.

Trevor's lashes flutter closed over those blue eyes, and his nose twitches. A whine start up the back o' his throat. "I got a headache, a real bad one. And my teeth throb like they gon' fall right out. Why's it feel like this?"

I bite my lip, brows furrowed. We ain't fed him yet; neither o' us explained how he gots to eat people blood to survive. A phantom ache hits my tooths, and I lean down to pat his hand. He snatch it back, lips curled, but I snarl and grip his wrist 'til he cry out and let loose the Bloodbud.

"No one growls at me." There's crunch, his bone bent sideways, but my grip don't let up even as he struggles back and wails. Dorothea whimper and slide 'way, but I don't pay her no mind, focus locked on Trevor.

Rumbles build in my chest and stay there, tooths out, and we locked like that 'til he settle down with little whimpers. When I let go, he whips his hand back to his chest and cradles it. The Bloodbud lay 'tween us and I nod at Dorothea to pick it up. She stays silent, then plucks the bloom into her hands and tucks it into the folds o' her dress.

Trevor rubs his wrist, then his eyes go wide, impossibly so, like he half-owl now. "It ain't broke no more."

Dorothea's head snap to him, then me. "Well, ain't that something. We *all* heal fast, don't we?" Her gaze seeks out mine.

The voices slither forward like they 'bout to answer her, but I swipe them 'way 'cause I don't want to listen to they hissing. "Yea, guess we don't break easy and heal quicker than a caught blaze." I turn back to Trevor, his expression still awed. He ain't that bad, I s'pose. Just new. "We gon' go live somewhere else. It's close to my family, but I own it, so they cain't get mad we staying there. It's my lily pad pond. Like my name, see? *Lilli*-an."

He don't do more than nod, lips puckered so he can touch his tooths with his tongue.

"We'll tell you all 'bout that once we move. Gots a lot to talk 'bout when it comes to hunting." I hold a hand out and lift him off the ground. He's warm, but not the way he was 'fore I infected him. Not the way it is when I touch them humans, they skin a pleasant burn.

Dorothea stalks to the edge o' the clearing, then swings back to us. Her skirts lift off and fan out, a ribbon o' color, and she look better than the hawk we named her after. More bright and alive.

Her hands twitch at her side. "Do we got to cross through town to get to your pond?"

I exhale then flop to the ground.

It's all the answer Dorothea need, and she nod. "We just wait 'til it dark then, so no one sees Trevor, nor us."

It a full day 'til darkness falls, and we spend the time in silence: Dorothea with her pine needles, me with my Blood-buds, and Trevor with his wrist and his tooths. When it's time and I got the Bloodbuds packed in a pouch at Dorothea's side, we huddle together and trek the path to the town. I pop out from the woods first, then scramble to the well. There people out, but they should mind they business if we mind ours. I close my eyes and listen, then take long sniffs with my nose. It smell like gravel and dust and manure and the faint scent o' people, with they jasmine and vanilla and charcoal and iron.

I wave the others to me. "I think we be fine if we're quick. Keep our heads low and just cut straight 'cross, then take the path to the Orchard. That's where my pond at."

Dorothea fidgets her fingers, her back and neck taunt. "Miss Lillian, people bound to see us. Me with my ..." her voice trails off, and she look at her hands like they hold the answer. I squint at them but don't see nothing. She shakes her head, then keeps on. "And Trevor just come with us yesterday. They still gon' be on the lookout for him, and his Paw been in town a few times. I'm sure the shopkeep's familiar with his looks. Maybe we should wait 'til no one out."

Her voice drip in a tone I don't like. It's a mix 'tween fear and command, the way her throat warbles even as she barks the words out. My eyes flash, and I snap my tooths at her. The thing 'tween us tingles, and she duck her head, face hidden by that pretty blue bonnet.

"My family at the Orchard, and we ain't got to wait." I let my lips curl up, then fold them down to hide my tooths 'gain.

Dorothea glance up, and I think she gon' apologize, but her hand snake out to grip my shoulder tight and her eyes bug. "He gone off."

My brows furrow as I spin 'round and squint. Stones drop down in my belly. It's Trevor. He's 'cross the town, a bolt in the twilight after a man that's just stumbled from the saloon. It be that Marcus guy, his Paw. Trevor gon' beg him to take him back. My chest squeezes, throat tight, 'cause I know that pain o' being abandoned and called a monster. I sprint from behind the well to take off after him.

Trevor's Paw gon' scoop his hopes in hand and crunch them all up under his boot. My chest aches, and a wetness coats my lashes. Just like Mama did when she said I couldn't come home. But I is; I'm gon' to our new home at the lily pad pond so we can be close.

"Trevor!" My voice bring 'nother person to the porch steps, this man less wobbly than Marcus, like he got his feet well under him. A few o' the people nearby stop to see what I be yelling 'bout. "Trevor!"

The boy stutters in his steps, and my throat loosens. He gon' come back to me. I cast a glance over my shoulder to see Dorothea right behind us with the pack bouncing at her hip. Then a strangled noise come from up 'head, and I wrench my gaze forward. The voices shrill while my belly flop.

Trevor's got his tooths in his Paw's throat, the two sprawled out on the dirt in a grapple. The boy snarls, then starts to whip his head left-right, left-right, left-right. Blood flies out in spatters, and the body 'neath him falls limp. My belly pitch, the scent at my own nose, and I stumbled over how good it smell, even with the faint burn o' smog.

Trevor still hadn't fed.

His tooths must've been so *angry*. The wetness in my gaze

disappears, sight now ablaze as I take in the blood that drip from Trevor's mouth and down his chin onto his tunic. Saliva builds in my mouth, and my tooths snap down.

Beside me, Dorothea growl, and the voices in my head roar. She take a step toward Marcus, his legs twitching where his body lie. I gasp and pant, try to say no, and her body still like she stepped in glue, then she twist her muddied gaze to mine like she's waiting for permission to move 'gain. The voices shriek and wail and hiss: *feed, prey, danger, run, feast, flee.* I growl into the dusk, my mind lit in chaos, and Trevor dips his head back into his Paw's throat so he can rip and tear and shred some more.

"Attack! Marcus's been attacked!" The man from the porch disappears inside as I whip my head 'round. There's a boom, then a hollow thunder as dozens o' footsteps ring out into the night from the open door. The few people that had stopped to watch scream and shriek. Two men, startled into stillness, now snap to and run after a nearby wagon.

I shove Dorothea in the back, then haul Trevor up by the collar o' his shirt and throw him 'head o' us. "We got to run." I shove them both 'gain when Trevor tries to turn back on the body, then we pick up the pace, my eyes wide, spittle on my lips from where I'm yelling. We need to get out o' here. There's a sharp *boom* in the distance, then something hit Dorothea in the leg. She trip and stumble, held upright by my fingers fisted in her gown. Trevor snarls, a word that sounds like *gun*. The voices unleash theyselves even as Dorothea staggers back upright.

I shake my head 'gainst the hissing. *Rip, tear, shred, flesh, blood, feast.* A hot light flares up my spine and down my legs, fear and the need to kill at battle with one 'nother, but we haul ourselves up the road. Trevor quickens beside me, his face and hands and torso covered in the blood o' his Paw. A nightmare. A beast. The gift swirls in its crooked way. A giggle burst up from me.

And once one let loose, they don't stop. Dorothea chokes,

mouth agape, then she start in as well. Trevor blinks, his legs a near blur as he keeps pace with us, his face coated in red, then his lips slide back to a grin. He howls out and sprints harder. And we laugh, heads thrown back, feet a storm o' harsh thuds that kick up dust, like we a pack o' coyotes singing to the night with our tooths come out, come alive, come together.

Family.

Screaming 'cause the hunt.

Won't take us long to reach our lily pad home.

17

A SWARM IN THE SKY

Ellie Hallivard

"—AN OUTRAGE!"

"—No Matriarch of mine!"

"—To ruin!"

The shouts clammer 'round me, an anvil at my skull, and I near wish the voices would clamber up to beat out the enraged witches that I've gathered in Mama's home. *My* home, now that she's gone. It's our council—myself, the Elders, and the head of every house—all settled near my hearth.

A brew bubbles in the cauldron over an open fire—Poultice of Discovery—and Mrs. Broussard checks its progress while I swipe beads of sweat from my brow. It's dawn, the sun already a blister where it pokes out over the forest edge, and the sweet trill of robins makes its way in through the cracked windows.

The instructions had been clear: only the Elders and the heads of house were allowed near the cabin. There's no one to overhear as we plan how to take care of the Forsaken.

"We should call on the Blackwoods—"

"This curse supposed to end us, this Forsaken—"

My gaze blurs as I watch them bicker, then I tap Mrs. Broussard. "You think we need blood of the kin, or will this do?" I extend my arm, where perspiration glistens. There're more yells, but Mrs. Laurelyn has taken on the task of calming our Clan so that, when the time comes, I can speak without interruption. Right now, my focus stays on the poultice.

Mrs. Broussard peers back into the grimoire, lain 'cross one of William's stools. My hand flutters to my heart, an absent gesture, and despite the chaos, the gift swirls in warmth and a smile flits 'cross my lips.

Mrs. Broussard shrugs, lips pursed. "Don't say it need to be blood, just a piece of the kin in leu of an item from the one to be discovered, but ..."

I nod and sigh. Blood is best. I stand from my own stool and peer into the poultice. It's close to a look to syruped sugar, opaque in hue, but it don't smell like it. There's a potent scent of burnt parchment and rose, mixed with a sharp sting that's likely from the broiled bees.

Mrs. Broussard wipes a fine powder from her hands, then peers up through thin, grayed lashes, her willow moss and kindling bright as the sun continues its ascent. "You sure there ain't nothing left of Lillian's?"

I sigh and pinch the bridge of my nose. The brilliant shine of her hair flits through my memory, how the stands fluttered 'round her neck yesterday in town. My teeth dig into my lip, and I look to the Elder. It would be better if there were. "No, Papa threw it all out while we prepared for the Matriarch ceremony."

Kylie'd been inconsolable, screaming at Papa, telling him he had no right to erase Lillian's memory. He'd been ghostlike, face a pallor that rivalled Opal's whitened coat, his gaze set on Mama's inkwell that still held her blood. My gut rolls, hollow save the soft rumble of the Ancestor. He burned it all, every last sheet and toy, like that would erase the pain our youngest sister left behind. Like it would bring Mama back to us.

"Well, then," Mrs. Broussard holds out her hand, and I lay my own in it, wrist down so the scarred flesh underneath sits ready, "our men grieve in different ways. Not our place to judge, but it does make the poultice less effective." She slides a knife 'cross. I hardly wince anymore, not after the countless times I've used this spot for Mama's medicine.

When I've bandaged the wound and returned to my stool, Mrs. Laurelyn looks to me and nods. The rest of the witches have gone silent, though an irate bog of injustice hangs 'round us. My teeth sink into my lips 'til I taste iron. Then, I begin.

"You all know the story Mama spread of Lillian. Of how she drowned in the pond at the back edge of the Orchard's land. The tale Kylie, Papa, and myself told you, too."

No one answers. I suppose I didn't need them to. This my second start to the meeting, as the first time I uttered these words, the room broke out in calamity. Still, it's eerie, the way they gaze at me, a den filled with willow moss and kindling, subtle shifts in the shades. Some lie more hickory than others, a deep umber in one or two, but in all the ways that matter, the ways that make us witches, it's the same. I swallow, glance 'round for a glass of water that ain't there, then look forward and continue.

"We weren't truthful in our tale, as you've heard by now. This year be the hundredth year of the Bloodbud curse that was set forth by the Blackwoods and Miriam Hallivard. We were meant to keep it from fruition." I suck in, the gift a wisp of cotton in my mind, like it wants to drag out and cling together by the faintest of threads, but I cain't fall apart now. "And we failed. Lillian completed the ritual from all those years ago. She's the Forsaken. But—"

Mrs. Orville stands from the rocker in the corner. Her hair falls loose from the hasty braid she wound it in, a curtain of ebony to frame her sharp cheekbones. "You and your Mama kept this from us. It a curse that could destroy the Coven!"

The rest of the assembled witches burst forward with they own words, some standing, others shaking heads or clenched fists. Mrs. Edinsburg slams her palm 'gainst the flat top of 'nother's stool. "What of the townsfolk? The disappearances? They been riled and riled … just a matter of time 'fore they swarm us. Hornets whose nest been kicked and stomped on!"

The gift swirls, and the voices raise up. *Command. Kin. Safe.* From within, the Ancestor growls, kneads its claws 'gainst my breast. I open my mouth to speak, but a *thud, thud, thud* rings out over the witches. The assembly quiets, heads turned to Mrs. Childress and her cane. Her upper lip curls down, her cupid's bow wrinkled in age, and her eyes pierce those gathered. "You will listen to your Matriarch."

"That," I cut in, a grateful nod sent in her direction, "or you may leave and take your kin with you." Mama didn't teach me all she wanted, but she did teach me many an important part of my duty as Matriarch. To ensure loyalty, she said, voice soft yet stern, is pertinent to maintaining order.

The few witches that be standing start to back 'way, then sit. No one exits my home. I play with a fringe in my dress, probably where a bramble caught hold then tore through. Never was good at speaking in front of others, but that's got to change now. "We was wrong to say nothing, and worse still to lie. Mama was sick, and I …" My voice catches. I flick my gaze out over the room, all these faces familiar. "I didn't know what to do. Mrs. Broussard said just today that our men mourn in odd ways, and mourning Lillian while she was gone but not gone, took its toll. Now that I'm Matriarch, I'm working to make things right."

Mrs. Broussard pulls the cauldron from the hearth and places it on a pan to cool. There's a pause, then she sniffs and addresses the room. "We started on a Poultice of Discovery just last night." The witches murmur, heads tilted together, but keep quiet otherwise. "By twilight, it will tell us where the Forsaken is, but we've yet to determine how to put her down."

I nod. "The spirit that took Mama said the Forsaken may be an eternal being. I don't think she'll die of age, if we take the spirit at its word." My mind races back to that moment in the Orchard, Mama's body slit open from my hand, the spirit gurgling and laughing while it claimed we the liars, that it told the truth. A shiver taps up my spine, and I blink 'way the images of pooled blood and fallen apples, of fangs and smoke and clawed fingers. If the spirit was true in its word, then Lillian ain't alone. "But I do think she can be killed. A dagger to the heart. And if that works on the Forsaken, it will work on the other Infected."

Swift as a tempest wind, a cacophony of voices breaks through the room; shouts of "more" and "doom" beat 'gainst my mind. Mrs. Laurelyn scowls at me, but I ignore her—the others have a right to know. I won't hold this secret any longer.

Mrs. Kindred hollers for quiet then clicks her tongue from where she leans 'gainst the wall, her arms crossed over her breast. "We knew this curse would spread if it came to be," she snaps at the others. Then, she pins her sight on me. "You know this 'bout the dagger, how?"

"The Ancestors." I don't say more, don't tell them it's from the trials, where I killed the figment of Lillian conjured to be my test. No one questions further, satisfied by the answer. "Once the poultice is complete, we'll need a plan to capture the Forsaken, then kill her and any others. If we can, the disappearances will stop and the concerns of the townsfolk should taper off. Plus, there's always the Poultice of Lost Remembrance to help them 'bout they way. But we need—"

The front door slams open, and Mrs. Kindred jumps 'way just before it smacks her, dough beneath a determined fist. I startle back, the Ancestor in my sternum ready to pounce while the gift spins up to my throat. A shocked gasp slides through the witches, a few even leaping to candlesticks and brooms like they 'bout to fight. But my heart stutters and a warmth slides through my body. I know who's at the door before my eyes adjust to the morning sunlight that blinds us from its abrupt entrance.

William.

He bursts into the room with Kylie on his heels. That solid chest heaves, green-grass eyes wide as he scans the assembly. I'm halfway to him before I'm conscious of the movement, and the gift scrambles to be closer, to bury itself in him and calm the wildness in his gaze. Kylie slides past me to Mrs. Broussard, and I reach William as he pulls me in. The witches 'round us holler, but I don't pay them any mind.

"It's the townsfolk," William gasps, his voice low and hoarse, cheeks flushed and tunic soaked through with sweat. He must have run here. "They on they way to the Orchard. Ellie, a man was murdered in town last night. Got his throat ripped out, and Lillian was there with the kid who did it, 'long with some other lady." He stops to suck in a breath. I grip his arm tight while the Ancestor *roars*. Slick terror races down my nape and into my gut in a white-hot wave.

I tug William in 'til we chest-to-chest, partially to appease the gift as it imprints at the edge of my flesh, and partially to keep 'way from the witches and they prying ears. He bends 'til his face right near mine. "And there've been disappearances. I didn't think 'bout it, not even when we was by the pond, but it's got to be Lillian, don't it? Even if it ain't, that's what they think. Madam Roux was hollering 'bout it in the square this morning while the men gathered. They saw your sister and just knew the Orchard was behind the missing people. Says you all bewitched the boy, too. They in a rage, Ellie, all loaded up with they guns and torches and coming up the Orchard path. I ran" —he gasps 'gain, then grabs my arm back—"fast as I could.

Caught Kylie at the edge of the pasture, and she brought me here."

William slumps a bit, his weight a sudden drop on my shoulder, then he's up tall, his arms flexed as he pushes me 'way from the door. "You just stay here. You and all the women. I'll find your Papa and gather the others. We'll head them off by the bend and stop them from—"

"William—"

"It's okay Ellie, we'll settle this right. Try to—"

"William," I snap. The Ancestor curls tight in my breast and snarls, even as the gift continues in its swarm to be near my William. He stops his rambling, green-grass gaze held by my own even as those strong fingers that built for the brutality of chopping wood and the gentleness of whittling it to art curl harder 'round my bicep. "This a matter for the witches. I'm the Matriarch. This my charge."

His brow furrow together, then he steps close. "Nah, Ellie, you—"

"I'm the Matriarch of the Orchard Clan." Touch gentle and firm, just as I am in my needlework, I remove his hand from it's white-knuckled grip. Pink rises to color each finger as it uncurls from my arm. "Go to the men, tell them what's happened, and gather the children. Once you've done that, meet me at the bend. Perhaps you can speak to the townsfolk with me." He stands still, like he wants to argue, so I push him 'way. There's silence 'round us, all the witches trained on our words, and William scans they faces. I'm sure he's met with a wall of willow moss and kindling. I soften my voice. "You know what the Orchard is, how we delegate. William, go."

He takes one step back, then 'nother. I think he 'bout to argue, but he surge forward to press a kiss 'gainst my temple instead. "I'll meet you at the bend."

Then he's gone, dashed out the door and back into the sunlight. I loose a breath and turn to those gathered 'round me.

The Elders and heads of house. Mrs. Broussard nods, and I return the gesture. The Ancestor settles in my gut, ready to heed my words just like the rest of them. I'm lightheaded with it all— the rush of charge and command.

"Heads of house, you're to return home, hide your poultices and grimoires, anything that might reveal our nature, and bring any Poultice of Lost Remembrance you've brewed of late to Ol' Molly. Ancestors, guide you."

The heads filter out at the dismissal, the Elders still at the hearth, and I rush to Mama and Papa's room. The bed's disheveled, quilt piled on the floor where it was surely kicked off. There's a glass of drink on the nightstand and an unused balm near Mama's spot. I bypass it all for the tiny cupboard in the corner. A musty draft filters out when I fling the door open, feeling at the bottom 'til my hand lights on a knob. The familiar false floor pulls up under my hands, and I grasp after the grimoire that's hidden within.

The *Opus lex Baeroot* lies heavy on my lap. Its leather binding coats my hands in a fresh layer of oil, the permanence of it specially crafted by a former Hallivard. A stinging scent of polish and copper force my nose to flare, but it's calmed by an after-aurora of daisies. My fingertips shake as they trace the gilded title on the cover, then I rock onto my feet and rush back to the Elders.

Mrs. Laurelyn has a map of the Orchard and the surrounding area, including the town, on Mama's desk in the corner of the common area. Its hobbled legs groan as she leans over the parchment. Next to her, Mrs. Broussard holds a flask of the poultice we brewed, its hue turned to a rosy pink that shifts to burnished bronze when hit by the sunlight that glints in through the window. She tilts the vial 'til the liquid slides out drop by drop, and the soft whisper of the Old Language fills the room as they chant together. The sound grates my ears even as the drops begin they trek 'cross the map, locating Lillian.

"Eleanor," Mrs. Childress hobbles to me, her cane a steady *clunk, clunk, clunk* on the wooden floor, "we need to leave. Go to the Orchard."

The Orchard, where I've sent the rest of the Clan. My eyes flutter shut and the Ancestor churns. "I'm not going to the Orchard." The tome grows heavier in my hands, its polish mixing in with the sweet smell of vanilla that hangs on the witch in front of me, the way dew clings to the grass on misty mornings. I cain't go with them to Ol' Molly. Not when I could stop the townspeople on my own.

Mrs. Childress opens her mouth to argue, but I narrow my eyes the way Mama used to. She wasn't questioned often—most of the Clan would heed her word without rebuttal—but I'm new to this and still trying to gain they faith. There's no reason for them to trust me save that I got the blessing of the Ancestors and passed the trials.

For now, that's enough, as her lips thin and she waits. "There's a spell in here. One used by Gretchen when a spirit possessed a townsfolk."

Her gaze slip wide. "You cain't," the witch starts, then slams her cane down. I jump, same as Mrs. Broussard and Mrs. Laurelyn. But they go back to they mutterings as they track Lillian. The cane rattles more as Mrs. Childress leans her weight 'gainst it. "That a tome of the Blackwoods. I doubt they know we got it, otherwise they'd have been after it. Nothing good in there, child, only black magic that require shards of the soul. Gretchen was a fool to cast on her own, even more foolish to risk mispronouncing the Old Language when she ain't never learned it. You got a member of the Inner Circle in your back pocket that gonna walk you through a spell? We sure cain't help."

My eyes slide to the other Elders, a slow enchantment rolling off they tongues. A frown deepens the crest of my forehead, but I open the grimoire anyway and flip through the pages. They lined in blood, the parchment brittle on my fingers, a sandpaper that bites the dead flesh of my hand, but I work my way through 'til I find what I'm looking for.

"Mama never knew I found it, but I've read these spells countless times. This is the same Gretchen used to wipe the memory of the humans. If William and I can catch the towns-folk at the bend, then—"

"Then you'll choke on your words, tongue twisted up and hung down your throat. Or you'll sell a shard of your soul. Ellie, we just lost your Mama, we cain't lose you, too. Kylie ain't groomed to be Matriarch, and there's not a Hallivard left aside from her."

"I know, but Gretchen didn't choke, did she? And there wasn't a Blackwoods here to help." I place my hand on her shoulder while the Ancestor slides 'round the gift, them two chasing one 'nother like an unending loop. "Matriarch's got a connection to the Ancestors, and *they* know the Old Language." There's a rumble; it breaks out a vibrato in my chest. A small comfort with what little time we've got left. "I'll go to the bend, head off the townsfolk with William. You gather the witches at Ol' Molly and ready yourselves to slip the Poultice of Remembrance to anyone who didn't come tonight, any woman or man that got left in town but saw the attack. We can fix this without shedding blood."

"And the Forsaken?" Mrs. Broussard cuts in, hands on her hips. "What are we to do 'bout her?"

Lillian. My throat clenches, rough, like I've dropped a spoonful of cinnamon in my tea and taken a swig. The map's set out, a stain of rose and copper visible from 'cross the room where I stand. If we wait 'til twilight, we'll find her. I tug at the fringe in my dress, teeth dug into my cheek, then exhale.

"The Forsaken ain't attacked us yet, but William seemed sure the townsfolk are on they way to see the Clan hurt at this very moment. We need to settle with them, then move to Li—" My words catch and my breath hitches. "Just a day."

Silence hangs 'round us. The hearth crackles where the flames continue to flicker, the wood yet to die out. Mrs. Laurelyn and Mrs. Broussard share a look, noses flared. Then, they deflate.

Mrs. Laurelyn rolls the map up and shoves it in a basket tucked under the desk. "You'd be a fool to use any spell out of that grimoire, Ellie. Brave, but a fool."

My knuckles rap the page. "Do you think it'll work?"

She hesitates, eyes trained on the burnished ink. "I think it worked for Gretchen. And that might mean that it'll work for you, but there's only one way for us to be certain."

A chill rushes up my spine, and I shudder with it. She put into words my own fears. What if there's a difference between myself and that former Matriarch? Am I strong enough? My mind races to Mrs. Broussard's words from before the trial: *you'll only pass if you're strong enough to ensure the Orchard's survival.* And I had. My shoulders straighten, chin lifted to gaze back at each Elder in turn. "This our one chance. If I fail, we may well have to fight the townsfolk. Unless you know 'nother option."

Mrs. Broussard's lips twitch, her brows furrowed, but that's all the answer I get. We ain't made to fight, the Orchard, and we been good at keeping our practices a secret. Only minor slips here and there, rumors and whispers spread by folks like Madam Roux. Lillian done hurt us in a way we didn't expect by turning the townsfolk on the Clan. And this spell be the only option I know of to calm them all at once.

We exit my home together. The sun's ablaze, at an apex now that we've spent the morning indoors, and I shield my face with the slight shadow my hand provides. The Elders leave, and I spot Kylie as my eyes adjust to the blinding rays.

"Where are we to go?" She tugs Opal's reins from the porch where she tied them. Her hair's pulled back from her face, tendrils of spun wheat left out to flutter in the breeze at her nape. There's a wildness in her gaze, a tremor in the scarred marks along her lips where she's chewed through. The anxiety and fear rolls off her and toward me. It sends the gift into a spin, upset at sensing a witch in turmoil.

I take the leather from her hands, and Opal shifts his eyes to me, lips puckered out like he expects an apple. "You're to go to the Orchard. Now." I pat Opal's muzzle, then move toward his saddle. "When I'm finished at the bend, I'll meet you there."

Kylie takes a step toward me as I haul myself up. "But—"

"No." I hold out my hand, a physical barrier to emphasize my words. "I need you in the Orchard." My heart compresses, like I've poured molten steel atop it and the metal's cooling to encase it. I need her safe. Surrounded by the others. *I cain't lose Kylie, too.*

She hesitates, on the tip of her toes, mouth open like she's gonna argue. To my surprise, she steps back and nods. My hands twitch, and there's a burn at the back of my eyes, like they gonna water. I should say something more. Comfort her, tell her it'll all be okay. But I cain't. She meets my gaze, a glimmer to her own sight like she knows what struggle I face.

Without 'nother word, I spin Opal to the road and send him into a gallop. The longer I take, the less likely it is for me to head off the townsfolk.

It ain't a long ride on Opal, a few minutes, nothing more. No one from the Clan is out, not even the menfolk, so William must've got them to gather the children as I asked. My hands tremble as I take the page for the spell out of my pocket, along with a poultice vial. It's complicated in its steps but not in its ingredients. The Old Language shifts and roils on the page like it alive, unable to be held down though it's ink and nothing more. I blink at it, then have to look 'way when my sight blurs.

Drink the poultice. Recite the words within thirty feet of all who need to forget. Then gag myself 'til I no longer have the potion in my system, that way *I* remember. And the final piece:

A shard of my soul, taken as payment.

I rub my hand over my breast. Will it hurt? It was nothing but warmth and solace for the poultice that bound William and myself.

I doubt this will be the same.

A steady *crunch, crunch, crunch* from behind catches my attention, and I whip my head 'round. Then settle, the gift a warm spear in my chest.

William jogs up the trail, his tunic matted and smeared in dirt, a sheen of sweat on his forehead and 'cross his arms. "They ain't come to the bend yet?" He stops at Opal and reaches out to pat the horse's flank.

I shake my head. "No, but they might be moving slow. How many do you think was coming?"

William inhales deep, eyes skyward as he thinks. A lone cloud passes over the sun. It's thin, like spread cotton, and the shade does little to stop the sweltering heat. "Twenty. Maybe thirty. 'Nough for a mob. Where'd everyone else get to?"

He ain't gonna like what I has to say. My teeth grit down on my cheek, but it don't matter. 'Cause my sight catches on a thin trail of smoke far over his crown. I squint toward it, then place my hand on his shoulder and lean out on the saddle. Dread coils in my gut and the Ancestors growls.

"William, what do that look like to you?"

He turns, then shields his eyes as the sun pops back out with a vengeance. "Chimney smoke."

The gift churns, then bounces from sternum to throat. The visions I'd seen, with fangs and smoke rear up in my mind. Even as we gaze on, the puff thickens, darkens, rises up to blot out the sky. William takes a step back to me, his hand moved to clutch my own on his shoulder.

"Ellie …," he starts, before the words fall 'way in horrified silence.

Our Orchard is on fire.

18

INTO THE SHADOWS AND FLAMES

Lillian Hallivard

MY POND just the way I 'member it, with the lily pads spread out like a green blanket to keep the water warm while a wall o' willows sway to the side, always in they dancing. Dorothea shuffles Trevor off to the bank without so much as a glance 'round like this place ain't filled her with awe and peace. Don't matter. My chest glows, lighter than it's been since I was Infected. Should my heart get any brighter, I'm gon' burn from the inside out.

The sun cuts a splice o' light through the thick foliage over-head. If I close my eyes, I can pretend it's Sissy here with me. And Kylie. And Mama. And Papa. Maybe even William 'cause he's like family, too. A smile tilt 'cross my lips as I think on the scene, my whole family here with me, ready to be this creature that make us better and faster and stronger. This Infected. It feel like I can live forever, then even more some.

Dorothea and Trevor splinter my thoughts as they squabble. A crease cuts 'cross my wrinkled brows. "What you two doing?" My tooths snap out, but I reel them back up to they spot in my gums. It used to hurt, how they'd slice through my flesh, but it just a pinch, now. Less a knick than when Kylie pricked my thumb that one time, Sissy snatching the needle and thread up with a scowl 'cross her lips and brows.

Dorothea shuffles 'round, then squints at the pond. "Gots to get the blood off him, Miss Lillian. Cain't have him walking with that stain spread over his tunic. And all that still left on his face and throat, too." She moves down a ways from the lily pads, nose wrinkled while she taps her fingers 'gainst her chin. "We can bathe in here just fine, though it don't got running water like the stream did."

My breath rips a ragged trail down my throat when she kneels by the water, then beckons to Trevor like she wants him to dip his body in.

"No!" I'm at her side in an instant, quicker than I used to be, and wrench her 'way from the edge. She staggers off to the side, gaze wide, and there a ripple in that space 'tween us, the one that let me feel her that tiny bit. It whines, struck frigid like a rabbit when caught by a rat snake. My chest burns at the fury o' my breaths. "Don't put *nothing* like dirt and blood in my pond. Got that? Nothing. This a good place. I don't want no stains here. Or any bodies."

Her mouth's loose and open, hands hung in midair still. Short, staccato waves o' hurt slither along my nape from her, gooseprickles on my arms to tell me she scared.

It takes a moment 'fore she speaks. "We ain't gon' eat here?"

My eyes take in the willows 'round the other side o' the pond, the lily pads that lie over the water to protect the fish, the pines and wildflowers that hide us from view o' the world. This place—it's safe. A plot o' peace. Like the pasture is for Mama and William is for Sissy.

I swallow hard and shake my head. "Nah, we ain't doing none o' that here. This … this be a sacred place, now. No food or blood or any o' that kind. We're gon' make this our home, so we need to treat it nice."

She don't say nothing for a moment. Her dark eyes follow 'round like mine had, a hawk in search o' answers, then she nods. "Okay, Miss Lillian. That sounds mighty fine. But I still need to do the laundry, and Trevor need to bathe, and we gots to eat somewhere, so how we gon' do that?"

Her gaze stay locked on me, open and ready. My teeth gnaw the side o' my tongue. Ain't no one ever watched me the way Dorothea does. It's the way the Clan looked to Mama, or how Kylie would look at Sissy when waiting for our morning chores. I set my shoulders back the way them both did, chin up and hands down at my sides so I won't fiddle with my yellow dress.

"There's a creek 'bout a mile west. I followed a trail to it once. Sissy got so mad when she finally found me." It'd been a dark day, the clouds all angry overhead with they rumbles and roars. We was soaked to the marrow by the time we made it home. "It's bigger than the one near the town, and it ain't as dirty, neither, 'cause no one really know 'bout it. We can use it, just like we used our old one, but we'll sleep here by the pond and spend our days with the willows."

Dorothea's eyes twinkle. "Alright then, Miss Lillian, it sounds like a nice plan. Trevor?" The boy startles, blue eyes a vast contrast to the murky green o' the pond. When he cast his gaze my way, I give him a grin. He rub at the dried blood on his chin, then startles when a few flakes flutter off. This a jumpy one.

Dorothea jerks her chin to the trail I pointed out, the one that goes to the stream, then waggles a finger at Trevor. "Come on, you're gon' help me get these stains out your clothes. We got to talk, too, 'bout," she pause, then gnaws the air like she chewing on words, "well, 'bout everything. Miss Lillian?"

She beckons me to follow, but I ring my hands in my dress,

then flick my eyes to the pond. "Nah, I think I'll stay here. With my lily pads and all."

They leave without much o' a glance back to me. On the other bank, them willows drape they moss over the pond in curly, wild tangles. A breeze drifts through and they dance, same as my hair where it tickles my neck and lifts to catch on my lashes. It ain't been brushed since Dorothea ran a comb through it, and that been over a week. I bet it all rampant and wavy, just like them trees on the other bank.

My eyes catch on the pond. The lily pads sit all delicate on its surface, and a ripple breaks the water every now and then. I'm 'bout to close my eyes, take a nap while Dorothea off to wash Trevor, when a shadow leaps to one o' my lily pads. Offset eyes stare out, big and black and round. My nails dig into the dirt on the bank and I lean forward, gaze stuck on the ridged back o' the frog.

It croaks, throat swollen, then not, swollen, then not, and keeps a steady watch on the pond. A water bug scampers right in view, and my tooths dip out, grin on my face 'cause that frog just been sitting and waiting for this. There's a pause, like the pond and willows know what's 'bout to be, then a rope o' pink flicks out, stretched 'cross the water for an eternity. The tip lands on a thin, gray body, then the bug's gone, gobbled on up like it ain't never been there to begin with. I cain't help the squeal that unleash from my lips. A film slide up those black eyes, then the frog leap into the pond with a *plunk*.

For the rest o' my wait, I watch the bugs that scamper to and fro on the water's surface, track the sharp glimmer o' scales when fish bob up near my lily pads, then flick they tails to drive back down to the murky shadows. No one taught me to swim. Not never. My tongue finds its way 'tween my tooths, and I bite down to hold it there. Maybe Dorothea could teach me to paddle, just the way our hounds do. Or maybe I can breathe underwater, now that I Infected.

I scurry to the bank and peer down. Cool mud squishes up 'tween my fingers, and there a wet patch at my knees that's staining my dress, sure as the spirits. Sissy would yell at me, her cheeks flushed and eyes alight. But she ain't here. Dorothea might be upset, too, but I know she won't gripe at me the way Sissy would. Nah, she'd just take me off to the shallow o' the stream so we can rinse.

There ain't a ripple to be had here at the bank. My face makes a clear reflection, hair a bright, fiery mass 'round my head. I pat it down and grimace. Wouldn't hurt for Dorothea to give it a good brushing, soon. My cheeks is pale with no rosy hue, though I don't look ghastly from it the way I'd think I might. And there's a sharp glint to my eyes, silver streaked through. That lightning I get to carry 'round with me everywhere I go. When I grin, my tooths pop down, and I look something feral, like a predator. My lips furl over, and the tooths snap back up.

I still ain't got an animal name. Dorothea's so good, her Hawk. And Trevor like a scorpion, small and forgettable, though I bet he just as special as the both o' us. Stung his Paw right good. Maybe he can get hit by wagons and feel fine. Or breathe underwater.

The pond's surface shifts, rings fanned out from a lone fish; my reflection shutter and warp, and the eyes that stare back up flicker. Right as I'm 'bout to tuck my face in, I catch a scent.

There's a prick at my nose. It wrinkles up at the faint tickle as I sit back on my heels and lift my chin toward the sky. Sunlight trickles through to hit the middle o' the pond, then casts its rays over my back. The way it's bright and warm makes my skin tender, but I shrug the tight sensations 'way and focus on that odor that ain't right. My nostrils flare, suck in a great breath, then spasm.

Ash and smoke. That's what it smell like. I whip my head 'round, the orange curls a mass that cling to my neck and hang heavy on my shoulders, a curtain in they own right. Every breath I take, the scent sharpens, grows thicker, like it's spreading quick. On my feet, I track the smell to the eastern edge o' the clearing. If I kept going, where would I be? The town? The pasture?

Pebbles pop up in my belly, and my eyes cow wide open.

The Orchard.

I'm in a sprint 'fore I think 'bout it, my feet quick and sure in a way they weren't when I was a witch. The pebbles grow to stones, and my heart clenches as it tries to beat harder, faster, stronger, too. What if Mama's there with the Clan, or Kylie and Sissy with the other witches harvesting apples? The voices leer in my mind and lash out like rattlers do, then I take off.

There ain't no sweat as I run, just an itch under my skin where the sun hit it. Like an old burn. When I reach the last threads o' the forest, my breath catch. The smoke's a cloud, dark and thunderous as it races up from the ground, and the stench rakes its way down my throat like claws. I cough and hack, but it don't clear the taste o' smog, nor do it help the raw scrapes o' every breath.

"Miss Lillian!" Dorothea bursts out from a nearby hedge, Trevor at her heels.

Her gaze catch the cloud, a blast o' charcoal in an otherwise blue day. The same blue as Trevor's eyes, clear and liquid-like. My belly twists all up as the voices start they leer. It's a raspy canter, ragged and excited all in one, like a candy that's sour when you bite in but got a sweet, juicy center.

Dorothea spins to me, hand out to grab Trevor and pull him in. "We gots to go back to the pond. Ain't no telling what caused that fire, but there bound to be lots o' people there to put it out."

Not people. Witches. The whole Clan gon' be there, circled 'round Ol' Molly to protect her. My *family* be by that smoke, my first family, and I ain't there to help. A whimper slip out my throat, high and pained. The stones in my belly churn, and even the hand I place over it to hold them in place don't help. "I need to get Mama."

"No, Miss Lill—"

Dorothea choke off as I grab tight o' that bond 'tween us and tug, my tooths out like I might dig them deep in her throat 'gain. Trevor slides behind her, his slim figure hunched to a quiver. She struggles, keeps bobbing her mouth as though she gon' try to speak anyways, then stops. The bond settles, and she chokes through a ragged inhale.

"You cain't stop me from helping Mama," I shrill. My hands curl to fists, and I stomp. The smoke pulses higher, spreads out to hold back the blue o' the day.

Dorothea's brows furrow and twitch, then she nods. "We'll all go. I ain't 'bout to leave you. We ... we family." The words come out shaky.

My tooths slide 'way. Eyes like damp clay gaze back at me, wary, yet certain. I take a step forward and pat Dorothea's arm, then Trevor's. He slips back out from behind her form. "Yea, we family."

I'm 'bout to smile, but a crash breaks out from the distance, followed by yelling. There's a boom like the one we heard right 'fore Dorthea got hit in her leg. That leg that was healed right up by the time we reached my pond. A snarl rip out my throat. *Guns.*

We cain't wait any longer. The herb garden sits off to our left, and I tear toward it, a shortcut to the Orchard that Kylie showed me when we got caught in a storm. It seems so long ago, though it ain't even been a few months. The patter-stomp o' Trevor and Dorothea keep pace after me, and we make it to the Orchard far sooner than Kylie and I ever did back then.

Those stones in my belly tumble and brick up. The fence line is covered in foggy wisps that singe my throat. Too many voices to keep track o' barrel together from the abyss o' the Orchard, they shouts at a crescendo. And above them all is the crackle and bang o' the fire. A darkness fold over us, like we've descended into nighttime, and in the center o' it all is flames.

They lash out in shades o' orange and yellow and gold. Already, my skin itches from the heat, though there ain't a drop o' sweat on me. It's like the edge o' sunset, but close 'nough to touch. 'Nother crash echoes 'round us, then a scream and boom. Was that Mama? Sissy?

I race to the fence, then slip through into the shadows and blaze. It don't take long 'fore figures rush past me. The first be a lady I don't recognize, her hem caught up like an ember that trail her as she sprints out o' the thicket. A branch falls from a tree at my right, sending ash up to tickle my nose. It scrape at my throat 'til my eyes water. The voices is shrill and frantic in they hisses, angry at the flames, but I keep moving deeper, like I'm on my way to skip circles 'round Ol' Molly.

"Sissy," I screech as I scramble forward. "Kylie! Mama!" My voice cracks on the last name, throat dry. "Sissy! Kylie! Mama!"

"Lillian?" a voice call back, but it ain't my sisters or Mama. It ain't 'nother witch. It's Sissy's William.

I catch a whiff o' pine dust and cider, then a shadow passes to my right. My head whips that way, and I squint through the plumes, but I cain't see nothing. "William?" The shadow stops, then rushes forward to me, and I break into a sprint toward it. "William! Where's Sissy and—"

A man lurches into view, his eyes glazed and cheeks flushed, a kerchief wrapped 'round his face to block the smoke. That's a smart thing to do. I grab the neckline o' my dress and try to pull it up to mimic him and block the stinging smoke, but it won't go. When his gaze lights on mine, the corners o' his eyes crinkle, like he's smiling 'neath the fabric.

But it don't seem like a good smile. The voices growl and crackle, the hair on my nape risen in apprehension, and I take a step back.

He follows me with 'nother step forward. "Well, if it ain't my day. A young witch to hang and set fire to."

Hang? What he talking 'bout? I whip my gaze to the smoldered shadows 'round us and squint. "Willi—"

My scream's choked off by a hand 'round my neck. It's tight, what little air I had squeezed out and closed off. He wrenches me from the ground like I'm an empty bushel o' apples. I grapple and flail. Where's William? My legs kick out, but the man got a good length to his arm. Sissy … Sissy will be here; she'll get me. The man's eyes crinkle further, they green dark 'nough to pass for the deepest shadow o' hedges. I try to suck in a breath, but there ain't no air, and my head's light and fuzzy.

The voices shriek and growl and hiss at me. They tell me to *take*.

To *kill, feast, rip, tear, shred, rise.*

A snarl rumble in my chest, then past his hand and out my throat. The voices trill. Heat flashes up my spine, and I *feel* the spark in my eyes. I think I might burn him with my gaze, but he don't cower back. 'Stead, he squints at me, and in the distance William's voice calls out my name 'gain, faded and distant, but it don't matter. The hand at my throat tightens further, so much so that if I were still a witch, it'd surely break something.

But I ain't.

My tooths snap down, and I grip his wrist and both hands and twist. There's a *snap*, then the pressure's gone from my throat, and I hit the ground on the balls o' my feet. The man screams and cowers back, his broken bones cradled to his chest. He looks like prey, weak and brittle and easy to take. To rip and shred and *kill*. The growl in my chest deepens and my belly fills with light, a joy brighter than the thoughts o' seeing my family 'gain. 'Cause this a hunt now, and there ain't nothing better than the lightning crash o' my fevered desire to feast.

A quiver rolls up my body. I smile wide, and my tooths slide down even further, they points no doubt glinting, even in the

smoke 'round us. I don't care 'bout the sting it cause no more—
I'm 'bout to soothe the burn in my throat.

The man stumbles back from me like he gon' flee, but he lose
his balance and topple backwards to the ground. His eyes widen
in the face o' my grin, and he digs his heels and elbows into soft
soil, scrambling 'way. "What are—"

When I lunge forward, my hands hit his shoulders first, and
there's a *thud* as his head snaps back on the ground. A scream
rips out his throat; the one I sink my tooths into. It blends in
with the panicked cries that surround us. The fire crackles and
roars and snaps just as the voices do, all happy and pleased with
the chaos.

He's got his hands in my hair, yanks at my dress, a desperate
fight to pull me off him, but I'm strong. My fingers dig down
into his collarbone, and it cracks from the pressure. He shrieks,
then gurgles. It don't matter. My belly in a rush o' *warm* and
good as the man's blood floods my tongue. It tastes like venom
and iron mixed with rose dew, like sugar-laced gun powder. A
shudder ripples up my spine, and my eyes flutter shut. I push
my face closer, and let my tooths sink in to the root to taste
more o' him. The hands that beat at my body slacken, then fall
limp to the ground.

Footsteps approach, the *boom-boom-boom* o' a sprint that's
coming straight at me, rather than passing by, and I lift my face
to snarl at the newcomer. This is *my* kill. My blood. My *feast*. I
blink up at the figure, can feel the silver that's settled into my
gaze pass over like a spark. The rose dew and electricity sizzle
in my belly, then settle when the shape steps close 'nough that I
can see through the smoke. I grin up as a scent o' leather and
sage fights through the charcoal sting. "Sissy, you came! I knew
you would. Now we gots to get Mama and Kylie safe."

She stares down at me, her face the same ash as those plumes
that choked me up earlier, sweat a mask on her skin, her hair a
matted mess and left sleeve ripped.

"Lillian," she breathes, that familiar willow moss and kindling a flurry from my eyes to my dress to the man at my feet. Her mouth slackens then clenches at her jaw.

My tooths drip in russet as I smile. We're gon' go find the rest o' the family. Take them back to the pond where it safe and the fire cain't get us. Brittle cloth crinkles in my hands as I yank the man to the side, then a flash catch my eye.

Sissy got a knife gripped tight in her hand.

19
EYES THAT BURN

Ellie Hallivard

THE NEW MAGIC in my gut roars, a creature with talons ready to rip my sister to pieces as she kneels before me. I cain't speak past the lump in my throat, not with how happy she is, a smile yawned open on her blood-stained face. My hand tightens on the knife in my hand, grip an acute ache as I struggle to either keep the weapon or launch it to a place where it ain't never gonna hurt her.

'Round us, the Orchard burns. It cuts deep in my heart, Ol' Molly's limbs aflame at the center of our home. The gift scatters in my breast, a flighty response to the horror that surrounds me. There's a distant blare, its pop dense and low. Guns from the townsfolk. Sweat trickles down my neck as smoke clogs my nose then claws into my throat. They've attacked us, set our very core on fire, but I cain't think 'bout that with Lillian here in front of me. Cain't think 'bout William and his warmth that furls in my chest, gone to help the men capture the humans before they cause more harm. Cain't think 'bout my Clan as they work to save Ol' Molly and put out the flames.

Lillian cocks her head. It's so familiar to the vision at the Matriarch trial. Her auburn hair's wild and unkempt, the yellow dress with my flowers all splattered in mud and grime and worse. Those tense brows lie furrowed and rosy lips pull down to a pout. My heart drops 'way to a hollow place that's been carved up like William's woodwork, the raw shavings sent to form thousands of splinters. I cain't do it—I cain't kill my sister.

She sits up on her haunches, and the movement makes her teeth glint. Sharp ones. Beastly ones. I suck in a shattered breath.

But *this ain't my sister*. Not this creature that's knelt over a mutilated man, his eyes rolled back and open, throat ripped and shredded like it's been mauled by coyotes. Her hand grips his hair and pulls the torn neck wider on display, like it's a subconscious act and she ain't even aware she's done it. Blood dribbles out the wounds, then spurts, like his heart's still trying to pump life through. A failed effort.

Lillian's fangs drip with it, her chin coated, and every now and 'gain a slash of silver sparks in her gaze. Something like lightning, except it strikes over and over and over 'gain.

She shifts and drops the head in her hands. They lathered in red, too. "Sissy, why you looking like that? It's okay, he ain't gon' hurt you. Tried to choke me off, but I got him. He cain't hurt no one else."

I gasp past the lump. My gut clenches on the Ancestor as it roars and stalks within me. She stands, the dress hemmed perfectly to the ground. My breath catches at the movement, and I hold the knife out 'tween us. I don't know which quivers more—my hand or my soul. "Stop! You need to leave. And don't you never come back."

Spittle flies out from my words. Lillian lurches as though I've already stabbed the knife to her chest. Shouts echo off in the distance, but I keep my focus. Her eyes widen, big and bright, so lifelike, though I know deep down that she ain't alive no more. My lips clench on a whimper. Ancestors, how did we get here? Kylie's life in my hands, Mama's blood never gone from my knife, and Lillian—Lillian's soul lost forever, even as she stands before me.

My hand clutches the knife 'til my knuckles go white, but my grip steadies. I'm to protect the Clan. Protect the Orchard. Protect my William.

The spirit rumbles an assenting purr.

"You don't mean that," Lillian says, soft as a butterfly's wings. The words barely reach me. "Just, go get Mama, Sissy. It'll be better, you'll see. I gots new friends, and they can be part of our family, and you all can come visit us at the pond! Mama will plait my hair and Kylie—"

"Mama's dead." I snap at her, heat risen in my neck to flush out along my cheeks.

Lillian reels. Her hands flutter out and 'round to grasp at an anchor but there ain't none. Her eyes blink a rapid flurry, lips parted. A wave of despair hits me, and I lean forward, rocked by the nausea. Is that grief in her silvered gaze? It cain't be. A lie, all of it. Just as that spirit said, we're liars, each and every one of us.

This more than a curse, these Bloodbuds and Infected. It's a nightmare, *my* nightmare, a continuous blasphemy that follows in my wake. I choke back a sob as my eyes clench shut. But it don't stop the water from welling in them, cain't tame the onslaught of loss and pain that rises in me. Even the warmth of William's soul connected to mine cain't break through that winter's air of loss. When I try to suck in, my chest heaves at the effort, and the exhale comes out stuttered and broken and wet.

I snarl at this thing that ain't my sister. I'm the Matriarch, and I won't let my Clan be brought to ruin by this Infected. This Forsaken. Cain't dishonor Mama that way. *Mama.* "She's dead. I killed her so the spirit couldn't take her body. You're dead. Kylie's in danger of the spirits, William's now bound to me and this chaos for eternity, and I have to protect what's left." My sight lands on the body she ripped apart and smiled over. The magic rears up in me, dark and strong and angry. "I have to protect them from you! You're the Forsaken that will destroy the Coven. You're the evil brought up by this curse. You're the monster that caused the townsfolk to attack our home. You, Lillian!"

The magic ignites and unfurls. It snakes down to my toes, a ripple of power that draws from me, then my gift, like it's dipped a hand into the Beyond. The spark surges up to my mind and out to my grasping hands. I don't know who lunges, me or the thing that once was Lillian but ain't no more, its talons out and poised. She's hardly opened her mouth to speak when I'm on her. The dagger slashes through the space that separates us and lands in her chest.

An inhuman scream rips out from her. It shrills higher than wind chimes tinkling in a summer breeze, dips lower than the whistle of a tornado—mayhem dropped in a mortar and beaten by a pestle. The screech pierces my sternum and drops me to the ground like I've been cracked open. But I cain't tear my eyes from her.

Lillian tumbles down by the bleeding man, the hilt of my blade stuck out from her breast. She grips her head and thrashes, the wails and shrieks that spill from her lips unending. They batter my skull. It pulses like it might implode, forcing my breath to ragged gasps, but I crawl forward through the agony, ready to end this before William comes after us, before the townsfolk find me weak by Lillian and end my life, before Kylie sees that I've 'nother of our family's lives on my hands, even if this is the Forsaken.

My elbows dig into the ground as I inch closer, coughs racking through me with each inhale of smoke and flame. Screams and shouts ring out 'round us, the occasional thunder of a gunshot echoing in the dark expanse we've been plunged into, but I keep my eyes on the dagger in Lillian's chest. If I can finish the curse, here beneath Ol' Molly and the watchful eyes of the Ancestors, perhaps the Coven will be safe. We'll regrow. Our center will survive. We're rooted deep.

Lillian convulses. I have to swallow down the bile that rises in my throat 'cause this may not be my sister but it looks like her. Just as that spirit that wore Mama's body and cackled as she bled from her throat still wore her face.

When I make it to Lillian's side, she stills. Her mouth lies slack, poisoned willow moss and kindling open, and her chest heaves in quick pants. It reminds me of the bunnies she'd chase. They bodies would convulse at the adrenaline of escaping her grasp. Our Little Lillian. I cain't help it when I brush the tanged halo of curls back from her face. A sharp sting settles in my eyes. Perhaps I'm crying, perhaps it's the thick smog that's settled 'round us.

Her gaze slides to me, the barest hint of a witch underneath that glint of lightning. "Sissy—"

"I know, I know." I place my hand on her forehead and soothe the words 'way. This is a beast, a monster. Lillian left this world the day she touched that Bloodbud, but we can both pretend she's here, pretend that I can give her a Rite and send her off to the Ancestors. My other palm reaches out for the dagger, ready to plunge it deeper, twist 'til it won't move no more. "It'll be quick, I promise."

Her lids flutter, and those long lashes brush 'gainst her cheek. She lolls her head to the side, brows furrowed, lips pursed and forehead crinkled in thought. "You tried to kill me?" It flows out in a whisper, a hint of disbelief at the end.

I want to brush my knuckles over her cheek, to hold her hand and hush the pain in her voice. Instead, I freeze. Lillian's face morphs. Her lips peel back, and those fangs slide down, a threat in slow form. The silver blazes in her gaze as she sits up, not even a wince on her face as the dagger jostles in her chest. There's little blood 'round the wound, like she ain't got enough in her body to bleed. Nothing like the man that's been tossed to the side, his neck twisted at an angle that brings bile to my throat. The talons in my sternum retract and the magic quivers in unease. It makes my gut churn.

Lillian looks down at the handle, carved by Papa, and pulls the knife out. A growl rumbles in her chest, low and deep, a predatory thing, and gooseprickles rise along my arms and down the nape of my neck. The red that should drip from the blade sits stagnant, like it's days old. Chills work they way down to the marrow of my bones as she sneers at the weapon.

What kind of monster did the Ancestors create? The rumble in my gut tapers off to a whine, like I asked a question it cain't answer. I try to swallow past the barren waste of my throat, but my tongue catches. If I turn and run, can I escape?

Lillian flings the knife 'way. It whistles into the shadows and disappears an impossible distance from us. Then, she's on her feet. And for the first time, I cain't see Lillian. Not in this twisted face of rage, hair a brazen inferno 'round her that wars 'gainst the flames that lick towards us, a tear in her dress from the dagger, blood raked 'cross her skin with her fangs on display and her eyes overrun in silver. She's predator. Neither witch nor human nor spirit—a new creation.

"You killed Mama?" Her voice hisses out like them vipers that slither they way to our porches. "You killed Mama! You tried to kill me." Her throat vibrates on a growl. "You ain't family no more. You a murderer worse than me. Dorothea, she's my family. And Trevor, too. But you and Kylie and Papa? Nah, you all ain't nothing but monsters that left me to die, then tried to stab me when I didn't."

She leans in to me, her lips furled back. My gut falls 'way and the ice settles in 'til I cain't move, frozen to this spot, hidden in the receding smoke with the face of my tormentor before me. Lillian's mouth opens.

This is it. She's to slit my throat open with her fangs, just as she did the townsman at our feet. A calm settles down on my shoulders, the magic all but hidden and cowered. Even the Ancestor is curled down in disbelief and defeat. I deserve this death. Perhaps, it's for the best. I set my gaze on Lillian, ready to go at her hand, but she stiffens.

Her chin tilts up to sky, and her nose flares and quivers, like she's caught a scent. The Orchard falls into its own well of time as she pulls back from me and stands tall. Then a figure darts out of the blackened bog. It's a woman, her skin dark as the smoke that surrounds us and glittering in the orange light of the flames. Lillian's at rapt attention, myself all but forgotten.

"Miss Lillian," the woman gasps, her eyes bugged out, "Trevor done attacked a group of townsfolk. He got 'bout three of them, but the others struck him with a flaming stick. He ... I think he ..." She sucks in, eyes a quick dart to me then back. "We need to get him."

Lillian lurches forward, gaze wide. The Ancestor barrels at my chest, roars and slams into me. The gift blots a frenzied shriek, and the voices drop in with they pleas. *Flee, run, hide. Forsaken, death, predator.*

My fingers tremble as I dig them into the dirt and scramble to my feet. The smoke's clearing out, likely the work of Kylie and the Clan Elders. I don't look back when I set off at a sprint into the thick wisps. This to be the second time I've fled from Lillian. It feels an eternity ago, that day at the pond when she melded her existence to the curse.

Just as before, I run. And just as before, Lillian calls after me, my name at her lips. But it ain't a frightened shriek she lets out.

This time, she roars.

Opus Lex Baeroot - Creation of Petal to the Beyond

*Ingredients to be gathered the night of a notable celestial marker.
Potency notes to be added after trials.
Poultice creates bloom which will form bridge to the Beyond. Intention, once
creation has been tested, is to add ingredient to Illumination of Prophetic
Divination and provide ability to access the Beyond without spirits.*

- Grave dirt, fresh lain
- Heart of infant, a few days old
- Heart of elder, near death's edge
- Coyote canines
- Bat skull
- Guts of Rattlesnake
- Meadowsweet, whole
- Claw of salamander

- Sage
- Web of a nightmare
- Splinter of soul from Creator
- Blood of witch possessed by spirit, from source
- Blood from daughter of possessed witch, first-born, from source

To be brewed under a moonless night.

Begin chanting "Ode of the Eternal" from the Opus lex Vexan.
Ensure smoothness of enunciation—those who mispronounce the
Old Language shall be punished through asphyxiation.
Continue chant throughout creation.

Set cauldron in hearth and sprinkle in grave dirt. Squeeze
blood from heart of infant and heart of elder into cauldron.
Continue to milk organs of blood until no more will come, then
bring to simmer. Discard of remains. Grind coyote canines
and bat skull to fine powder, then add to brew. Stir thrice
clockwise, thrice counterclockwise.

Hold rattlesnake over cauldron and slice open soft underside,
stripping of innards. Bring poultice to boil. Discard of
remains. Mince meadowsweet and add to brew. Stir in claw of
salamander. Allow to sit until boiling slows to individual,
tar-like bubbles. Crush sage in hand and sprinkle over
poultice. Allow to sit until brew froths.

Settle web of a nightmare over poultice. (Make notations of
whether web of nightmare from creator or possessed witch gives
greater potency.) Offer forth splinter of soul to create initial
opening into the Beyond.

Complete the remainder of the poultice as quick as possible to lower contact with spirits.

Stir in blood of witch possessed by spirit until poultice takes on a gray tone. Remove blood-source immediately after hue changes. Stir in blood of daughter until poultice transitions to boysenberry hue. Remove blood-source immediately after hue changes. Cease chanting. Bottle brew.

Poultice to be used similar to seeds. Plant five teaspoons of brew in garden to create one bloom. Care for with sunlight and water.

Continue making notations as poultice is created to further accuracy of recipe.

Warning to Creators: this poultice is of black magic. It will tarnish the soul due to splinter that is offered to the Beyond. The creation of too many poultices invoking black magic will cause negative symptoms, such as lack of protection against possession, loss of emotion, inability to separate reality from falsities, and, in serious cases, an implosion of magic. These are only a few possibilities. Refer to Opus lex Vexan for full list of recorded symptoms and conditions related to black magic.

20

BONDS BROKEN AND FORGED

Lillian Hallivard

MY SKIN TINGLES, flushed in an anger I ain't never got lost in, 'cause Sissy tried to *kill* me. A grumble rip out my chest, and my tooths throb. The panic and terror that sparks off Dorothea to me sends the voices to a hiss. I shake my head like that'll rattle them loose, but they just get louder.

The smoke 'round us loosens its tight grip on the air. My legs tense and quiver, gaze set on the spot 'tween the trees where Sissy bounded off through, like she a bunny. I want to chase her. Catch her. A growl turn over in my throat, then slide to a whimper.

She killed Mama. The next whine brings Dorothea's hand to my shoulder, and I lean into her. Mama ain't never gon' brush my hair 'gain. She ain't gon' arch her brow at me or make me warm cider in the winter or sing hushed lullabies at night when it's storming and I cain't shake the tremor o' fear in my breast as I burrow under the covers.

And it's all 'cause o' Sissy.

The whines taper off, and I spin to Dorothea. Her eyes still that dark clay with a hint o' silver, but they wide in fright. "Miss Lillian—"

"We gots to get Trevor and go." I push past her and lift my nose to the air to sniff for him. My smelling gets better every day, but the smoke makes everything sting, then leaves it fuzzy at the edges. "Where he at? I cain't get any o' that copper, lemongrass, and rose with this charcoal 'bout us."

Dorothea don't say nothing, just nod toward the direction she came from, then takes off. I follow after her, Ol' Molly at our backs, 'til we break out past a row o' limp trees. A screech splits out into the Orchard, different from the shouts that been constant since we got here. I whip my head to the left, then follow the shrill screams Trevor makes.

My tooths drop down, and the voices dance in my mind, poised to strike. Figures appear, clearer and clearer as the fire settles. I don't know why it's going down, but my skin cools with every second that passes, and the tightness in my nape loosens. Up 'head, the cries and whoops o' humans greet me, and I push harder, my feet a blur 'cross the ground as I move faster than I ever did when I'd race them boys by the pasture.

Then, I see him. My legs near crumple out 'neath me when I take a sudden stop, the slow beat o' my heart dropped low to my belly. Dorothea slide to a halt next to me.

Trevor's trussed up to a tree with so much rope, it look like he fell asleep for a hundred years and got buried in vines. He thrash 'gainst them, tooths out as he screams and tries to launch himself out at the group; the humans shout and stab they sharp plows and rakes at him, whoop and grin in a slimy way that be like the first man I feasted on by my Bloodbuds. Heat lashes up my spine to coil behind my gaze and my fingers curl to claws.

I gon' rip they throats out, feast on them one by one for hurting my brother. My new family. The voices chant in a rampant fury and cheer at the rage I let spread through my bones. *Rip, tear, shred, kill, blood, prey, feast, rise.*

My gaze narrows, the lightning in it a prick that bring a grin to my lips. Then, a flash of orange leap out from the crowd o' humans.

A torch gets tossed the few feet 'tween the townsfolk and the tree Trevor's bound to, and the flame leaps to devour the kindling at the ground and flies up the trunk. A boulder hits my chest, burrows in so I cain't breathe. The fire flicker and dance up, up, up in a way I ain't never seen. So fast. It lick over Trevor, and his skin *shrinks*, tightens and curls in on itself, then *rips* as it blackens. Shudders wrack my body, but I cain't take my eyes off him. His screams pitch to fever heights and splinter the Orchard with a flat chord o' death. The flames eat everything up, tree and flesh, Trevor's blue eyes lost in a casket o' smoke and fire, wrapped up in black and gold, a monarch butterfly with its wings ripped clean off and left to suffer.

Then the shrieks stop. Dorothea quivers at my side, and in front o' us, the humans holler out a brazen celebration.

"They killed him," she whispers, then her voice grows thick and angry. "They burnt him alive like he weren't just a boy."

Her words slam into me, make me double over. Bile rises in my throat. So much I been clinging to, Kylie and Sissy and Mama and Papa. Like I still they daughter. Like I just a girl. It was a mad thing to do.

"He was Infected. He was so much more than just a boy," I say. My hands curl to fists. "We so much more than we once was, Dorothea. You and I. Trevor, too." I flick my gaze back to the townsfolk. There's a subtle pinch as my tooths slide 'way. I let my lips quiver, then furl up, my nose wrinkled in a silent snarl. "He's gone, but we ain't. And these people gon' pay for what they done."

The weight in my chest spread out, drags at my shoulders, then slides to the edges o' my body. Dorothea's bold eyes find mine. They dart back and forth 'tween my lightning and kindling, then she sends a final glance to the burning tree and nods.

We stalk toward the fence o' the Orchard, back the way we came so we can go to the pond, our sanctuary, when I catch a lone scent up 'head. A scent o' cider and pine.

"Dorothea," I start, a feral glee dancing in my belly, "go on. I'll meet you back home."

She startles, then opens her mouth like she gon' argue. My narrowed eyes and warning growl is all it takes to have her scampering to the left and over the fence.

It take less than a moment to reach that scent. William's got his face wrapped up in cloth and stomps 'round on the grass like he's in some sort o' crazed dance. It crunches up 'neath his boots, all blackened and burned. When a desperate spark pops out and catches a new spot, he rips a rag from the ground and throws it on the budding flame to squash it.

A smile grow 'round my tooths, and I dig the toe o' my boot to the ground, like I can crunch up all my aches, too. My hands curl up, and a funny little sweep o' warmth runs 'cross my spine. We've lost Trevor, Dorothea and I. We need a new brother, and I always knew William would join our family eventually. Though, I thought it'd be with Sissy.

A flush o' anger rips up in my breast, and my tooths ache to pop out, like they doused in rage with me. My mind shifts back to Sissy with her knife. I bet she used it to kill Mama, just the way she tried to kill me. Pain slices through my chest and I groan, but it ain't from no wound.

I lost Mama.

But I can have William.

He don't know 'bout the witches, but maybe if I tell him, he'll understand. A brother. A real one. If I Infect him, it'll make my new family stronger. I dip my tongue over my tooths as a seed o' twisted glee takes root in my gut.

If I Infect him, I'll hurt Sissy.

William's gaze roves the ground, brows furrowed as he paces. He don't notice me 'til I'm right at his side, my fingers gentle as I prod his arm. The touch sends him into a leap, and he spins, eyes widened. If he didn't have his lips covered, I bet they'd be parted. When those green-grass eyes spot me, they grow larger, like apples theyselves. His head flicks in a rapid shake, like he got water in his ear. "Lillian?"

My name spills from his mouth all throaty and raw. A bass croak. My lips pull down and I squint at the kerchief 'round his face. The smoke must have got past it, and I know that ain't good. He cain't be hurt now that I claimed him as my brother.

William takes a step back, rakes his eyes over my body 'til they settle at my chin, still caked in blood. "Lillian … what did you do?" He sucks in a breath and holds his hand over his chest, right near that spot where his heart beats. My eyes flick to it, snap to his throat where all them veins flutter and flare. When he speaks 'gain, I tear my gaze back to his. "Where's Ellie? If you hurt her …"

I snarl at William's words, and he pulls back, brows stitched together. It take an effort to roll my lips down and taper off the grumbles. He don't know what she did—cain't know—but I'll tell him what she is. A murderer. Someone that trying to pick off her family one by one. If she got him, then there's no doubt she'd hurt him to. But my family, we'll keep one 'nother safe.

I swallow hard, then clench my eyes shut. Oil dribbles down to my belly, and I whimper. When did I lose so many people? So many I loved? I couldn't keep Trevor safe. But now I know, now I can do better.

I cain't lose no one else. I'm at William's side in an instant, a sure grip on his wrist so he cain't run like Sissy did. He tenses when I stand on my toes and tilt his chin to look in my eyes, same as I done to so many, but this different. William ain't food, he's to be one o' us. Infected. "Sissy gon' be here soon, I'm sure. But you ain't to be with her no more."

William's cheekbones twitch, like he's frowned under the fabric. His eyes lose focus for a moment, but not the way I'm used to. He don't go slack in the jaw and nod along with my words.

I tighten my grip, and he winces, but he don't pull 'way. 'Stead, his hand comes up to rub over his ribs and heart, like he's got a pain there. My gaze narrows, and I lean in closer to look into the green-grass o' his eyes. "William, you gots to listen to me, okay?"

He stills, then dips his face like he's agreeing with me.

I lick my lips and start 'gain. "You gon' leave Sissy."

He blinks a slow pass, those dark lashes 'gainst his cheeks for a moment too long, and his hand pushes harder to his chest. Why ain't it working? It's s'posed to work! My shoulders hunch, and my tooths slip out. I ain't leaving without him. He's human, it shouldn't be different from the others. My jaw tenses as I pull him down, then I push my forehead to his, our sight as close as it can get. "William, you gon' come with me. You gon' follow me back to the pond."

His form sways. Then that gaze goes all hazy in the way I need it to, glassed over like he lost in thought.

"Okay," his words come out muffled, "I'm gon' follow you to the pond."

My grin splits wide, tooths out and open as I release him then step back. He swallows, then moves forward to close the distance. It's worked, it seems. The voices grumble in assent, an echo in my mind. I take 'nother step 'way, and he follows. That pine and cider hangs 'round us, the smell that's all William and nothing else. When I'm sure he ain't gon' turn and leave me, I trudge out from the Orchard and start my way back to the pond.

It takes longer with William, his kerchief now loose 'round his neck. I gots to tell him to keep following me a couple o' times, but he don't rub his chest or frown the way he did near

Ol' Molly. Maybe she got something to do with it? Mama used to say she the life o' our Orchard, the place where we can get closest to the Ancestors. Though, I ain't a part o' that *we* no more. A lump builds up in my throat, and I push my lips together. They wobble anyhow.

I ain't never gon' see Mama 'gain. A sniffle works its way out my nose, and I rub at it. There's a constant clamber from behind me where William walks. I try to focus on the snap and crack o' twigs from the brush, but I cain't. Not when Mama's eyes peer out from 'tween the trees, and her laugh trills every time a bird chirps.

She's gone.

Goose prickles rise along my arms, and my throat burns from the way I try not to swallow or breathe. Tears cloud my gaze. Mama ain't gon' meet Dorothea. She won't never come to the pond to brush my hair or listen while I tell her how good it feel to hunt. I won't hear her lullaby 'gain or get hushed into sleep when it storms outside, the wind beating our shutters the way Dorothea now beats my laundry 'gainst boulders.

I brush 'way the few drops that roll down my cheek. It's Sissy's fault. It's *all* Sissy's fault. My lips pull back in a snarl, and William stutters behind me. It takes a moment to get him to follow once more. When I look at him, that knotted sense o' pleasure wraps up in my belly 'gain. Sissy took Mama, so I'll keep William.

William, with his green-grass eyes that crinkle at the corners when he smiles. The one that dimples his cheeks and draws his shoulders forward to pull others in. No one's got a smile like William. I always liked him, the way he good at making chairs and porches and beds with his hands, like they crafted for building. How he brought me sweets, a sly wink my way as he slipped them in my hands then left to be with Sissy. There ain't no one better to be my brother.

We reach the pond to Dorothea. She a vibrating line o' fear

and power and madness that stalks back and forth by my lily pads. The hammer o' her emotions hit me like a bottle that filled with water then shattered over my head. It make me reach out to William like an anchor, my slender hand wrapped 'round the thick flesh and bone o' his wrist. I still ain't used to this bond we got, Dorothea and I.

When she spots William, she snarls. Her tooths snap down to glint in the fading sunlight and silver flashes 'cross the depths o' her burnished eyes. "You got one o' them townspeople. We should rip him apart for what they did to Trevor, Miss Lillian. Leave his body at the edge o' town for them to find, then run. Leave this place for good and never come back."

My hand tightens on William's wrist without thought, growls in my throat, and he cries out when the bones snap. She lunges even as William yanks 'way from me to cradle his wrist to his chest. There's a moment when I think she 'bout to rip his throat out, and I'm gon' have to bite her 'gain, send her in convulsions to the ground, but she pulls up short just as she reaches William.

Quick, thick pants burst from 'tween her lips as she waits, eyes locked on William's throat, then she tilt her head to me. "Miss Lillian, please, let me do this for Trevor. You said we was bold, strong; and yet he dead. What the point if we ain't to protect ourselves?" The words slither low, so soft I know William ain't heard them with his human ears. But they a crisp plea to my own.

I gnaw on my cheek. Dorothea right, what's the point if we ain't to do something with what we is? My eyes search out William. That's what I'm to do here, hurt Sissy for what she's done to me. The townspeople should be hurt, too, for taking Trevor from us. Near the pond, the willows drag they branches in a shallow brush 'cross the ground. A caress. I step back to wrap my hand 'round William's nape. His eyes have lost most o' they haze, brighter than they was a few minutes ago.

"You right, but not him. This is William. He was Sissy's, but ..."

My words choke off, and I bite back a stammer. *But she tried to kill me, so I took him.* My belly hurts, the way it used to cramp when I was a witch and hadn't eaten nothing all day. But it don't tell me I need food no more. I nudge closer to his side and hope he'll wrap an arm 'round me. He don't, just blinks and rubs his brow. He'll come too, soon, pull back from me and try to run. My fingers clench 'til they dig in and bruise.

"Don't matter, he ain't Sissy's no more. William's gon' be our new brother." I tilt my chin up to look at him, my hair draped to one side. It brushes 'gainst my cheek, and I cain't help but wish it was Mama here, 'stead, so she could push my curls back and plait my hair the way she liked to do. It hangs loose and heavy since I got Infected. William's gaze catches mine. "Ain't that right? You gon' leave Sissy for us?"

His lids flutter, and he grimaces, that same hand at his chest as 'fore. It rubs circles 'round his heart, pressed in so that the shirt bunches up. My lips tug down, and I move 'way. Won't matter in a bit—he'll be one o' us.

The Bloodbuds is still laid out where I left them, under the moss to stay safe from the sun. They all nice and pretty, my blooms, with petals velvety gray like thunder and bright red leaves that mimic the setting sun. My hand hovers over they stems as I examine each one, then I glance back to William.

He should get the largest o' the bunch. William's tall and strong—I bet he gon' be able to rip a tree out the ground. Not a willow, those too big, but a dogwood, maybe, or one o' them trees at the Orchard. Definitely not Ol' Molly. Ain't nothing gon' be able to get her roots up, not ever. My finger pets over a petal, and I cock my head 'gain.

William's kinda like thunder. Right now, it's that plume that's miles 'way, when we running 'bout to get the hens in the coops and the horses safe in the barn. It grumbles and barks, but it ain't too loud.

I sweep the Bloodbud into my hand and clutch it to my chest.

When he's one o' us, William's gon' be like thunder as it crashes overhead, a boom that shakes the bones o' houses and sends children to cower under the covers they mama's made for them. The kind that brings the ground to heel.

William's green-grass gaze lights on the Bloodbud as I hold it out, and he walks to me, just like all them people follow me when I tell them to. Only this time, he's set on the bloom. When he reaches out to pull it from my palm, the voices start they screeches. It don't make me hunker down, though. Nah, this a victory call, like the cry o' hawks as they circle high in open blue skies. And when he plucks it from my palm, eyes wide and pupils thrown black to overtake the green-grass, the voices *howl*. I want to throw my head back and join in, but I cain't take my gaze from William.

The way the hair along his arms stands up tall and his body shudders a violent, savage ripple that floods over his skin. As the green-grass hue floods back in, even bolder than 'fore, a dash o' silver in them. How his jaw drops open and a thin trickle o' blood falls to his bottom lip as new tooths slide down. His scent change. It's all pine and cider one moment, and the next, there's no more crisp apple, replaced by a undercurrent o' stagnant air on a winter's morning. I grin, hands twitching at my side as excitement blossoms in my breast.

Then, William's head jerks. The Bloodbud slips from his fingers and lands 'tween us with a dull thud. The voices draw back and hiss. I jerk 'way. What's gon' on? This didn't happen with Dorothea or Trevor. I don't think it happened with me. My belly rolls, and I send wide eyes to William's throat when he throws his head back and screams.

Dorothea rushes to my side, mouth agape and shoulders hunched. "What's wrong with him? Why's he wailing so?"

I don't know. My hands clutch at my hair, tug and rip at it as William crumples to the ground and seizes at my feet. Did I kill him? My brother? A whimper slips out my throat as pinpricks o' ice slide through my chest. All the veins in his neck lie raised and angry, and his hands claw like fiends at his shirt, over his heart, that same place he's been messing with since we was in the Orchard.

Maybe I broke it when I took him from Sissy. That's what Mama told me happened to Kylie when that older boy from the Orchard said he didn't like her back. She'd cried and cried, and Mama told me she was suffering from heartbreak.

But Mama also said it would pass, and it did.

'Nother wail breaks out from William, then a sob. His body lurches and thrashes. The shirt rips when he gives a violent tug, and he digs his nails into his skin 'til the iron tinge o' blood settles in the air. "Make it stop!" He gasps and chokes back on a broken cry. "Make it stop!"

I'm on my knees in the next moment and pull his hands back from his chest. A snarl rumbles out from him, his tooths bared, and I cain't help it when I wrench his wrists and flash my own in his face, then bite down on his throat, just like I did Dorothea. He sucks in, then goes slack. Silence filters 'cross the pond. Dorothea whines, and there's a thud, like she's dropped to her knees. As I release my tooths and pull back, William pants 'neath me, his eyes clenched shut and lips twisted together.

My growls tumble 'way, then I let his arms loose. They fall back to the ground and flop the way they might if all the muscle been stripped out and left to rot. My belly sinks 'neath the pebbles that line its sides and pile all the way up to my chest.

"William?" I brush his hair back like Mama or Sissy would, even though it ain't in his eyes. It's s'posed to soothe, either way. "William, you okay now? You gots to feel better."

He don't answer, but his chest ain't heaving the way it was. That seems a good sign. My hand keeps up its work to comfort him. When his eyes flutter open, there's still that green-grass coat, but there's also a lilt o' more, a shard o' silver in they midst. They flit over my face, then pass up to the canopy. No one speaks; the voices even hushed theyselves to an off-key hum. I hope he don't hate me. I hope I ain't lost William, too. My hand trembles on his forehead, then stops.

The touch has William's eyes back on mine.

"Yah, I'm okay," he rasps. Then, he smiles. It crinkles his eyes and dimples his cheeks, but it's better than 'fore. His lips pull back to make way for his tooths, and his nose scrunches like he's caught a scent. My own lips slide wide and loony to greet his grin.

He smiles like a predator.

21

A SPLINTER OF THE SOUL

Ellie Hallivard

IT'S LACERATED, split open and left to bleed a slow death. My forearms shake where I plant them in the cool soil of the Orchard, down on my knees, and let my forehead drop to rest 'gainst the dirt. Tears leave streaming, salty trails down my cheeks, but I don't scream or wail or pound my fists 'gainst my breast. It ain't like when I lost Lillian or Mama. This a hollow feel, like someone scooped out my heart and dropped it in the lake to feed them fish there. Gone. Empty.

The smoke has cleared from the Orchard, a thin veil of ash still in the air to tickle our throats. 'Round me, witches curse and cry out and whimper. My people.

Ol' Molly was spared, the Elders at her side soon after the flames began to lick 'cross our home. The same cain't be said for much of our crop. I dig my nails into the soil, end up with a ball of burnt grass that crinkles in my palm, then gasp out a shuttered breath.

"Eleanor," a voice calls from above. My shoulder tucks in

toward the ground, but Mrs. Broussard carries on. "Eleanor, we need to go after the townsfolk. Many died here today, but most of them returned home. They'll be back. And the Forsaken, the boy that was like her ..."

The Elder stutters off, but I know what's there in those silent words. Lillian's spread her curse, and we've no idea how many there are. Much of the Clan saw the child as he tore through townsmen like they was corn stalks in his way, eyes silvered, body red with blood and flesh and sinew. A shudder hits my body, and I force myself to rise. Mrs. Broussard's willow moss and kindling settles on mine when I'm on my feet.

"Fire killed him." My voice comes out harsh, like I've inhaled a hearth's worth of smoke, but I don't think that's why it's broken. My hand comes to clutch at my chest, the gift and Ancestor furled 'way to leave me in my own misery. "It should kill the Forsaken, too. I'll deal with the townsfolk on my own. How many ..." I stop and breathe in deep, glance 'round to the dried husks and skeletal trees that once gave this place a taste and smell of crisp apples. It's nothing but ash now. "How many did we lose?"

Her face falls, chin tilted down to hide the downtick of her lips, but she cain't do nothing 'bout the sullen crinkle 'round her eyes, nor the sheen to them. "Four. One witch and three men." She spits to the side then scowls. "Humans and they *guns*."

My lips tremble, and I cough in place of a sob. Her count's wrong. "Five. One witch and four men."

'Cause my William's gone. A shriveled inhale skips its way down my throat, a quick *hit-release-hit* like when my sisters and I would skip stones 'cross the lake when we was younger. I felt him ripped from me, how it took part of my soul and left me barren. The gift grows cold, falls as far from me as it can, though it still a part of me.

I cast my gaze to the Clan that surrounds us. There's nothing for them to do tonight, the moon finally having overtaken the sunset. It casts a dark haze on the bones of our Orchard, lights the trailing smoke like mist. "We was attacked," I call out, then pause 'til the bodies still and voices drop 'way, "and we remain. But this ain't over. The townsfolk will be dealt with, and so will the Forsaken. But not tonight. We need to regain our strength. Tomorrow morning, the Clan will meet in my home. Men, you're to gather kindling, firewood, oils … anything that will burn, and anything we can carry. For now, return home and be with those you love."

'Cause more of us will perish before she's dealt with. I spot Kylie off to the right, Papa's arm slung 'round her shoulders as they support one 'nother toward the gate, then walk beyond my sight with Opal behind them. Mrs. Broussard draws closer as the Clan follows my orders. "Tomorrow might be too late—"

"We have to hope it's not." I place my hand on her arm, then nod 'cross the way where Mrs. Childress and Mrs. Laurelynn watch, they faces cast in the half-light of the moon. It's nearly a full one, waxing, so close to a powerful source, but not at the right height. "Can you have the Poultice of Discovery ready for tomorrow when we go after Li—the Forsaken?" My teeth dig deep into my cheek at the lapse.

She hesitates, gaze searching for something in mine, then sighs. With a final nod, Mrs. Broussard leaves me.

The Orchard's nearly empty, some of the tree branches still crumbling when a lone breeze shifts through, they limbs tender to its touch. I make my way to Ol' Molly, her embrace a thick, wide expanse, like she's set out to cover and protect us all. A task I've failed in over and over 'gain with my family. She's cool to the touch, bark rough 'gainst my palm. "I'm sorry. You put your faith in me, and I couldn't stop her. I couldn't keep the humans from our home. I couldn't"—I choke, then hiccup on a sharp breath—"save my William."

Her leaves flutter in the hushed wind, but otherwise, she

don't move. I sigh and drop my forehead to her trunk. "I'm gonna cast the spell tonight. I know it's black magic, but there ain't nothing else I can do. If the townsfolk don't remember, they won't seek revenge. And if I don't make it ... well, at least I'll be with my William in the Beyond."

The Ancestor lurches, then falls down 'gain, like it's too weak to stay afoot. It's a silent, lonely walk home. No one's out, dim candle light filtering from windows in every home, like we fear the dark, too, after what's happened in the day. If my chest weren't empty, I'd go to them, each one, and reassure them that we'll be safe. But I walk past they porches one-by-one 'til I reach my own.

"Kylie?" I call out as the door closes behind me. It clicks into place with a solid thud. "Papa?"

My sister enters from the back hall. "Papa's gone to the pasture." Her willow moss and kindling glints, hair frizzed out from its plait, and she's got a pair of riding boots on that track mud 'cross our home. A haunted part of me wants to reprimand her for it, the old Ellie that used to fret 'bout such things. I eye them in defeat and tuck that girl 'way.

"He'd be safer here with us."

"Would he?" Kylie's gaze sharpens, her mouth a brittle point. Her nose flares, then she sighs and collapses into an armchair near the hall. The bruises beneath her eyes deepen to smoldered crescents. It takes me a moment to realize she's thinned out just as I have, that her brows hang heavy and her pallor's a shade gray, different from the sun-kissed tan that's always a sweet blossom 'bout her cheeks. She's aged and hurt, too.

I perch on the desk chair. It creaks as my weight pools in. My first thought is of William, and I slam him 'way before I can lose myself to the grief. "Of course, he is. Here in our home."

Kylie huffs a laugh and shakes her head. She nudges a knot in our wood floor with her boot then clenches her hands together. The skin blooms white, like she's shoved the blood 'way with how hard she presses them into one 'nother. When she looks up to me, her gaze has hardened, the way it always did when she'd come to a decision she knew I wouldn't like. My breathing thins out. "Do you mean this house, or the Orchard? Ellie, we lost Lillian and Mama. The townsfolk attacked. There's more of those Infected out there. Most everything but Ol' Molly's been burned to the ground—"

"But we continue on." I stand and move to kneel at her feet, put my hands 'round hers 'til they loosen, then hold them there. "We the Orchard, Kylie. They ain't pulled our roots up, not yet, and if we stay strong then they won't be able to. We'll grow 'gain"

I pull her hands apart and grasp them in my own, even as her shoulders sag down. Her magic trickles out to touch mine, then cowers back when the gift whirls 'way.

"Maybe the Orchard can remain, but I won't be here to see it." She slides her hands from mine and tucks them in her lap.

"What?" She's still a witch, a Hallivard. My sister. She's of the Orchard. "Kylie, you're—"

"Leaving." She stands as she cuts me off, and I catch myself on my palms before she can knock me over.

A faint scent of vanilla wafts through the home as I scramble after her when she disappears into the back hall. Mama always smelt of vanilla and beeswax with a hint of mint. Nostalgia hits my gut, and I double over. It gives Kylie enough time to grab her packs, a knife that mirrors my own attached to a holster at her thigh. The room spins, fear punched through my chest to fill the hollow place William left behind. "What 'bout Papa? You cain't just leave him. He's lost so much."

She stops in the doorway, hand on the knob. My eyes bug out at it. If she twists her wrist, opens that door, I'm alone. Kylie chews her lips, brows drawn together in a single line. "Papa's coming with me. He's the one who said we should leave, get 'way from this place, and I agree with him." Her free hand wraps 'round my arm, and her nails dig into the tender skin on its underside. "Come with us. We're heading north, 'way from the Coven for good. He says they building up there, factories and railroads and such. There'll be plenty of work, and we'll live in the city."

I'm shaking my head as she speaks. Leave the Coven? Our Clan? The Orchard? My thoughts flit to Mama's pasture and the way Opal likes to roll in the dirt and steal apples from my pockets. To Ol' Molly and her lumbering limbs. To the Ancestors and the magic that lies imbued in the ground here after all this time. To my people, huddled in they homes, waiting for me to guide them come morning. I step back, and her hand drops to her side.

Kylie's lashes flutter closed. A small, fragile smile greets me when she opens them. "I told Papa you'd stay. You're so much like Mama, sometimes I cain't even look at you."

My throat clenches, stung by a hundred bees and swollen straight up. "And you've always been like Papa."

We stare at one 'nother, a chasm of silence 'tween us. Then, she turns from me and opens the door. My stomach drops low. "Please. Please stay." The words breach the yawning rift, soft as a breeze.

Her shoulders tense, head tilted down. "May the Ancestors guide you, Ellie. I love you."

Then, she's gone. The door shuts with its heavy, wood-born thud. It rings in my ears, turns to a sentencing toll. My hands quiver, spine bent in terror and pain and the slick, fiery notion of *alone*. They all gone. Mama and Lillian, Kylie and Papa. William. A tremor sweeps up my body, and I cain't stop the way I shake and shake and *shake*, like I'm laid out in the back of a wagon as it travels a terrible, rocky terrain.

There's so much I cain't do, but in the midst of it all, there's something I must. Mind numb and body spent, I return to Mama and Papa's room. Is it still theirs, even if they ain't here no more? I force the thought 'way. Yes. It'll always be theirs.

The grimoire's just where I left it, tucked down in the cupboard under the false bottom. That very same place Mama and, my guess is, many of the Matriarch's before her kept it safe. I run my fingers over its gilded title, the *Opus lex Baeroot*, then pull it from its hidden place and flip to the page I need. The flat of my palm rests over my heart, and I reach out to the Ancestor. "Are you with me?"

It shifts from down in my stomach, then slides upward, a soft nudge to my magic with its own. The gift unfurls with it and glides out to my fingertips.

It's a short spell, for all its power. Simple and subtle with a steep price—a shard of my soul. I breathe in deep, rake my eyes over the text one last time, then tuck the tome 'way in its hiding place. Should anything go wrong, I don't want to hand the *Opus lex Baeroot* over to the townsfolk.

When I exit the house, it's quiet out save for the alto chirp of crickets and steady hum of the cicadas. A wet heat envelops the night. I brush the strands of hair that stick to my forehead back, then start my trek to the pastures. Kylie and Papa took Opal, I'm sure. Perhaps 'nother horse as well. They'll be gone by now, well into they departure from the Orchard. The empty depths of my heart grind and ache.

I'll have to make do with a mare from 'nother witch. My fingers twitch at my side, and anxiety bubbles in my gut. This has to work. The Ancestor threads its way to my nape like a cloak, shielding me from my doubts.

I'm halfway to the pasture when the gift lurches. It fans out, coats my arms and sends goose prickles along them. My strides halt as I glance 'round to the shadows that shift and move, an attempt to warn me of what's come. The Ancestor rips up from my gut, a bear of a thing, to beat at my chest. The fire it unleashes makes me choke, that burn in my sternum an inferno to consume me.

"Wha—" I gag at the way it shreds my flesh and bone from the inside, then burrows deep to my soul.

"Sissy."

My gaze snaps up, and there she is. Lillian.

She's timeless like this, bathed in the moonlight, cast in shadows that send the angles of her face to pointed divots. Ethereal. Like she ain't aged a day from the moment she touched the Bloodbud. Maybe she hasn't. She ain't human. Ain't a witch, neither.

Echoes of that spirit's laughter ring in my mind as she advances on me. Her dress hangs bright 'round her, a beacon, and the little flowers I sewed in the hem mock me as she nears. The sight of them sends pinpricks of pain along my temple as I think of what our family once was. Happy, joyful, stubborn. *Alive*.

"Leave!" The word hitches as it comes out my mouth, chord bent by the battle inside me. She cain't be here. *She cain't be here*. Not before I cast the spell. Not before I help my people one time, just *once*, and die as something more than the Matriarch who brought death and worse. My gut plummets and the Ancestor roars.

Lillian's head tilts, her burning eyes backlit by the starry sky. It makes the silver in her willow moss and kindling glint like a thousand needles "That's all you want, for me to go and never, ever come back. You gots Kylie and Papa and the Clan. That's fine. I gots a new family. A better one. And my brother, he ain't happy with you. Say you put something in him that burns."

A chill slips up my spine even as I step back to create distance between us. Has she made more Infected already? "What you talking 'bout? I ain't done nothing to no one. Mama didn't let us brew curses, you know that, even if you ain't really Lillian no more."

Her lips curl back, and she snarls at me. Those fangs glint, and the gums they stick out from is pink and angry. She can have me, be angry with me, but not yet. I open my mouth to say as much, but she's on me in an instant. My scream catches in my throat. One moment, I'm looking down on her slight frame, the next, I'm gasping for air, vision blurred as it tries to take in the night sky overhead.

Lillian's got her hand at my throat, and I scrabble at it, rake my nails 'cross her skin and buck my hips to try and fling her off. "Lillian," I gasp out, "don't do this. Not yet. The townsfolk—"

There's a gurgle and crunch as she presses down on my windpipe and cuts the air off. But I cain't stop fighting. I won't never stop. Even as my eyelids flutter, a mimicry of moths' wings, and bright starbursts flash 'cross the backs of them.

"You ain't gots to worry 'bout the townsfolk, Sissy. They killed Trevor, so they gon' suffer like him. Dorothea and William already on they way out there. But I wanted to come see you. Tell you 'bout my new family, so you can hurt the way I've been hurting."

She loosens her hand. It's almost worse, each breath I take a flame in my throat. But my body's ice. My heart and soul. Even the gift's grown chilled. I wonder if this what Mama meant when she'd tell Papa she felt cold. So cold. "What you mean, William? He's dead. I felt it when he left me."

My hand goes to my breast, rubs the place that empty and hollow. She tracks the movement and narrows her eyes. "That's the one. The spot William say burns like red embers. He ain't dead, just Infected. And he *like it*. Just the way I knew he would. The same way I knew you would, but you don't get to touch the Bloodbud no more. Don't want you in my family."

Blood roars in my ears. It blocks out whatever Lillian's still saying where she hangs over me, fangs out, hair a wild, tangled halo of auburn.

William ain't dead. He's worse, stolen from me. The Ancestor howls and wriggles 'way even as the gift splinters. I won't see him in the Beyond. We won't be together if he's this thing that's alive and not, lifeless and not. Our eternity's been ripped out from under us, and Lillian's to have me believe he's *happy* that she changed him.

I scream and launch myself forward at her, grip her shoulders and throw her to the side. Her eyes bug out wide, a shock that makes her look so much like our Little Lillian who squealed in joy when she saw her first poultice. She tumbles back of her own accord. It's probably the only reason she's moved, knocked over by her own surprise more than the weight I throw into the movement.

My sister's gone, and this monster that's left has taken *everything* from me. The Ancestor digs its claws into my breast, roars with me as I snarl in her face. There was so much black magic in that tome. I read it over and over 'gain but never thought to memorize the spells. None of them save what I meant to use on the townsfolk. Nothing that gives me a final chance to save the Orchard from Lillian, to rid them of her and keep them safe.

And yet, there's a flicker in my periphery, the gift a static rage. I think it's just as shattered as I am over William. But then, words flicker into sight like a vision. They shift and coil like they cain't quite sit still where they've been etched into the shadows, cloaked in that misty visage the gift gives.

"You're a monster. And I ain't your sister." I spit the words at Lillian, then the Ancestor wraps itself 'round my throat as the Old Language spews out. "En veratum nox abeaus. Leux valum en at horatium nateau lux therat spirit-abeat."

The words scrape they way from me, burn my throat as they pass forth, and my tongue curls over each one like it wants to reel back in and lodge itself in my esophagus. But the Ancestor pushes forward and I follow, allowing the gift to guide me. With every sound, my soul blackens and twists, thorns dug in 'til it tears right in two and leaves me as less than I was. So, so different from the black magic that tied me to my William. I cain't help the shrill laughter that bubbles up.

Lillian snarls at me, the silver in her gaze a bright gleam, then throws her head back and howls. "What did you do? What did you do!"

Exhausted, my body heavy, I roll off her to the gravel path. "Possession. I called on a spirit to possess you. May not kill you, but it should leave you weak enough for the Clan to finish you off." My eyes flutter shut as Lillian snarls and shrieks and pants next to me, her body thrashing 'gainst whatever spirit's trying to get in. There's a steady scent of winter's air on her, the lone aura of an empty bird's nest—still and stagnant. It mixes in with the crisp breeze and cut grass that surrounds us for a sinister harmony. I wonder what I smell like to her. Probably rotten and feral.

Lillian shrieks beside me, claws at the air 'round her, though I don't see nothing there. Then, she stills, her breathing labored. I turn my face to look at her. The gravel bites into my cheek. "Perhaps we were meant to die together."

She don't speak, just lies there. I'm 'bout to lift my hand, brush it 'gainst hers, when she bolts upright. Her chest flutters, a rapid rise and fall, like what I imagine a hummingbird might look like if it ever slowed down long enough for me to watch. Then, she turns her eyes on mine.

They a bolt of rage, strung up in silver that flashes and flares. My breath stutters. Even the Ancestor shudders. Moonlight drips down on her, and the stars create a fiery backdrop to her flaming hair. But it's those fangs I cain't tear my gaze from. They glint and spark in the night.

"No, Sissy. We ain't."

The gift retreats even as the Ancestor slumps, defeated. My thoughts slow, body numb as Lillian bares her canines and sinks down on my throat.

It ain't at all like I thought it'd be. There's no pain. No fear. A warm buzz washes through my veins and settles in my gut. And I should be frightened. I know it. But all I can think 'bout is that Kylie did good, her and Papa. They gonna be safe.

And soon, I'll be with Mama.

22

THE VIPER

Lillian Hallivard

I THRASH 'BOUT, flop and scream while the voices wail they scraping song o' *kill, predator, wraith, rip, tear, shred.* My tooths still out, Sissy's blood on them. She lie off to the side with her throat open, the willow moss and kindling that hurt me left wide and vacant.

Sissy killed Mama. Tried to kill *me.* Then when she couldn't, she tried to have me *possessed.* A growl unfurl in my chest then rumble out my throat.

I don't think she could see it, but I can.

The spirit's a broken thing, made up o' cotton-thin wisps that flicker like chimney smoke, though it's hue be o' sheep's wool, 'stead o' that dark charcoal that pinches and burns. Makes it harder to see the spirit with that light color, but it's there. The mouth yawns open like it wants to gobble the world on up, and its shape twitches, then shifts, a dizzying pattern that make it hard to catch.

"She dead," I shriek, then bat at it with fists when the cloud dive for my chest to burrow down in. My hands catch on the wisps and hold. It's a mist in my palm, icy bits that cut into my fingers, and though it ain't solid, there's something there that I can grasp onto so I can keep the spirit back. "Sissy's dead. Her words don't mean nothing now. You cain't do this!"

My skin ripples with gooseprickles while them voices rage and fit. But the spirit don't stop. It just shove itself at me. A chill touches my breast, then dips in. Goes deeper.

Screams work they way out my throat, the raw anger in the voices now drenched 'cross my heart. The spark I got in my eyes flashes and burns, then I launch myself toward that cold. My nails dig into the odd grip I got as I rip and tear and shred. A sharp, piercing ring echoes 'round us as the spirit's mouth drops even wider. Shudders form a tingling path down my spine at the thing's voice. It's like the spirit shrieking down low in a ravine, and I'm standing all the way at the top.

Tremors steal up my body, iron hot in rage. I'm a poker that been held in the fire, then left on the floor to singe a hold right into the base o' a home. A sudden jerk o' the spirit pulls the chill from my breast. The mist struggles in my hands even as that ice leaves my palms and fingers raw, but I don't let go. Just like them townspeople gon' pay for what they did to Trevor, and Sissy paid for what she did to Mama, this spirit 'bout to pay for what it trying to do to me.

My tooths throb and ache in my mouth, anxious for me to bite. So, I does.

Soon as they sink in, my body go rigid. Pain light up my gums then races to my mind and all the way down my spine. It's like chewing on metal, like letting it slice clean through blood and flesh. My eyes bug, nails clenched into that mist as it spins and thrashes, tries to break free, but we cain't move. Neither o' us. We're here, bound together 'til someone fades or dies.

The chills starts to spread 'gain, slide along that path in my breast and spine, then tap up, up, up towards my mind. Once caught there, the voices set in with they hisses. *Rip, tear, shred, feast, kill, rise.* My eyes clench shut as I focus on them and they strength, let those words sink in. The silver blaze in my sight prickles.

I picture Dorothea, her lips spread wide to show her tooths while she says we strong. I see Trevor, tied to that tree in the Orchard while the flames ate him. Then I think on William, seizing on the ground as he changed, how he fought through the pain and the hurt that Sissy put on him 'til he was a blossomed thunderclap o' power.

My eyes snap open, and I shove back at the ice. It don't budge, so I grit down on the spirit and *bite.* The mist shudders as my tooths cut lower, then I do as them voices says. I rip and tear and shred. My head snaps back and forth in violent flurry, like I a hound that's got a possum in its jaws and wants nothing more than to snap its neck.

The chill whips back so quick I stumble, then the spirit falters. My hands slip and punch forward through empty air, but I grapple back on that icy mist. 'Nother piercing ring echoes 'round us in the night. I bet the spirit's scream be heard by mutts for miles 'round, even as the witches and humans sleep. But I tune it out and listen to the voices as they chant and hiss, a victory in the way they wrap 'round my mind then slither to my nape.

It take one more bite, then the spirit shrieks, and the ice in my gum disappears. My tooths clack down hard on one 'nother and the spirit shatters and crumbles in my hands, falling to the ground in shattered pieces o' dust that glint like the stars overhead, harsh to gaze at, but hard to look 'way from. My chest heaves and the voices shriek with they thrills, but I cain't look 'way from the spirit as, bit by bit, those glittering remains vanish.

It's dead. I can tell. The way it screamed, how the cold fled entirely and the busted pieces o' it vanished as I watched, how the voices shriek and hiss a celebration. A giddy bloom folds up in my chest even as I drop to my knees and pant. That thing them witches fear so much, even more than me—I can hurt it, maim it, make it dead.

My lips pull back in a loony smile, the one that show my tooths. They buzzing from the spirit, a good kind o' sting, one that make them feel more like energy than bone. The pink o' my tongue slide over they smooth surface, now cleaned o' Sissy's blood.

I turn to face her. She still there, laid out 'cross the ground, the russet moved down to cloak her breast and the gravel 'neath her. My feet move 'fore I think 'bout it, then I'm knelt next to her. The stain soaks up in my dress and makes my knees sticky. Sissy would have huffed and groaned over the mess, but Dorothea gon' be right fine to wash my clothes and scrub my skin in that way she does that make it pink and prickly.

They gots to be in town by now, Dorothea and William, finishing off them townsfolk one by one. My new family.

My fingers hover near Sissy's face, the willow moss and kindling dull in the light o' the stars overhead. I don't touch, just trace a hair's breadth over her cheek bone, her nose, her temple. Only when I reach the wisps o' hair that have fallen 'cross her face do I touch. I brush them back, same as she done to me even as she was trying to hurt me. Don't know why she did it 'cause I don't feel no different doing it now. My nose scrunch up, and I pull my hand back.

Sissy ain't been my family for a long while.

I'm 'bout to stand when her skirts rustle. Maybe it a lizard or a frog. A grin split 'cross my face, and I snap my hand out to catch it 'fore it can get 'way. The thing wriggles and fights where I got it caught up in the fabric. It's too dry to be a frog and too long to be a lizard. I'm careful to keep a good grip on it as I pull it free.

The viper's jaw is gaped wide soon as I got it out from under Sissy. Its scales is a muddy brown mixed with copper and hickory and amber. The eyes track me, body tense, and the slick tail whips back and forth. When it swings high 'nough to reach my slender arm, it wraps 'round my wrist and holds on. I try to switch hands, gentle, 'cause if I grip too hard I might break it.

Just as I'm reaching forward, the viper lunges, its fangs out, and sinks them sharp tooths into my hand. It don't hurt bad, a prick if anything, but my eyes bug wide anyhow. I twist my wrist as its tail wraps tighter and its fangs grip harder in my flesh, like it gon' hold on 'til I drop dead with its venom.

Same as I did with that spirit.

Warmth blossoms up my breast and settles there, then dips into my belly. The voices hum an off-tune melody.

This what I be, what my animal name is. Viper. 'Cause I lunge like this and fight like this and hold on like this, tooths and body and all. Dorothea gon' like it, I know.

I don't budge the viper, knelt here by Sissy, and when it do release me, I set it on the ground and stand, then watch it slither off to the line o' trees 'cross the way, like it know just where home is.

A rumble starts up in my chest, but it's more a coo than a growl, a dove 'stead o' a coyote. Sissy was a threat to my new family—y Dorothea and William—But she ain't no more.

The Clan can have they fits and the Coven can wreck they-selves—I ain't worried.

I can make people do what I want them to. My bones all firm, even when a wagon roll over them and they should shatter. The voices hiss and growl, all twisted up in my mind, the trees warped in what might have been a vision if I could have them anymore. But I ain't a witch nor a human.

I be more. I can kill them spirits that the witches fear so bad.

My lips slip wide for my tooths, my fangs. I stand and skip the rest o' the way to town where my family be. My new one. My better one. This family o' Infected that I gon' grow and grow and grow like them willows that as ancient as the Ancestors.

I'm a willow too, now.

I gon' live for an eternity and longer.

THEY BURN they sting they like that thing leaving iron taste along reddened tongue and though it keep a harshest scent my nostrils twitch in they open glee leaving me to wonder why this grating smell and brazen flavor make the voices scream like fevered things all wild and happy while my hands crush bone and my belly sing and my tooths point out point down point bloody forever to sting like them bees that all angry

ACKNOWLEDGMENTS

Creating the first installment of the *Willow Moss and Kindling* series was a tangled web of blossoming ideas, devious characters, scrapped remnants for further novels, and, of course, a curse.

I wanted to broach many questions and examine them within a supernatural setting. What comes first: family, duty, or loyalty? On the topic of monsters (which fascinates all readers and writers of horror) I cliff dived into the same question posed by Mary Shelley during the enlightenment: what creates a monster? And last, at least in this tiny space I have to speak to you on a personal level, is the question I pose to readers: who do you believe to be the monster within the world of Willow Moss and Kindling? Who would you fear?

This novel wouldn't be here without the faithful—and occasionally rude, Coven bless her—conviction of my grandmother. You're my best friend. This tale, and all those to follow, is for you. I love you.

To my readers, I hope I did this story justice and gave you a vibrant, macabre world to love. I hope you root for these characters as much as I do. I hope your expectations were met with every twist and turn and impetuous monologue. You're as ominous as the Ancestors that watch over each and every clan of the Coven. (And I'm certain as the spirits you *clucked* your tongue a time or two at the Hallivard sisters.) Be well as we continue on.

To my parents, thank you for throwing me into this land of creation from the beginning. Mama, going to work at the school library with you started off my love for reading and the written word. Those weird, printed lines and curves and dots let me travel to worlds unimaginable. Dad, going to work with you at the move theatre put into bright perspective just how *big* story-telling could be. I love both of you.

To Dr. Milakovic, you get a special shout out here for opening my eyes to so much of the world. You sit firmly on the throne of my enlightenment.

To Kelly Colby and CDS Publishing, thank you for this chance to chase my dream. You're the snarky comments that tore vignette novels to pieces, still saw something worthwhile, and convinced me to build it back up into a series. I think there's some witchery involved . . . but we'll turn a blind eye.

And to my dear writing partner, JM Jordan, thank you for patiently sitting through the excited spit balling of ideas, the frustrations, the venting, the dangerous amounts of caffeine I fueled my body with. Thank you for believing in me when I didn't believe in myself. Thank you for always sticking around. I couldn't have done this without you.

ABOUT THE AUTHOR

Taylor Shepeard is a Houstonian author who focuses on the dark and twisties that make up the psychological dilemmas of humanity. She examines how the tiny nuances of her characters incite action in the world. When she isn't writing, she's lounging around with her dog or teaching impressionable high schoolers.

OTHER TITLES BY CURSED DRAGON SHIP

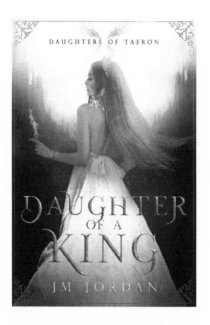

All their precautions failed and the Darkness came.
Huldah and Flora must stop him before he consumes
them all.

When magic is rediscovered in a land devoid of it, one set of twins must compete to earn the right to be called True Heir, a title that means more than either imagined.